WHEN'S THE WEDDING?

DREAMING OF SAYING 'I DO'...

OLIVIA SPRING

HARTLEY PUBLISHING

First Edition: March 2021

www.oliviaspring.com

Follow Olivia on Facebook/Twitter/Instagram: @ospringauthor

Dedicated to my darling PD.

CHAPTER ONE

Ah, Paris.

Don't you just love it?

The food. The culture. The sightseeing. I adored it all.

As I stood at the top of the Eiffel Tower, taking in the breathtaking panoramic views with Miles' arms wrapped around me, it was easy to understand why it was known as one of the most romantic cities in the world.

The sun was setting and I could see the gorgeous orange light touching the tops of the French capital's coolest landmarks. Notre Dame, the Grand Palais—even the bends in the river Seine.

Miles and I had started the day on a high, waking up legs and arms entwined underneath the crisp white sheets of our king-size bed in the fancy boutique hotel he'd booked.

We'd enjoyed breakfast on the balcony, devouring fresh, buttery, flaky croissants and pain au chocolat whilst sipping on a cheeky glass of champagne. A little tipsy and feeling frisky, we'd stumbled back into bed to work off those calories, then set off for a day of sightseeing.

We made sure we visited some of the most popular tourist haunts. Taking in the stunning art at the Louvre. Window-shopping hand in hand along the Champs-Élysées, where the clothes cost more than a whole month's salary. And now we were finishing the day here: at one of the most iconic monuments in the world. Miles couldn't have planned this better if he'd had the entire production team of *Say I Do* working with him.

Yep. This had been the perfect day, and I had a feeling it was about to get even better.

I'd dreamt about this for what felt like forever. Getting to this point definitely hadn't been easy. I'd kissed *way* too many frogs along the way. But now, as I stood here, ready for my moment, I could say that the prize of finally finding my Prince Charming was worth all those years of heartache.

Any minute now…

I'd imagined my reaction at least a million times in my head. The shock. My hands covering my mouth as I gasped with surprise. The tears of joy as Miles slid the ring on my finger.

The ring—how exciting! What would it be like? A big classic diamond, or something smaller and understated? Yes. That was more my style. Neither of us were into flashy bling. He'd know I'd prefer something more simple and elegant.

'Shall we go over here?' Miles gently released his arms from around my waist.

'Okay!' I said, trying to contain my excitement and practically skipping ahead to the other side of the viewing platform. He was right. The views were even better from this position. The engagement photos would look *amazing*. I stood still, watching him walk slowly towards me.

'So, I was wondering…'

'Yes…' My eyes widened.

'There's something I've been wanting to ask you all afternoon…' Miles took a deep breath, then suddenly dropped down on one knee.

OMG. This was it.

It was finally happening.

The butterflies began dancing in my stomach, the blood racing through my veins.

'Would you…' He glanced up at me.

'Yes! Yes! Yes! *YES!!*' I replied excitedly, staring into his gorgeous dark brown eyes. I didn't even need to let him finish his sentence. I knew I wanted to take our relationship to the next level. To become official partners. To spend the rest of our lives together. Right now, there was nothing I wanted more than to be his wife.

'You would? So you don't mind going back to the gift shop to get my dad the T-shirt we saw earlier? Excellent!'

He swiftly tied his shoelaces and stood back up.

Oh…

Hold on.

'I felt bad about asking, because you did say I should just get it, and you were right.'

My stomach plummeted.

Miles was still talking, but I was in a daze, trying to take in what was happening.

'I know it's a pain to have to go all the way back because it's been a long day, but the guy said he only had one left in his size. If you're too tired, we can just go straight back to the hotel. Alex?'

'Huh?' I came to my senses and regained the ability to speak. 'Um… no… it's fine.'

'Brilliant! Dad's gonna love it. You're the best!' Miles pecked me on the cheek. 'Shall we take some more photos? Such amazing views.'

That hadn't *quite* gone like I'd hoped.

I'd thought Miles was finally going to propose. I mean, everything seemed so right. The setting. The sunset. This would have been the perfect scene for our real-life romcom.

Maybe that was my problem. I'd spent so many years bingeing on romance novels and films that I had my head in the clouds, dreaming of the perfect proposal.

I shouldn't have got carried away. I should've realised that I wasn't Julia Roberts or Meg Ryan starring in a big Hollywood romantic comedy. This was real life.

And life with Miles was great. Our relationship was solid, so there was no need to worry.

We'd get engaged one day.

It was going to happen.

When, exactly?

Now *that* was the million-dollar question…

CHAPTER TWO

I pressed the home button on my phone to check the time.

6.23 a.m.

Why was it that whenever I could have a lie-in, I always woke up early? I sighed, then glanced at my left hand. Yep. My ring finger was just as bare as it had been before we'd gone to Paris.

I winced, thinking of how silly I'd been, getting my hopes up like that. Then I remembered why I'd booked the day off and winced even more.

I'd taken annual leave because I'd thought I would be basking in the happiness of being newly engaged.

Today, I'd imagined Miles and I would wake up gazing into each other's eyes, then enjoy some *morning delight.* We'd have a lovely breakfast together, and after he left for work, I'd pictured spending some time looking through my wedding planning folders, making a shortlist of a few suppliers I planned to contact.

Next I was going to meet my friend Stacey for lunch so

I could share all the details about Miles' romantic proposal and get some wedding planning tips. Then I'd hoped to spend the rest of the afternoon going to the wedding appointments I'd set up.

Cringe.

I'd arranged to go and try on dresses at a bridal boutique in central London, then meet a florist, followed by a visit to a bakery I'd spotted on Pinterest for a mini tasting.

Even though I knew we wouldn't have set a date until we'd visited venues (which I'd hoped we could start doing next weekend), I'd still wanted to get the ball rolling. It was never too early to get suppliers in place. If I had time, I'd also thought I could call my hairdresser to book a wedding hair consultation.

I had everything planned. And now I'd have to spend the morning cancelling it all.

Unless...

Maybe I could still go after all? Trying on some wedding dresses might cheer me up.

Then again, standing there all dressed in white knowing I was no closer to getting the proposal I'd been dreaming about for years probably wasn't a good idea.

Talk about embarrassing. I wasn't sure what was worse. Jumping to conclusions about getting engaged, or that time I'd rushed to a meeting but decided to go to the toilet first and hadn't realised that, in my haste, I'd tucked the back of my skirt into my tights, so I'd been flashing my knickers to the whole office. *Jeez.* At least they were my good ones and not the big Bridget Jones granny pants I used to wear when it was that time of the month. Thankfully the receptionist had pulled me aside before I'd stepped into the boardroom to meet the big bosses, but it was still mortifying.

Hmm… Maybe that was worse. At least no one had seen me make a fool of myself in Paris, and I hadn't exposed my bum in public.

Anyway. Enough wallowing. With all the thoughts swimming around my head, I knew I wouldn't be able to get back to sleep, so I might as well get up. I gently climbed out of the king-size oak bed and tiptoed across the soft charcoal carpet into the en suite bathroom.

I quickly brushed my teeth, then ran my fingers through my chocolate-brown hair. It was growing. Nowhere near as long as the extensions I always used to wear before getting a pixie cut. Now it was a kind of choppy bob. I quite liked the new length.

After heading to the kitchen, I opened the chrome fridge and saw the bottle of fancy champagne staring back at me. I'd snuck it inside just before we'd left for Paris so it would be nice and chilled, ready for us to celebrate this morning.

We won't be needing that now.

It's fine.

Absolutely fine.

Right. Just because we weren't celebrating our engagement didn't mean I couldn't cook us a nice breakfast. After all, last week Miles and I had reached our second anniversary.

Following years of failed relationships (well, most of them only lasted one night, so didn't even warrant using the 'r' word), I'd reached a landmark.

We were happy together. That was an achievement in itself. I shouldn't be feeling disappointed. I should be over the moon. *Grateful.* I'd finally found *the one.* My Mr Right.

I took out the smoked salmon, eggs and avocado and put them on the white marble worktops. The kitchen décor was very neutral. Sleek dark grey cupboards with chrome handles and white tiled flooring and walls. Since Miles had asked me to move in, I'd added little bits and pieces like plants, bright blue crockery and accessories, just to try and inject a bit of colour.

I opened the freezer and pulled out the pastries I'd hidden at the back. Normally we just had toast or cereal for breakfast, but before we'd left, I'd popped to the supermarket to get something special.

Pain au chocolat was Miles' favourite, so I thought it'd be a nice reminder of our weekend away. I loved how when you cooked the pre-prepared ones in the oven, the warm chocolate oozed from each end. *Yum.*

Whilst the pastries were baking, I flicked through the post that had come when we were away.

Oooh. A new edition of *The Perfect Bride* magazine.

I ripped it out of the plastic packaging and sat down at the kitchen table.

An engagement ring special!

As much as I'd hoped that I wouldn't have needed to look at this section today because I'd be too focused on thinking about wedding rings, I couldn't resist.

I was more excited flicking through the pages than a pervert looking at porn. So much beauty in one place. This was orgasmic.

There were white gold, yellow gold and rose gold rings. Every kind I could imagine. Round-cut, oval-shaped, emerald-cut, radiant-cut and princess-cut. I was in heaven.

I grabbed a pair of scissors from the kitchen drawer and started removing the pages so I could add them to my wedding folder later.

A stunning three-stone diamond ring instantly caught my eye. The platinum band had one diamond in the centre, flanked by smaller ones on each side. It was gorgeous, and the price was surprisingly reasonable too. Having a mega-expensive ring didn't interest me. I just wanted something simple, classic and pretty. Yep, this was ideal.

'Morning beautiful!' Miles kissed me gently on the lips. 'You're up early!' Cuddles, our British shorthair, followed him into the kitchen and wrapped herself around his legs, purring loudly. I didn't blame her. I felt like doing the same.

'Morning…'

God, Miles looked *hot*. He had dark stubble on his cheeks, and he hadn't put in his contacts yet, so was wearing his glasses, which gave him a sexy Clark Kent vibe. His black boxer shorts clung to his solid thighs, and as for his chest… yum. I didn't think I could ever get tired of admiring it. So broad, solid and smooth. *Damn.* I pulled my mind out of the gutter and brought myself back in the room.

'Yeah,' I continued. 'Thought I'd cook us a nice breakfast. I'm doing eggs, avocado on toast and I've put some pains au chocolat in the oven so they'll be nice and warm, just like at that patisserie we went to.'

'*Mmm*, my favourite. I can smell the chocolate already. Thank you!' He picked up Cuddles and started stroking her blue-grey fur. 'And smoked salmon?' Miles glanced at the packet on the kitchen worktop. '*Very posh.* Are we celebrating something?'

Ouch.

I wanted to say, *I hoped we'd be celebrating our engagement*, but I thought better of it.

'Our anniversary, of course…' I plastered on a smile.

'*Awww.* That was last week. Not that I'm complaining. This will be a great extension of our amazing celebration in Paris.' Cuddles jumped out of his arms as he opened the fridge. 'Champagne too? *Wow.* Let's save that for tonight, after work, so we can both enjoy it properly.' He pecked me on the cheek, then glanced over my shoulder. 'What are you reading?'

'Just a magazine that came in the post. Look at these engagement rings.' I showed him one of the pages I'd cut out and pointed. 'Aren't they gorgeous?'

'Very nice. I mean, I don't know much about rings, but they look, er, *sparkly*.'

'I think they're *stunning*.'

'Yep…' Miles paused. 'So, do I have time to have a shower before breakfast, or should I wait until after we've eaten?'

Not *quite* the response I was hoping for…

'You've got time.' I tried to sound upbeat but felt like a deflated balloon. 'The pastries are almost done, but I need to prepare everything else. Should all be ready in about fifteen minutes.'

After his shower, Miles returned to the kitchen and we both devoured breakfast.

'That was delicious.' Miles rubbed his stomach, then looked at his watch. 'I'd better go.' He picked up our empty plates, rinsed them off quickly and put them in the dishwasher. 'Got anything nice planned for your day off?'

'Um, not much.' *I did, but…* 'I'm meeting Stacey for lunch and then we'll see. Might go to the gym or just relax at home this afternoon.' After all that great food in Paris and eating so much this morning, I definitely should do some exercise, but I wasn't feeling that motivated.

'Cool. Thanks again for an amazing weekend in Paris. *So* romantic.'

He planted another soft kiss on my lips, clearly oblivious to the thoughts swirling around my head.

'You're the one that organised everything.'

'Well, it wouldn't have been any fun without you! Enjoy being a lady of leisure. See you later.'

'Yep.' I smiled. 'Have a good day at work.'

I sighed.

Yes. Miles was right. It *was* an amazing weekend. And it *was* romantic. It just wasn't the romantic weekend that I'd dreamt of.

CHAPTER THREE

That was the last of the appointments cancelled. It was so awkward when the lady at the bridal store had asked if I wanted to reschedule. Before I could stop it, a loud 'yes!' had flown out of my mouth. *Again*. Note to self to use that word more carefully in future. Especially when at the top of iconic buildings.

Naturally, she'd then asked me when. But I had no idea. Next week? Next month? Her guess was as good as mine. I politely said I'd call back once I knew, because my schedule was just *crazy* at the moment. She probably realised I was telling porkies, but was sweet about it and said she'd be here whenever I was ready, which was a relief.

The good, non-embarrassing news was I'd just arrived at the little Italian restaurant near my old workplace and was going to meet Stacey for lunch. I knew she'd be sympathetic and know the right things to say.

When I'd texted her to let her know the proposal

hadn't happened, she'd asked whether I wanted to cancel. Although I wasn't feeling my best, I said I'd be fine. I had been looking forward to catching up, and an hour with her was sure to lift my spirits.

'So good to see you!' I quickly walked towards Stacey. She was sitting at our favourite table by the window.

'You too!' She got up and gave me a big hug. 'Feels like it's been ages!' Her shoulder-length blond hair looked like it had just been cut, and as always she looked effortlessly beautiful. She was dressed in a pair of wide black trousers and a loose cream blouse.

'It *does*! So strange not seeing you every day. I miss our morning coffee catch-ups.'

Stacey and I used to work together selling exhibition space at M&E UK Media Group, a trade publishing and events company in central London. Whilst she'd joined two years ago, I'd been there ever since I'd left uni, so a whopping fifteen years. Towards the end, it had felt more like I was serving a prison sentence. I was so glad I'd escaped that hellhole three months ago and had found my dream job.

'Me too. It hasn't been the same since you left. Believe it or not, Steve has become even more annoying.'

'*No way*. Steve is one of the most annoying people on the planet, so that's impossible.'

'You'd think so. But his clichés and management speak have got worse. The other day he said we needed to organise a *thought shower*. And when I presented my ideas in the meeting, rather than just asking everyone what they thought, he said: "Let's run it up the flagpole." Then—now *this* was the classic—after dismissing everyone's suggestions and before he started boring us with his own, he said: "I'm going to stir-fry an idea in your think wok and let's see what sizzles."'

'He *didn't*?'

'Oh yes, he did.'

'*Think wok*? Jesus. Who even talks like that?'

'I know, right?' Stacey sighed. 'Why couldn't he have just said "what do you think about my ideas?" like a normal person? And I heard he's considering putting a timer in the kitchen to make sure no one takes longer than five minutes to get a cup of coffee.'

'No way!'

'The guy's a dick. Next he'll be timing how long we spend in the loo.'

That would be just like Steve. If there was an award for Britain's Most Irritating Boss, he would be a prime contender.

'I'm *so* glad I left. No offence, but that place was becoming toxic.'

'It is. I'm glad I won't be there for much longer.'

'Thinking of leaving?' I asked.

'Yeah, something like that… anyway, enough about stupid Steve. Tell me what happened in Paris!'

I filled her in on the non-engagement.

'I feel so disappointed,' I sighed. 'Every time we go somewhere romantic, I know I shouldn't, but I get my hopes up that a proposal is coming. And then when it doesn't, I feel conflicted. On the one hand, we always have an amazing time together, but on the other, it's like since we moved in together a year ago, we've kind of stalled. Miles knows that getting married is important to me, but he doesn't seem any closer to proposing.'

'I know it must be gutting.' Stacey squeezed my hand. 'Especially when everything seemed perfect with the Eiffel Tower and the Parisian skyline as a backdrop, but I think you just have to be patient.'

'I have been. The beginning of our relationship was built on patience. Not many people wait six months before having sex.'

'Nope, but holding out for your Mr Right paid off.'

'Yeah, it did, and I'm so grateful you recommended I followed the advice in the book. But I hoped that, like you, I'd be married by now. I wish Laurie Love had written a sequel on how to make your boyfriend put a ring on it!' I laughed.

'Normally finding *the one* is the most difficult part.'

'True. Sometimes when I think back to how my life used to be, dating all those losers, I feel bad for wanting more. Like I'm being ungrateful. I mean, my relationship is happy and fulfilling in literally every other department. Miles is supportive, kind, funny—we have so much in common. And the sex is fantastic. Apart from not being hitched, everything feels right.'

It really did. Part of me thought maybe I was asking too much. If everything else was pretty perfect, why push it? *If it ain't broke, don't fix it*. But I'd always wanted to get married. Just like I had professional goals, I had goals for my personal life. And marriage was one of them.

'You two are great together,' said Stacey.

'Yeah. We get on like a house on fire. And it's not like the whole wedding thing is completely one-sided. We've spoken about marriage and Miles has said he wants it too. But if he does, what's he waiting for?'

I just didn't get it. When we'd decided to go exclusive

and discussed the future, I'd said I'd love us to commit to marriage within a year, and Miles had been fine with that. I knew it would take time to plan the wedding afterwards, but I'd hoped at least he'd propose.

Then, after we'd been dating for a year, Miles had asked me to move in with him. Of course, I'd jumped at the chance. The more I thought about it, the more it made sense for us to live together before getting hitched. It would give us time to see how well we handled being around each other full-time and how we coped with any challenges that came our way as a couple. So I hadn't minded waiting a bit longer. Plus, I'd reasoned that I couldn't exactly nag him about the whole 'marriage commitment in the first twelve months' thing considering he'd waited six months to sleep with me.

One thing I *had* said, though, was that I didn't want to be living with him for 'years', as in more than one, before we got engaged, and again, Miles had seemed like he was on board. So now that we'd just celebrated twelve months of cohabitation and our two-year anniversary, I didn't understand why he hadn't popped the question.

'When was the last time you discussed it?'

'Last month. We were walking past a church, and a bride and groom were at the top of the steps kissing, with all their friends and family around them throwing confetti. It was beautiful. And I said something like: "That will be us one day."'

'What did Miles say?'

'He said, "Yeah. Soon."'

I remembered the excitement pulsing through me. I'd been so happy to hear that. I'd known there were only a few weeks to go until our anniversary and that we'd be going to Paris not long after that, so I'd been convinced it was going to happen.

I could hardly sleep the night before our anniversary. We'd gone out to dinner at a lovely Chinese restaurant in town to celebrate, and when the waiter kept hovering, I was sure it was because he was waiting for a cue from Miles or something.

I decided to leave the table in case they needed time to set things up, so said I was going to the ladies'. I waited ten minutes, just in case, but then I thought if I stayed in there much longer, they'd think I was taking a dump, so I quickly went back outside. When I got closer, I saw there was a bottle of champagne and two fancy red opaque champagne flutes. My heart began to flutter.

After Miles raised a toast *to us*, I tried to scrutinise the glass as I slowly sipped the bubbly, just to double-check there wasn't an engagement ring at the bottom. But I soon realised there were no hidden extras.

Then, when we were given fortune cookies, I hoped I'd crack open mine and find a ring with a personalised message saying *Marry Me, Alex* inside. But instead it said: *If you eat something and nobody sees you, it has no calories.*

Although it wasn't what I'd hoped to see and it gave me zero insight into my future, at first it made me smile because I'd wolfed down three extra prawn balls when Miles went to the gents'. But I'd gladly accept thousands of extra calories if it meant I'd get the proposal.

I was disappointed at the end of the night, but I comforted myself with the fact that we still had Paris. *Yes,*

I reasoned. Why would Miles propose at a restaurant when we'd be going to the most romantic city in the world a few days later? It was sure to happen then. Except we all know how that turned out…

'You just have to trust him,' said Stacey. 'Just let nature take its course.'

I *did* trust Miles. On the one hand, I was still hopeful about getting a proposal soon, but at the same time, I was worried about taking up an indefinite residency in limbo land. I felt a shiver run down my spine as I imagined myself in a constant state of anxiety. Always wondering whether today would be the day.

'The thing is, I know I need to be patient, but I've heard about so many women who waited for years and nothing happened. Today, I was scrolling through an online forum where they were chatting about how hard it was waiting for a proposal. I just wanted to get some reassurance to stop myself from fretting. I came across a post from this lady, I think her name was Jolene, who'd been fobbed off for fifteen years. *Fifteen!* Her boyfriend constantly told her they'd get engaged *soon*. First he needed to find a good job. Then when he found one, he said he needed to make sure they had enough money to pay for the wedding.'

'Well, that's important. Weddings aren't exactly cheap.'

'I know.' I'd been saving up for years and had a decent amount set aside. Miles had savings too and a great job working as a paediatrician at a hospital in East London, so money couldn't be the issue. 'Anyway, then this guy's sister got engaged and he claimed he was going to propose that same weekend, but didn't want it to look like he was just copying them. But two years later, he *still* hadn't proposed! In the end, after getting tired of all the broken promises, Jolene gave him an ultimatum: marry me or I'm leaving. And do you know what he said?'

'No. What?'

'He wasn't ready! I mean, *come on*! This woman had wasted fifteen valuable years waiting and hoping and *nothing*. In the end they broke up, and by then, it was too late for her to start a family.'

'Maybe they both weren't on the same page. Maybe he didn't really want to get married. Who knows? Just because this Jolene waited years doesn't mean you'll have to. It's still fairly early on in your relationship.'

I knew that was true. I was aware that it might seem like I was overreacting. After all, it wasn't like five years had passed, let alone fifteen. But that was the thing with time. It had a habit of flying by without you realising. That was how situations like Jolene's happened. A few weeks quickly became a few months. A few months then became a few years. And then *boom*. In what felt like the blink of an eye, a decade had disappeared. Gone. Then a decade and a half…

I explained my concerns to Stacey.

'At the end of the day, you made what you wanted clear early on, Miles said he's on board, so I just think you have to believe that it will happen.'

'And if it doesn't?'

'Then you'll have to decide whether marriage is a deal breaker, and if it is, and it gets to, say, this time next year and you don't seem like you've got any closer, then you'll need to have a serious talk with him.'

'Next year?' I didn't want to wait another twelve months for things to happen. That was too long.

'I've been where you are, Alex, and if a traditional proposal from your boyfriend is what you want, then I don't believe there's any tricks you can use to make him propose faster. If you want the marriage to last, there's no point forcing Miles to propose before he's ready. It'll only end in tears.'

'I definitely don't want to force or nag him into it. I'd like the proposal to come from Miles. For him to want to do it on his own.'

That was important to me. Look at how Bridget almost permanently ruined her relationship with Mark Darcy in *Bridget Jones: The Edge of Reason*—by being pushy about getting engaged. *No.* Proposals should be unexpected and romantic.

I could talk to Miles openly about everything. Work, life, sex—even stuff like the discomfort of constipation or how good it felt to pop an angry spot (naughty I know, yet *so* satisfying). But if I had to ask Miles to propose, it wouldn't count. It'd lose the whole meaning.

We'd spoken about marriage in general and discussed *general* timings, but asking directly '*When are we getting married?*' and pushing him to tell me a specific date would be too desperate. I wasn't going to say, 'Darling, please can you propose to me next Saturday at the top of a London skyscraper like the Shard with a thousand red roses and a string quartet?' Where was the romance in that?

A proposal needed to be natural. It had to appear spontaneous. Even if it took weeks for him to plan.

Yep. If I wanted a traditional proposal, it looked like

there was only one option. Just like I'd done before, I just had to be patient. Stacey had been right before about how to find a man, so she must know best this time around too.

The famous saying promised that *all good things come to those who wait*. And I hoped that in this case, it would really be true.

CHAPTER FOUR

Back to work today.

I didn't mind too much, because for once in my life I'd achieved the miracle of finding a job that I actually loved. So rather than dreading the day ahead every morning like I used to, normally I woke up with enthusiasm. Not *skipping down the street, arriving at work two hours early* kind of enthusiasm. I wasn't completely crazy. Just, you know, the *spring in my step, happy to be there, looking forward to new challenges* kind. And after the last couple of days, it would be a good distraction.

I stood outside the bright red stained-glass door and rang the bell. Still felt weird going to work in a house. It was no ordinary home, though. It was three-storey, five-bedroom Victorian townhouse in Clapham, which had been converted into the Happy Dog Hotel. And I was the recently appointed marketing manager.

After spending over a year job hunting, trying to follow my dream to work with animals, applying for hundreds of positions and receiving rejection after rejection, I'd felt like the cat that got the cream when I was offered the role.

I was having a stroll on Clapham Common when I saw this tall, blondish woman in her mid-fifties walking several adorable dogs, and I had to stop to say hello. We got talking and I asked her if she'd had them for long. The lady, who told me her name was Marigold, or Goldie for short, explained that they weren't all hers. She was taking care of some of them for the week whilst the owners were on holiday.

Goldie went on to tell me all about her hotel, which she'd founded two years earlier. I said it sounded amazing, gushed about how lucky she was to work with animals all day and grumbled about the fact that I'd been trying to find a job in that field for ages. I'd tried the marketing departments of all the zoos in and around London, animal charities, and vet chains. You name it. And I still hadn't had any joy. The closest I got was an interview for a fundraising role at Battersea Dogs and Cats Home, but someone else pipped me to the post.

Then she told me she was looking for someone to help them get more customers and asked if I'd be interested. Did teenagers love TikTok? I nearly bit her hand off there and then. After a couple of very informal interviews with her and Jada, the business and finance director, she told me the job was mine. I couldn't believe my luck. And so here I was. Feeling like I was living the dream.

I'd barely stepped through the door before the welcoming committee, aka *the siblings*, leapt up to greet me.

Scooby, a Jack Russell, yelped with delight and flashed me his trademark smile. I remembered when I'd come here for the first time, it had freaked me out a bit when I'd seen him flashing his teeth, but he was harmless.

Flapjack, a cute little Westiepoo puppy, jumped up with excitement, clutching a pair of frilly red knickers in his mouth, and Princess, a black Labradoodle, clung to my leg.

'Hello, lovelies!' I ruffled Flapjack's furry white head, then bent down and scooped Princess up from the floor and gave her a big cuddle. 'How you doing today?'

Scooby barked enthusiastically to confirm all was well.

'They're good,' said Goldie. 'Flapjack's up to his normal mischief. I did some washing this morning, and as you can see, he's pinched my undies from the basket again.' She rolled her eyes. Flapjack had a thing with socks and underwear. Sounds gross, but apparently it was because they carried Goldie's scent. 'Come on, handsome. Hand them over.' Flapjack looked up at her and whimpered as if to say, *Do I really have to?* Then he spat them out and lay down on the floor by Goldie's feet.

Jada laughed as she joined us in the hallway. I noticed she'd just had her hair done. Her jet-black braids hung beautifully past her shoulders. 'The knickers *do* look pretty eye-catching, though, to be fair. Are they new?' she smirked.

'That's for me to know and for you *not* to find out…' Goldie winked. 'Anyhow!' She turned to face me. 'Enough talk about my undies. So!' Her face lit up and she clapped her hands with excitement. 'How was Paris?'

Oh God. I really shouldn't have mentioned that I thought Miles was going to propose. That was what happened when you spent eight hours of your day at work. Sometimes you revealed far too much about yourself.

Jada looked at my left hand and then her face fell.

'Um, maybe you can tell us all about it later,' she said quickly. 'I'd love to hear all about the places you visited and of course *the food*. Actually, I picked up some chocolate croissants from that posh coffee shop round the corner. If we have them now, they might still be warm. Let's go to the kitchen to taste them and you can tell me if they're as good as the ones in Paris.'

So kind of Jada to rescue me like that. I didn't think I could have stomached any questions about the non-existent engagement. I was still feeling like a plonker.

The penny appeared to drop with Goldie too and she patted my shoulder sympathetically, like she was trying to console someone who thought they'd won the lottery, then remembered they'd forgotten to buy a ticket.

'Okay.' Relief washed over me. At least now that they both knew nothing happened, hopefully they'd avoid quizzing me. I looked at the clock on the wall. 'It's only 8.47, so there should be enough time to sit and have a coffee before I start at nine.'

'Remember, you don't have to worry about clock-watching, Alex.' Goldie reached for her bright yellow coat and pushed her arms through the sleeves. 'This isn't some sort of bootcamp. We're family here. Our foundations are built on trust. If you need to start a few minutes later to gather your thoughts, no worries. What's important is the work you do. Not how many minutes you sit in the chair.'

It felt good to be valued for a change. I was so used to being constantly monitored, like in my old job.

'Thanks.' I smiled.

'I got a vegan croissant for you, Goldie. Want me to save it?' said Jada.

'Oooh, yes, please! What a treat! I'll have it after I've taken these darlings for their morning walk.' She zipped up her coat and rounded up the troops.

Jada and I came into the kitchen and sat down at the rustic reclaimed wood table. I loved hanging out in here. It was so bright, airy and huge. Almost twice the size of our kitchen at home. It had mint-green cupboards and dark wooden flooring, and the back wall behind the stove was decorated with red, blue and green tiles. Suited Goldie's colourful personality perfectly.

As well as the kitchen, downstairs there was also a living room, playroom and toilet, plus a garden. Upstairs, the bathrooms and bedrooms were spread over two floors and one of the bedrooms had been converted into an office, which was where Jada and I worked.

'Thanks for saving me back there.' I poured coffee into two mugs.

'That's okay.' Jada rolled up the sleeves of her burgundy polo neck jumper. It was quite warm in here. 'I saw the look on your face when Goldie asked about Paris and just put two and two together. Want to talk about it?'

'Do you mind if we don't?' I said gently before taking a bite of my croissant.

'That's cool. I know we don't know each other that well yet, but like Goldie said, this isn't like a normal workplace. We've always wanted anyone working here to feel like they're family. Nice family, though, not the ones you only see once a year and it still feels about as fun as putting your head in a blender.' Sounded like how I felt about my parents. 'So if you ever need to talk…'

'Thanks. Really appreciate it. So…' I sipped on my coffee. Who've we got in today?'

'The new guests from last week, plus Lady Gaga and Casanova.'

'Great!' Casanova was a French bulldog and a regular guest who didn't go anywhere without his 'girlfriend', a cuddly toy called Lulu. Lady Gaga was a Chihuahua who I swore had a bigger wardrobe than me. She cried like a baby if ever she was 'naked'. Her owner, Trixibelle, always insisted she wore a different outfit every day. The hotel was quite literally her catwalk. Her owner often travelled, so Lady Gaga was typically booked in for fortnightly or monthly stints.

As well as Scooby, Flapjack and Princess, who lived here full-time, there were also two cats, Bonnie and Purdey, plus Mr Chilli, a parrot Goldie had recently rescued.

We normally had at least four or five other guests each day. Because we were a small team, as well as doing our own work, Jada and I helped out with feeding, walking and playing with the dogs whenever we could, which I loved. And on weekends when we weren't here or on really busy days, Goldie's friend Viola stepped in to help take care of them.

'Yeah, it's quite a good crew for a Tuesday. Speaking of good, how's the croissant?'

'It's nice, but if I'm honest, not a patch on the ones I had in Paris.'

'Thought you might say that…' Jada winked.

I stepped inside the hallway, put down my umbrella, hung up my coat, then took off my boots. As soon as I'd left the hotel it had started raining, so I was glad to be home.

Today I'd had a productive day at work. We'd confirmed two new bookings for a couple of dogs which came from the Facebook adverts I'd set up.

The main part of my job was raising awareness of the hotel and attracting more customers. So working on new ads, doing social media, updating the website, that kind of thing.

I got to do loads of other stuff too. As well as managing the marketing and helping Goldie with the siblings sometimes, I also answered the phones, handled enquiries and took bookings for extended stays or our doggie day care service. That was what people like Casanova's owner used if they were at work or away for the day and wanted their furry friends to be looked after.

Making client follow-up calls to find out how their dogs had enjoyed their stay was also my responsibility. Those calls were great for requesting testimonials and getting repeat bookings too. I loved that my role was so varied.

Time to think about what we should have for dinner. I went into the kitchen, opened the fridge and looked at the options. I sifted through the stack of ready meals. Thai red chicken curry, fish pie, pasta bake… *Decisions, decisions.* The supermarkets did so many good dishes. Not as tasty as something cooked from scratch, obviously—especially as they put far too much salt in them—but at least zero effort was required. I decided on the family-sized shepherd's pie, peeled off the plastic film and popped it in the oven.

Now that dinner was taken care of and there was about

an hour before Miles got home from work, it was time for my favourite hobby.

I went into the lilac-coloured spare room, opened a storage box in the corner and pulled out my secret wedding planning folder.

Every time I looked at the white cover with pretty blue and orange butterflies, it made me smile. This was my file of dreams.

I'd had it for years. It had originally started as a kind of scrapbook when I was younger. Whenever I spotted a dress or something in a magazine, I used to just rip pages out to use for inspiration. For the day when I'd finally get hitched.

In my twenties, the scrapbook had got bigger and bigger. Those were the years where I was young, naive and optimistic and thought I still had lots of time to find my Mr Right. When I'd hit my thirties and realised that things weren't quite going to plan, I'd packed it away in the loft, because rather than making me happy, it had become a reminder of what I didn't have.

I'd thought I'd be married with kids by then and be happy. But nothing could have been further from the truth. One disappointing relationship followed another. Men came and went like shoppers through a revolving department store door. Fuckboy after fuckboy. How could I even think about planning a wedding when I couldn't even get a man to stay for breakfast?

But then Stacey had introduced me to Laurie Love's book, *Six Months to Love: Seven Sure-Fire Steps to finding the One*, which promised I'd find my Mr Right if I followed her advice—and it had literally changed my life.

I was reluctant at first. After all, one of the steps

involved 'keeping my pussy padlocked for six months', as Laurie delicately put it. I was allowed to date guys, but not sleep with them for half a year. *Six long months*. I thought it would be impossible—I mean, before then, I'd never gone more than a month or two without sex. Plus, I thought there was no way a man would even consider waiting that long to get jiggy. Usually our bedroom gymnastics would happen after a few hours or at most a few days. But then I'd met Miles. And surprisingly, he'd agreed to wait.

A couple of months after we'd done the deed, I'd decided to go into the loft and take the box down again. There *was* hope. There was a chance I might get my happily ever after, after all.

Since then, I'd been building up the folder. Especially after Miles had asked me to move in with him.

I generally took it out when he wasn't here. Miles knew I collected bridal stuff, but he probably didn't realise how much. Because I'd had it for so long, the folder had become pretty huge, so I reckoned it was best to keep it out of sight so he didn't think I was a wedding-obsessed woman or something.

Living together was a positive sign that things were getting serious. Knowing that we were one step closer to making things official, I spent about an hour on it maybe once a week after work, then probably a couple of hours on Saturday afternoons.

I'd stock up on the latest bridal magazines and pore over the pages, dreaming of my big day. Making notes of suppliers and cutting out wedding dress designs before filing them in my folder.

It had dozens of categories. All separated with colour-coded dividers. There were sections for everything—venues, rings, photographers, cakes, flowers, dresses, hair, make-up, invitations, the ceremony, reception, décor, table decorations, honeymoon ideas… *everything*. It all went inside. I liked leafing through the pages. Feeling the paper. It was like flipping through a coffee table book. I found it relaxing.

And of course, I had digital folders too, so I'd save loads of wedding inspo pics to my bridal boards on Instagram and Pinterest.

It had become my new hobby. Back when I was single, I used to spend my evenings watching romcoms or reading romance books. Now I was all coupled up, I was planning my own fairy tale.

Speaking of which, I just realised I hadn't watched *My Fantasy Wedding* for a while. I checked the time. If I worked on my folder in front of the TV, I could squeeze in an episode before Miles got home.

I took the folder into the living room, put it on the comfy charcoal sofa, then sat down. I loved this room. It was one that we'd decorated together after I'd moved in. Before, it just had plain white walls, so I'd suggested we jazz it up a bit by adding a blue feature wall. Blue was my favourite colour and Miles liked it too, so it was perfect.

Like the dining room and hallway, it had dark wooden flooring. I'd also bought some colourful cushions and a couple of paintings, which gave the room a bit more personality. There were still some other bits and pieces we thought we'd like to do to the house, but I was comfortable here. It felt like home.

Cuddles came and curled up beside me. 'Ready to watch some lucky couple get married?' I said, stroking her fur. I took her purring as a yes, picked up the remote, selected the show and pressed play.

The couple in this episode had always dreamt of having a big Disney-style wedding, so they had been given a fifty-thousand-pound budget to make their dream come true. That was the thing I liked about this programme. It gave ordinary people the chance to choose a dress and venue they wouldn't normally be able to afford. *So lucky.*

It isn't all about having a fairy-tale wedding, though, I said to myself as I added a page I'd cut out from a magazine with this season's hottest princess ball gowns to my folder. Yes, that was important. I mean, who hadn't imagined what it would be like to wear a beautiful wedding dress and walk down the aisle? But it was about more than that. For me, marriage meant security. Sharing your hopes and dreams. Having a lifelong partner who'd be by your side, no matter what.

Marriage to me was the ultimate celebration of love. It was a formal declaration of how much you adored another human being and how much they adored you.

After getting zero love from my parents and most of the men I'd dated, marriage was proof that someone loved me enough to make the greatest commitment and make it official.

Yeah. Some people might not understand it. Especially as marriage was less common these days. But I didn't care. It was a personal goal. Something that was important to me. Something I truly valued. And something I'd dreamt about for far too long to just give up on.

CHAPTER FIVE

I took two pizzas out of the freezer and quickly popped them in the oven.

It was Wednesday evening. I'd just got home from work and my cousin Roxy was coming around for dinner.

Roxy was one of just two family members I was in regular contact with. We normally met once a month, and when she'd suggested last week that we see each other this evening, part of me thought it would be perfect timing. Even though she wasn't into lovey-dovey stuff, I was excited about being able to share my big news with her. *Just goes to show that things don't always go according to plan…*

Right on cue, the doorbell rang.

'So where's lover boy, then?' Roxy stepped into the hallway and kissed me on both cheeks. She must have noticed that Miles' coat was missing from the stand. After unzipping her knee-high heeled boots, Roxy straightened her black leather miniskirt, then tossed her fiery red hair over her shoulders.

'Gone to the gym. Miles thought we might want some time to catch up alone, so said he'd leave us to it.'

'*Smart man.*' Roxy followed me into the living room and plonked herself down on the sofa. 'Nice to hear he's not letting himself go. My ex was no Dwayne Johnson when we met, but boy did he pile on the relationship pounds after we got shacked up. His gut had more rolls than a bakery. I probably wasn't any better, though.' She shuddered. Roxy had worked hard to lose weight after her divorce. 'But it was his fault for making me so bloody miserable. The only pleasure I got during that marriage was from the biscuit tin.'

'It's easy to put on weight when you're happy in a relationship too.' I put two glasses on the coffee table and poured a G&T for Roxy, then a glass of rosé for myself. 'When it's cold outside like it has been lately, coming home, eating dinner and curling up on the sofa together is much more appealing than trekking to the gym.' Although I used to do exercise classes two or three times a week, I hadn't been for at least a fortnight.

'But being loved up also means you shouldn't have to go to the gym for a good workout.' She winked, then let out her trademark cackle. *Classic Roxy.* Always a one track mind.

'Yep!' I grinned, thinking about the *exercise sessions* Miles and I had had in Paris. That was definitely one of the highlights of our weekend away.

'And how are things in the nookie department? I know how sex goes downhill once you're living with someone and have to start picking up their smelly socks, listening to their snoring, smelling their eggy farts or hearing them take a dump. It's easy for the attraction to go down the toilet. Excuse the pun!'

Not the best mental image I'd had today. But Roxy was never one to hold back with her graphic descriptions.

'All good on that front. Miles is really tidy, and thankfully he doesn't snore. And he even puts the toilet seat down. It's a miracle!'

Miles did have a bad habit of leaving the lights on in every room he went in, though. Sometimes it felt like the house was lit up more than Harrods at Christmas. But I'd heard of boyfriends with some awful habits, so in the grand scheme of things, it could be a lot worse.

'Bloody Nora! That really *is* a miracle. My ex *never* put the toilet seat down. Not once. And I was constantly cleaning up his piss stains from the bathroom floor. You'd think a grown man would have learnt how to aim his dick so his wee went inside the toilet instead of everywhere else. Mind you, he was useless at doing anything with his cock. Couldn't find my G-spot either!' There went her cackle again.

'Thankfully, Miles located that a long time ago…' I smirked. 'Things are great. In the bedroom, living together, it's just…' I took a sip of my rosé. 'I know you won't understand, but I just wish he'd hurry up and propose already. Make everything official.'

'WTF? You're not *still* obsessed about this whole proposal, getting married bollocks, are you?' Roxy shook her head like a disappointed parent. 'Don't tell me you were expecting Miles to get down on one knee in Paris?'

'It's not bollocks!' I deliberately avoided answering the question.

'I'll take that as a yes, then. *Oh, darling*. The only time you should be happy about a man getting on his knees is to go down on you. *Trust me*. I've been married and it's not all that it's cracked up to be. Actually, that's the understatement of the century. Marriage was hands down the worst experience of my life. Getting divorced and being footloose and fancy-free, on the other hand, was the best. Now I can do whatever and whoever I want, whenever I want. No cleaning up after anyone. No expectations. Just total freedom, happiness and hot sex!'

'You *can* have hot sex when you're in a relationship too, you know.' I rolled my eyes. 'In fact, it's better because there's that bond, that connection. It's more special. I don't want to be footloose and fancy-free. I *want* the fairy tale. Marriage might have been your idea of a nightmare, and being single might work for you, which is fine. But my dating days were awful for me. The stress, the uncertainty, the arseholes. *No, thanks*. There's no way I'd want to go back to that. I'd love to be Miles' wife.'

'Why, though? You've already shacked up with him. What's the point of tying yourself down legally with marriage? Spending all that money on a poncy wedding dress, throwing away thousands on hiring a venue, a massive cake and a shitload of food so a bunch of people you hardly know and probably don't like can come and stuff their faces? All that for a little piece of paper?'

'It's not just a piece of paper!'

I really didn't agree with that argument. Was a degree certificate *just a piece of paper*? Was a driving licence *just a piece of paper* or plastic? *No*. Of course they weren't. A driving licence was a passport to freedom that meant you could go wherever you wanted. A degree certificate was proof that you'd committed to studying something at university for three years or more. It was a celebration of reaching a milestone. It was a big achievement.

Yes, people could get great jobs without a degree. *Yes*, people could get around by using public transport or booking an Uber. *Yes*, people could be in a serious relationship without getting married. But the point was, a marriage certificate was concrete proof that Miles was totally committed to me. It was a tangible representation of our love. That document made things official. And that was what I'd love to have. A formal declaration that Miles and I were committed.

I knew that all marriages weren't perfect. Take my parents, for example. They fought like cat and dog.

An image of my mum throwing a plate of dinner at my dad when she found out he'd cheated on her suddenly flashed into my mind. That wasn't a pretty sight. Not least because the Bolognese sauce had gone everywhere. My brother Nick had had to step in and restrain her before she picked up a knife. So yeah, clearly there were men like my dad who didn't take the whole commitment thing seriously. But despite that, I still believed in marriage. I still believed that getting hitched meant that we'd stick together through thick and thin. That we were in it for the long haul.

'I love you, honey,' added Roxy, 'but you're crazy! Look at the statistics. Even if Miles proposed and you got married, that doesn't mean it will last. Chances are you'll be divorced before you've even managed to pay off the credit card bill. Why not spend that dosh on a nice holiday or put it towards a bigger house or, I dunno… *anything* except a bloody wedding! You might as well get a pile of money and throw it down the drain.'

I didn't know why I even bothered having this conversation with Roxy. She clearly thought that a wedding was some sort of dark magic ritual where a loving relationship was suddenly transformed into a destructive one.

Roxy was against any form of commitment. Her experiences with her controlling ex-husband had scarred her for life. She'd got divorced just before her fortieth birthday, and four years on, she was still loving being footloose and fancy-free. Staying with the same guy for more than a couple of months was enough to make her run for the hills. So the thought of getting married again was about as appealing as a fifty-year prison sentence.

'I disagree. It was your horrible husband and your relationship that was the problem—you can't blame marriage. I *love* living with Miles. I *love* being in a couple. I *love* the idea of being husband and wife. Having that partnership and feeling like I'm part of a team. The fact that we get to face challenges together. Miles is *the one*, and I know I want to spend the rest of my life with him.'

'Each to their own.' Roxy shrugged her shoulders, realising we were never going to agree. 'Well, if you're convinced he's your Mr Right and you want to go ahead with all this fairy-tale crap, then what's stopping you? Just get hitched and be done with it!'

'I'd love to, but…' I stopped myself. If I told Roxy I was waiting for him to propose, she'd think I was weak. A disgrace to feminists worldwide.

'Oh, let me guess: because you're waiting for *him* to do it!' She rolled her eyes.

Busted.

'Well, yeah.' I bowed my head.

'JFC! Jesus fucking Christ. Get with the programme,

Alex. It's the twenty-first century. If you want something that badly, you don't have to wait for the man to pop the question. Take control and do it yourself. This isn't one of your silly romcoms or a Disney movie. Women do it a lot more these days. You don't want to hang around for ten years hoping he'll pull his finger out. The sooner you get married, the sooner you can move on if it doesn't work out.'

How romantic.

She had a point about the waiting bit, though. Reminded me of poor Jolene.

'It *will* work out.'

'That's what *every* wannabe bride thinks! It's not like anyone gets engaged thinking, *Yay, I'm going to spend thirty grand on getting married and then after three years of bickering and not being able to pay the bills, we'll hate each other's guts and get divorced*! Everyone thinks they'll be different. That *their* relationship will go the distance. Look, I know you think I'm being a Debbie Downer about the whole marriage malarkey, but I'm just trying to be a realist. You're my cousin and I love you. I don't want you to go through the same crap that I did.'

'My relationship with Miles is nothing like the one you had. Miles is kind, loving and considerate. The man waited six months to sleep with me, for God's sake. That speaks volumes.'

'*True*. Still don't know how either of you pulled that off, but if he did keep his dick in his pants the whole time, then *kudos*. Anyway, do whatever you think's best, darling. Just trying to look out for you, that's all. Think about what I said, though. What's the point of torturing yourself every time you go out to dinner or on a weekend away, wondering if he'll propose when you can quite easily do it yourself? Yeah, his friends will probably take the piss out of him for the rest of his life and he'll feel completely emasculated, but he'll get over it. Things are changing. We want equal rights at home and in the workplace, so why shouldn't a woman be able to propose to a man?'

She was right, of course, but that wasn't what I wanted. Yeah, some people might condemn me for it, but I liked the tradition of a man proposing. The getting down on one knee. The whole shebang. I'd dreamt of it. As far as I was concerned, wanting that didn't make me any less of a feminist. Women still had the power to accept or decline the proposal. I could believe in equality and appreciate traditional values at the same time.

'I'm not saying a woman shouldn't. It's just I'd like *him* to propose to *me*. There's nothing wrong with that.'

'Like I said, whatever floats your boat, darling. But if that's what you want, you need to put a time limit on things. Give him an ultimatum or something to give him a kick up the arse. Otherwise before you know it, you'll be forty and still waiting to get married and have kids. It can happen, of course. I've got friends that have popped out sprogs at that age, but the reality is that it's harder the older you get. So if all that domestic ball and chain, husband with 2.4 kids bollocks is what you want, you have to get the ball rolling. *Pronto*.'

If only.

I wished I could take action. Wave some sort of magic wand to make it happen quickly, but an ultimatum was too strong. Miles was the best thing that had ever happened to me. I didn't want to chase him away.

As much as I disagreed with Roxy's views on marriage

and preferred Miles to propose rather than doing it myself, I did at least agree that maybe I should start thinking about doing *something*.

I didn't know what exactly, yet. But I was sure if I thought about it long and hard enough, the answer would come to me.

CHAPTER SIX

Hard to believe it was Thursday night already. This week was flying by.

I'd had another great day at work. I'd spent most of the afternoon going through pics of the siblings and uploading them to the website, which was fun. When I'd first arrived, Goldie and Jada had had a website, but it was pretty basic and they hardly had any images. I'd suggested we get it completely redesigned, and thankfully, they'd agreed.

I'd booked a professional photographer to come and take photos of our furry friends in different settings and scenarios around the hotel. So some of them chilling on the sofa, eating, playing in the garden—that kind of thing.

I also thought it was important to show more photos of the team interacting with the guests. Dogs were more than just pets to their owners. They were family. So it was understandable that they'd want to know who would be looking after their fur babies. We needed to reassure them that they would be in safe hands. So I asked the photographer to include a few snaps of the siblings sleeping by our feet or curled up on our laps or snuggled up beside us. We got some good shots of Goldie giving them pampering treatments too.

Getting that website up and running had been one of my most satisfying projects so far and it was going well. But I needed to find a way to do better. Bring in more customers. I knew the business wasn't earning as much as it should be, and Goldie needed some extra cash to invest, so I really wanted to help her make that happen.

It was time to switch off from work stuff now, though. Tonight, I was meeting Miles for a work drinks thing. To be honest, I'd rather we just curl up together on the sofa with Cuddles. But Sandeep, one of Miles' colleagues, was celebrating his birthday, so a group of them were going to the pub and partners were invited too.

When I arrived at the pub, I looked around, but there was no sign of Miles. This place was a pretty traditional British pub, with a wooden bar, tables and chairs, burgundy-and-white checked carpet and matching walls. Standard stuff. It was right near the hospital, so Miles and his colleagues often met here.

I smiled at a few people I recognised. Might as well get myself a drink whilst I was waiting.

'Glass of rosé, please.' The man behind the bar nodded and swiftly poured the wine. I sat down on the stool and took out my phone to keep me company.

Actually, I should message Karen. Get the goss on how her new romance was blossoming.

Me

Hey you! How'd the audition go? And how's things with the new man? Xxx

. . .

Karen, who'd been my best friend since we were teenagers, had moved to LA almost two and a half years ago to pursue a career as an actress. She'd had a few small parts. Nothing major, yet, but she seemed to be making a lot of new connections, and apparently in Hollywood it was all about who you knew, so that was good.

A few of those connections had been romantic too. And she'd recently started dating a director. In her last text, when we were in Paris, she'd said things were going really well. She was due to call me the next day to elaborate, but I hadn't heard back from her, which in a way was a relief. I'd also told her that I thought Miles was going to propose in Paris, so I wasn't in a hurry to share the news that he hadn't. Karen wasn't always good at calling. Especially since she'd moved. But I understood that with the time difference and everything, it was tricky to find a time for us both to talk.

Same with Nick. He was living in Australia with his wife and kids. Still couldn't believe my brother had three and I hadn't even popped out one yet. Well, at thirty-eight he was a couple years older than me, so I supposed it would balance out by the time I was his age. I hoped so anyway. That was the kind of thing I told myself whenever I felt like I was being left behind everyone else in life.

Me

Nicky!

How's it going? Should we video call soon? I miss your face. Let me know when's good. Tell Cate and the kids I said hi! Xxx

. . .

I scanned the pub again. Nope. Miles wasn't here yet. It wasn't too loud in here right now, so I'd give Audrey, my seventy-nine-year-old ex-neighbour, a quick call.

I used to see her at least a couple of evenings a week, but since I'd rented out my house and moved in with Miles, I saw her about once a month. She wasn't one for text messages, so calling was best.

I dialled her number.

Ringing.

Ringing.

Answerphone.

Hi, Audrey, Alex here. Just thought I'd say hi and see how you're doing. Would be great to catch up soon. Call me when you can. Bye.

Oh well. What to do next?

I clicked on Instagram, then scrolled through my feed.

Wow, I said to myself as my eyes fixated on a post from one of the bridal stores I followed. *Look at that dress.* It was *gorgeous*. I zoomed in to take a closer look. It was a stunning big princess gown with a sweetheart neckline. That was *definitely* getting saved.

I clicked on the bookmark icon under the pic, then saved it in the Wedding Dresses Inspiration collection I'd created.

Just as I was scrolling through the images, mentally oohing and aahing at their beauty, someone came up behind me and tapped my shoulder.

'Alex!'

'Oh, hi, Tabitha, how are you?' Tabitha was a surgeon at the hospital and married to one of Miles' colleagues slash friends, Humphrey.

'Oh my God! So did it happen, then? In Paris? When's the wedding? Did Miles propose?'

Bloody hell. I'd forgotten that I'd told her too. *Me and my mouth.* Looking at wedding dress photos in public probably didn't help. She must have seen my screen.

In my defence, the reason I'd mentioned our trip was because the last time we'd met, she'd asked me exactly the same question: *When's the wedding?* And because I hadn't known what to say, I'd blurted out that we were going to Paris soon, so you know, maybe it *could* happen.

Ugh.

I hated when people asked me when the big day would be, like I wasn't already agonising over a proposal.

Initially, I hadn't minded as much because I was always thinking, *Any day now. Any day now, he'll propose.* But as more time passed and my chances of getting engaged started to feel more elusive than receiving an invite to have afternoon tea with the queen, being asked *When's the wedding?* Felt like someone stabbing me in the heart with a pair of rusty scissors. And even though I'd been asked whether he'd popped the question dozens of times, I still struggled to find the perfect response.

I mean, obviously the honest answer was *No, he hasn't, and I have no idea when he will.*

And man, I would *love* to say:

By the way, you asking when we're getting married actually makes me feel really shitty, so kindly mind your own business and if it happens sometime this century, I'll be sure to let you know.

But of course, that would have been rude, so I couldn't. Instead I had to do what I was doing now. Grit my teeth and smile sweetly.

'Not yet, but we had an *amazing* time in Paris!' My voice was so high-pitched all the cats in London could probably hear me. 'Have you ever been?'

'Paris? *Of course!* Humphrey has taken me there several times. It's the *perfect* city for a proposal. I mean, Humphrey proposed to me in New York, in Central Park, which was incredible. We had a horse and carriage and everything. *So romantic.* But if he hadn't done it there, I would have *loved* a proposal in Paris.' *You and me both, love.*

'Oh, hi, Jilly! Come and join us!' Jilly was Miles' colleague Benedict's wife. She spotted Tabitha and came rushing over. They threw their arms around each other and Jilly greeted me with two cheek kisses.

'Hi, Jilly,' I said. 'How are you? How are the kids?' Jilly had three children under the age of six, including a two-year-old, and was always marvelling about the new things they all did or said. Last time she'd told me that, since she started potty-training her daughter, every time Jilly went to the loo, her little one would cheer, clap and say, 'You weed on the potty, Mummy! *Good girl!*' That made me chuckle. Talking about their latest antics should fill up at least twenty minutes of conversation and avoid any more Paris proposal talk until Miles came to save me from what I was increasingly worried might turn into an engagement inquisition.

'They're great, thanks. My parents have got them, so tonight Mummy can get drunk—*woohoo!*'

'Which is *exactly* why we won't be spending the whole night talking about our children!' said Tabitha.

'Cheers to that!' Jilly clinked her glass against Tabitha's.

'So Alex and I were just talking about getting engaged!'

'Oh yeah! You went to Paris at the weekend, didn't you? So did Miles pop the question? It's about bloody time he put a ring on it! Have you set a date yet? When's the wedding?'

Dear God. Here we go again.

Deep breath. Deep breath.

You'd think that because almost a whole working week had passed since we went, they would have forgotten all about our trip. Surely they'd realise that if we *had* got engaged, they would have heard about it from Miles or their own husbands by now? Then again, a lot of Miles' colleagues were men, and so as sexist as it might sound, something told me that going home after work and gushing about our romantic weekend away probably wasn't at the top of their to-do lists.

'No! Not yet.' By now my smile was so forced, I was sure my face was about to shatter like a pane of broken glass.

'When are you thinking of, though? A spring wedding? Getting hitched in summer means the photos will be *gorgeous*. Or winter! Yes! Winter weddings are *so* romantic! Benedict and I got married in December and it was lovely. Bloody freezing, mind you, but I'd rather be cold than have sweat patches and look all shiny in the wedding photos. I suppose it all depends on the venue. Do you have somewhere in mind yet?'

Oh God.

When I'd said 'no, not yet', Jilly had clearly thought that I was talking about setting a date rather than the fact that Miles hadn't proposed at all. Talk about awkward.

'No, I mean, we're not engaged. *Yet…*,' I added hopefully.

'Oh…' Jilly's eyes widened as she realised she'd put her foot in it. 'Oh well, I'm sure it'll happen soon. I mean, I had to wait six months for Benedict to pull his finger out and propose. How long have you been together?'

'Two years.'

'Oh…well, still early-ish days, I suppose, although we were already married with a baby by that time. At our age, people get engaged faster, don't they? Nothing like the realisation of middle age to push you into action and get stuff done. Only feels like yesterday that I was in my twenties, and now I'm forty-three. *Goodness*. Before you know it we'll be collecting our pensions. And I'm sure you don't want to be struggling down the aisle with a walking stick or Zimmer frame!' She threw her head back, laughing so hard you'd think she had front-row seats at a comedy show.

'I think I've got a few more years before I collect my pension,' I snapped. What was wrong with her? I was thirty-six—barely in my mid-thirties. Not a teenager, granted. But talk about exaggerating. Especially that stupid comment about Zimmer frames. Not many people needed them in their sixties.

Anyway, there was no way Miles would make me wait decades before he proposed. At least I hoped not…

'Of course you still have time,' Tabitha added. 'I'm sure it'll happen. One day. If you like, I can ask Humphrey to have a quick word with Miles later? Or maybe we can drop some hints tonight, to hurry things along a bit for you?'

Hmmm... *Now we're talking.* Although it would look

desperate if I asked Miles myself, if it came from someone neutral, that couldn't hurt…

'Talk of the devil!' said Jilly. I looked at the door and saw Miles approaching with a group of colleagues.

'Hey!' Miles planted a kiss on my lips and I instantly felt lighter. 'Sorry, we got held up.'

'No worries,' I said as Tabitha and Jilly's husbands also joined us. Both men kissed their wives on the cheek. Two minutes ago I would've been so happy for Miles to rescue me from the awkward conversation. But now Tabitha was going to see if they could give him a gentle nudge, I was feeling a lot more positive.

'So, Miles!' Tabitha clapped her hands together like she had important business to discuss. 'Alex was just telling us all about Paris…' Ooh, she didn't hang about. *Nice one.* Straight in there.

'It was great,' said Miles, 'It was so—'

'Miles!' shouted Sandeep from across the bar. 'Could you give me a hand with the drinks, mate?'

'Sure.'

Dammit. Just as they were about to quiz him.

Miles headed to the other side of the bar and started passing several pint and wine glasses round to his colleagues.

After that, everyone mingled with others in the group. Jilly and Tabitha were in a deep conversation with some other wives for most of the night, so they never got around to speaking to Miles. Although they didn't bring up the proposal again, when Miles was chatting to his boss, two other women I spoke to later did. And I definitely hadn't mentioned it to them.

It wasn't just because we'd come back from Paris.

Whenever there was a social gathering, this always seemed to happen. Someone would always mention the 'm' word. People couldn't help themselves, and I hated the awkwardness of it all. If I wasn't bothered about getting married, then maybe I wouldn't find it so frustrating. I could just brush it off. But I couldn't.

My stomach sank. I didn't think I could bear another two years of being asked when we were going to tie the knot.

My conversations with Roxy and Stacey swirled around my head. Surely there must be a way to speed up the proposal process, gently, without driving Miles away.

Maybe Tabitha was onto something with the hinting idea. I could ask Roxy to mention something to Miles. Then again, she had zero filter, so she'd go too far.

Hmmm, who else could do it? If she didn't get around to it tonight, I could ask Tabitha at the next work gathering. There was bound to be another one before Christmas.

In the meantime, I'd ask Miles if he wanted to watch one of my bridal shows with me one Sunday instead of a romcom. Just something subtle like that. Nothing too crazy or demanding.

That way, I'd kind of still be waiting patiently like Stacey recommended, but by dropping an occasional, very subtle hint every now and again, I'd be taking on board Roxy's advice about doing something too. Sounded like a good compromise.

Yes.

Taking a softly, softly approach with a few light suggestions could still get the job done.

At last I'd found the perfect solution.

CHAPTER SEVEN

I *loved this.*

Afternoon walks on Clapham Common with the dogs. Although it was a bit chilly, it still felt so good to be out in the fresh air rather than cooped up in a stuffy office like in my old job.

I definitely had that Friday feeling. I was in a brilliant mood. This morning Goldie and Jada had approved my idea to run a competition to find the Happy Dog Hotel Hero Dog of the Year. Yay!

I was so lucky that they were open to my suggestions and gave me a lot of autonomy. So far, the ideas I had implemented, like the website and advertising on social media, had been working. But I knew I needed to do more to get new customers. Especially if the company was going to invest in opening another site next year.

I'd always loved animals, but working here had really shown me what dogs meant to their humans and how much they enriched their lives. That got me thinking. I reckoned there had to be loads of them in the area who'd done amazing things. Guide dogs, therapy dogs, ones who'd helped their owners through tough times—all sorts.

So I thought it would be cool for us to shine a spotlight on them by running a competition. As well as giving the animals and their owners recognition, it would also raise awareness of the hotel and help spread the word in the community.

I still had some details to finalise, but I was thinking that the winner's prize could be a one-week complimentary stay at the hotel, plus a £200 donation to their chosen dog charity. We could then have a weekend stay as second prize and doggie day care for the third winner.

It'd be good to give them trophies, a certificate and a doggy bag of treats too, and all entrants could get ten percent off services at the hotel.

Roxy had put me in contact with her friend Sophia, who was a PR guru. When I spoke to her on the phone at lunchtime to get some advice, she suggested getting the local media involved and having a local celebrity dog owner as one of the judges, which was an excellent idea. I had a good feeling about the whole thing. Just thinking about it gave me goosebumps. It was so exciting.

My new role really was a dream. Yes, I was earning less than before, but I was confident that would change if I kept bringing in more business. Plus, because it was still local, I was saving a shedload of money. No commuting into central London and paying to get the tube every day. It was just a thirty-five-minute walk to the office, which meant an extra half an hour in bed in the morning. And I got to take cuties like these out every day. Still couldn't get my head around the fact that hanging out with them was considered *work*. Definitely another perk of the job.

Goldie took all of the siblings out for a walk in the mornings (how she managed to keep several dogs together without breaking a sweat was a miracle). Then Jada and I would take turns to bring the younger ones out again in the afternoons. Today I had Scooby, Flapjack and Princess. I could handle three siblings. *Just.*

Goldie had trained her dogs really well and they were used to me, so letting Scooby and Flapjack off their leads was fine, but as a rule, although they were able to run around unleashed in the hotel's garden, we never let any guests do the same on Clapham Common unless we had the owner's written permission. The Common was an open park surrounded by busy roads. And because there weren't any big gates or fences, we had to be extra careful.

That was one of the reasons why Goldie was so keen to do up the place she owned in Surrey as a new site for the hotel. I hadn't seen it myself yet, but apparently it was a big farmhouse, with loads of outdoor space for them to run freely. It sounded perfect.

Flapjack and Scooby zoomed ahead. Princess and I followed them and found Flapjack playing with what looked like a glove someone had dropped and Scooby sitting obediently at the feet of two men drinking beer on the park bench, wagging his tail.

Aha.

I spotted a packet of opened crisps beside them. That was what Scooby was after. Always thinking about filling his stomach, that one. As I got closer, I saw the man frowning at his friend.

'How strong is this beer? I might be dreaming, but I could have sworn that dog was just smiling at me…' He rubbed his eyes. I guess it wasn't every day you saw a dog with a grin that was bigger than the Joker's.

'Come on, Scooby. You too, Flapjack. Time to go home.' I put their leads back on and started walking back to the hotel.

I felt my phone vibrating. I tied the leads tighter around my hand and picked my phone out of my pocket with the other.

It was Karen. After I'd messaged her last night, she'd replied to say she was just about to go out on date number seven with her new man. Things seemed to be hotting up.

I reckoned it was around seven in the morning in LA right now. And Karen was video-calling, so they must have had fun. Maybe she was just on her way back home… I was excited to hear how it all went. I answered the call.

'Good morning, dirty little stop-out!' I laughed.

'Hey!' She tossed her long blond hair over her shoulder. I still wasn't used to it being that colour. Karen had naturally dark hair, but had started dying it when she'd moved to LA. Must cost a fortune to maintain.

'Are you still at lover boy's fancy house?' She was sitting outside on a sprawling balcony with the beach behind her, and I could see the waves crashing in the distance. Definitely a step up from the views in Clapham Common.

'I am!' She grinned like a Cheshire cat.

'So your date went well, then?'

'More than well!' she screeched.

'Where did you go?'

'Well, first he took me for a late lunch at Gigi's, which is like *the* hottest restaurant in town. It takes like months to get a reservation, unless you're connected or a mega star like Kimmy K or Kylie.'

'Is Kylie big in the States too? I remember how much you used to love her music.'

'Not *that* Kylie, silly!' Karen snapped. '*The* Kylie. Kylie Jenner. As in, sister of Kimmy K—Kim Kardashian?'

'Oh... right. Sorry.' I'd heard of Kim, but I couldn't remember the names of all the others. I clearly hadn't been *keeping up with the Kardashians*.

'Anyway, as I was saying, so we went to Gigi's and had the most delicious meal. You know, champagne, oysters—the works. It was like—*A-MAZING*! Next thing I knew, he took me for a helicopter ride. You know, like in an *actual* helicopter he'd chartered just for us. So after a while, he tells me to look down and on a beach and there it was! Written in the sand. And then, and then it happened!! It happened, Alex!' She jumped up and down.

'What happened?'

'*This!*' She shoved her left hand in front of the screen. 'THIS!! *Will You Marry Me?* was written in the sand. He proposed! We're engaged!! I'm getting married!'

OMFG.

My mouth fell to the ground. I managed to catch the phone before that fell too. As if sensing my shock, Scooby barked loudly. If he hadn't brought me back to my senses, I probably would have dropped all of the leads as well.

Pretty sure that Karen had just said she was engaged.

That she was getting married.

To the man she'd been on seven dates with.

Seven.

As in the number after six.

Not seven dates over a long period of time either. Seven dates over what? A month? Six weeks? Probably not even that.

She cannot be serious.

I'd been dating Miles for two years and nothing. And Karen met a guy and was engaged less than six weeks later.

Six weeks!

What the hell was going on?

Why, God? *Why*?

Karen posted *constantly* on social media. At least four times a day. Now she was engaged, she'd be doubling down on posts. I could see it now. The trips to jewellers, venues, wedding shops… it would all be documented. Her wedding joy would also become a constant reminder of Miles' non-existent proposal, which was bound to make me feel like shit.

Now what was I supposed to do? I couldn't mute or unfollow my best friend. I always commented and liked every post. *Always.* So there was no way I could stop showing them love. That would really upset her. She lived for those likes and it was all part of her profile building in Hollywood.

Christ almighty.

No. This was wrong. I was being a bad friend. Selfish. I was thinking about myself.

I must not be jealous. I need to be happy for her.

That's right. Think happy thoughts. Happy thoughts… happy thoughts…

'That's…' Too soon. Crazy. Ridiculous. *Nope. Come on, Alex. Happy thoughts… happy thoughts…* Take two:

'That's *amazing*!' *Keep it going*… 'I'm soooo happy for you, Karen! I can't believe it!'

That was definitely true. I really couldn't.

'I know! I mean, I had no idea he was going to propose! You'd think after being proposed to so many times, I would have had some kind of inkling, but this time, *nothing*. Not a clue! It was brilliant. So romantic. Just perfect!'

Talk about twisting the knife in.

Yes. It was true. This was probably Karen's fourth or fifth proposal. I'd lost count. There was Ricky when she was twenty-one. She'd turned him down. I think because she didn't like the way he chewed. Then Sylvester. I can't remember the other guy's name, but this was definitely the second one she'd had since she'd been in LA. And she only went there a couple of years ago.

The last guy I thought was a keeper, but she broke the engagement off after he decided to leave the film industry and go on a voyage of self-discovery in Asia and wanted Karen to come with him. Not a chance. Karen was determined to make it big in LA and wasn't going to give up on her dream for anyone. Looked like it had paid off. Her career was gaining momentum, and now she'd bagged herself a fiancé too.

How come Karen picked up proposals like Ed Sheeran collected number ones, and in my thirty-six years on this earth, I hadn't managed to rack up any?

'I'm glad for you. It really does sound romantic! And *so… so* … unexpected. I don't mean to be a party pooper or anything, but don't you think it's a bit quick?'

It was a reasonable question to ask. My mind flashed back to when I dated that awful guy Luke who'd spoken about getting married on the first date. He often referred to me as his wife and I thought he was serious, so fell for it hook, line and sinker. *Silly me*. All he wanted to do was get in my knickers and add me as another notch on his bedpost. I wouldn't want Karen to get hurt like that. Although, seeing as they'd already slept together, it couldn't be that. Maybe this *was* the real deal after all…

'It *is* soon and I wasn't expecting a proposal so quickly. What can I say?' She shrugged her shoulders. 'I just must be the kind of woman that men see as wife material or something and just *have* to propose to.'

Ouch.

Now I felt like Tyson had just punched me in the gut.

'Yeah…'

'When you know, Alex, you just know. Chuck isn't one of these dithery types that *says* he wants to get married but then just dates you forever without committing properly. He's a go-getter. If he sees something he wants, he goes for it. He knows I'm a catch and said he wanted to prove how devoted he is to me by putting a ring on it ASAP before some other lucky guy snapped me up. Isn't it just *awesome*?!'

Battered and bruised, my poor stomach sank like the *Titanic*. Maybe I was being overly sensitive, but it sounded as though she was making a dig. Like she was implying that Miles was just stringing me along. *Not cool.*

'It is…,' I managed to reply.

'Oh yeah.' Karen put her hand over her mouth. 'How about you? Did Miles propose in Paris?'

'Um… no…' I winced.

'*Awww. Poor Alex*. Sounds like you need to light a fire under his arse. Don't just hang around. Anyway, hon'—

she leapt up from her seat, all smiles again—'better run! I've gotta go through the pics the photographer took last night so I can post the announcement on Insta and my website before lunchtime.'

Of course she does.

'Oh, right, yeah. Nice.' I couldn't think of anything else to say. I was still trying to wrap my head around it all.

'This is going to be *brilliant* for my profile. Might be time to start thinking of hiring a publicist to get us a massive feature in one of the glossy magazines about the engagement. I'm sure *everyone* will want to hear about it. Chuck is a big deal over here. Could even lead to some bridal companies reaching out and asking me to do some sponsored Instagram wedding posts. Or they might ask me to be the face of their brand! So exciting!'

'Yeah!' I tried to mirror her enthusiasm.

Karen started waving and blowing kisses—obviously with her left hand rather than her right, so I could get another good look at the giant diamond on her finger. 'Talk soon, honey!'

'Congrats again!' I replied just before she hung up. I dragged myself over to a nearby bench and plonked myself down.

Scooby, Flapjack and Princess gathered around my feet and looked up at me. Scooby rubbed his face against my leg and whimpered. Princess jumped up on my lap and started licking my hand. It was as if they all knew I was upset and were trying to console me.

'I'm okay, guys. I'll be fine.' Flapjack barked as if to say, *Yeah, right. Whatever.*

There was no hiding from them.

Of course, I wasn't okay. I was crushed. Jealous. And

ashamed of myself for letting the green-eyed monster dominate my thoughts. But I couldn't help it. It was how I felt.

Why couldn't it be *me* who was getting engaged? When would it be me? When was my wedding going to happen? When would *I* get to say *I do*?

Karen didn't have to worry about how long she'd have to wait for her man to put a ring on it. Proposals just fell right into her hands. Unlike me, she clearly was doing stuff that made men see her as wife material. If only Miles thought of me in the same way.

Maybe she was right. Maybe Miles *was* just stringing me along. If he *was* serious about our relationship, if he really believed I was a catch, then like Chuck, he'd propose. But he hadn't.

Although I wanted to believe otherwise, I couldn't help but wonder whether Miles was totally committed to me after all.

CHAPTER EIGHT

I walked the dogs back to the office in a trance. It still hadn't sunk in.

I tried to do some work, but I couldn't focus.

'You okay, Alex?' Jada frowned.

'Yeah, just got a bit of a headache.'

More like *heartache*.

'I've got some paracetamol if you need it?'

'Thanks, I should be okay. I'll just go and make a cup of tea. Fancy one?'

'Nah, I'm good.'

I got up and headed down to the kitchen. Just as the kettle boiled, my phone pinged. Then pinged again. And again.

I had a feeling I knew what the notifications were and that I shouldn't look, but it was like the phone was a magnet and my hand was suddenly made of metal. Before I could stop myself, I'd reached into my pocket and unlocked the screen and was glaring at Instagram.

There they were.

A series of back-to-back proposal posts from Karen.

The first one included at least half a dozen photos. There was a picture of her gasping as Chuck proposed, one of him sliding the ring on her finger, followed by another with her arms draped around his neck (of course with the lens zoomed in on her left hand).

There were also beach shots: one with *Will You Marry Me?* and another with *She Said Yes* written in the sand with the beautiful sunset behind them.

I slumped onto the kitchen bench before my legs gave way.

Karen was beaming. *Of course* she was over the moon. This was a wonderful thing. I was happy for her. I *was*. I was just gutted for me.

I couldn't help it. I'd spent practically my whole life dreaming of experiencing that moment. And *boom*. Karen gets a proposal faster than you can say *engagement*. I knew life wasn't fair, but that really took the cake.

I sighed, plucked a tea bag from the jar, popped it into a mug and poured hot water over it.

My phone pinged again. I looked down at the screen. Another post from Karen. This time, boomerang videos in her stories showing her flashing her ring and Chuck dropping down on one knee. If this was day one, God only knew what the next how many days and months were going to be like as the countdown to them getting married continued.

One word sprung to mind: torture.

It was funny. Not funny, *haha*, funny as in weird. I followed loads of strangers and random brides-to-be on Instagram and watched their bridal plans unfold all the time. And although seeing the build-up to their wedding niggled sometimes because I wished it was me, I was able to handle it. I'd save their posts for inspiration and mostly just got on with my day.

Yet even though her proposal had only just happened, I could already tell that watching Karen's fairy-tale wedding come to life was going to be hard. Maybe it was because it was happening to someone close to me. Somehow that made it more real. I felt more wounded emotionally. Like someone with a ten-carat diamond ring had slapped me across the face.

I took the tea back up to the office. As hard as it would be, I had to try and get some work done. At least that would take my mind off things.

Thankfully, the last couple of hours of work had flown by. I was now walking home and after giving myself a good talking-to (which unsurprisingly attracted some concerned looks from passers-by who thought I'd completely lost my marbles), I decided two things: firstly, Karen was one of my best friends, so no matter how much it hurt, I would be happy for her and support her. I wouldn't let the green-eyed monster and my own failure to get engaged ruin our friendship.

And secondly, despite what Karen tried to imply, I knew Miles was *the one* and that he loved me. I believed he *was* interested in marriage, but for whatever reason, he was taking his time to propose. So like Roxy and Karen had suggested, it was up to me to give him a bit of a nudge. Help make things happen.

I know Stacey recommended being patient, but I'd tried and it wasn't working. It was too passive.

The more I thought about it, the more I realised I couldn't just wait for a proposal to drop into my lap. That was like saying I wanted to get in shape but sitting on the sofa eating pizza all day and expecting the pounds to magically fall off my hips. Or saying I wanted to run a marathon but never even attempting to jog fifty metres to the end of the road. There was no point just talking about what you wanted in life. The actions had to follow the words.

I'd wasted too many years waiting to find *the one*. It was only when I'd followed a plan and stuck to it that I was rewarded with my Mr Right. Otherwise Miles and I might never have met.

The Six Months to Love challenge was about being proactive. Yes, patience was involved when it came to having sex, but otherwise it was about controlling your destiny. Whilst I was happy with my relationship now, securing a proposal would be a good investment in our long-term happiness.

Although Miles had said we'd get engaged *soon* and it sounded promising, it wasn't concrete enough. I needed to speed up the process. Find a way to encourage him to formalise our relationship. Then I could finally begin putting everything from my planning folder into action and get going on the organisation of my dream wedding, and Miles and I could start the rest of our lives together. *Properly*.

I couldn't waste another moment. If I really wanted a husband and babies, I had to take things into my own hands. Create a plan and follow it. Just like I had before.

Then I could finally have the proposal and family life I'd always dreamed of.

Not *sometime in the near future*.

Not *soon*.

Once I'd decided on the best plan of action, I was sure our engagement would happen *fast*.

CHAPTER NINE

This was perfect. I had the place to myself for the whole afternoon. Miles had gone to play tennis at a special indoor club with his friend Todd, which had given me plenty of time to work on 'Operation Proposal'. I could probably think of a snappier title, but that would do for now.

As soon as Miles was out the door, I'd put on my fluffy pink dressing gown, made myself a big mug of hot chocolate and snuggled up on the sofa with Cuddles, a blanket and my iPad, ready to take action.

Unlike before with Laurie Love's book, I didn't have a pre-made plan to follow, so I needed to create my own.

I'd started doing my homework as soon as I'd got home last night. I looked online and flicked through multiple bridal magazines, hunting for advice on how to get your boyfriend to propose quickly.

After pulling together yesterday's research and spending a few hours on it this afternoon, I finally felt like I had some direction.

There wasn't one complete approach that I agreed with, so I decided that instead of following the experts' advice to the letter, I'd cherry-pick the best information and interpret it in my own way. After all, every couple was different, so it made sense to personalise the advice to my own situation. I wasn't a robot. Just because they were experts, I didn't have to follow *everything* they said.

A lot of the tips were contradictory. Be his partner in all things… but also give him space. Do everything together… but also go away alone or with your friends so he can imagine you on a beach flirting with lots of men. *Crazy.*

That wasn't the worst of it, though. Some of the advice was *so* bad. For example, in one of the articles, it said if your boyfriend was dragging his feet, you needed to make him realise what he was missing, then he'd rush to propose. They suggested you could do this by starting to date other guys to show him that you had options. But that was taking things *way* too far. *Of course* I wasn't going to do something stupid like that.

Other features said to bag yourself a husband, you needed to 'look hot at all times'. You know, sexy clothes, always made up to the nines, never a hair out of place, twenty-four-seven. But I didn't believe in doing that either. My days of having long hair extensions, always wearing short skirts and heels and piling on the slap every day were over. Miles had seen me *au naturel* loads of times. I was confident that he liked the way I looked and didn't expect me to be immaculate like some of the guys I'd dated.

No. Not all advice was good, so this was going to be a tailor-made and logical strategy. Rather than some complicated seven- or ten-point plan, mine was going to be nice and simple.

I'd worked out that everything useful could be summarised in three easy steps. If I wanted Miles to commit to me properly by proposing, I just needed to follow the Three C's and a ring would be mine. First up was…

1) Convince: I needed to show Miles that I was wife material and that asking me to tie the knot with him would be a smart move. Clearly Karen and Stacey had some inbuilt *marry me* magnet that I sadly hadn't been blessed with, so it just meant I had to put in a little extra work. You know, by demonstrating how *wonderful* it would be to live with me. *Forever.*

So that meant no nagging (everyone knows how much men hate that), keeping the place tidy and having a nice home-cooked meal ready for him when he got home.

And *no*. That absolutely did *not* mean I wanted to become a passive Stepford housewife. I wasn't talking about having a feather duster surgically attached to my arm or slaving away ironing Miles' boxer shorts and socks. I just meant not complaining about him always leaving the lights on like I knew I was guilty of, being more attentive and cooking nice meals. That sort of thing.

Note to self that when I say *cooking*, I meant *proper* food. Making meals from scratch. Because my new job was local and I didn't have a long commute anymore, I got home an hour before Miles did, so I already took care of dinner during the week. It made sense. But I'd become a bit complacent.

When I'd looked in the fridge and freezer earlier, it had been stacked full of pizzas and ready meals. Apart from the breakfast I'd made on Monday, I couldn't remember us having anything fresh the whole week. I bet that wasn't how Miles had grown up with his adoptive parents, Ron and Mary.

Look how happy he was when I made a little bit of effort with the smoked salmon, eggs and stuff. Imagine if I could make him feel like that every day. I mean, he was hardly going to be in a hurry to propose if he thought we'd be existing on fish fingers and chips for the rest of our lives. No. I could do better.

Anyway, there was nothing wrong with trying to take pride in our house and looking after my man. God knows I'd waited long enough to find him. Plus, it was following the old-fashioned values Laurie Love recommended in her book that had helped me to attract Miles in the first place, so it stood to reason that it could help with securing an engagement too.

Yep. This was sounding like a solid first phase. A nice gentle way of encouraging Miles to want to propose on his own, without me directly pressuring him. I'd think of some other things to help convince him too. Must be loads of ways, but at least I had an idea of the direction I was going in.

Hopefully, this phase would be enough on its own to convince Miles that I'd make the perfect wife, but just in case it wasn't, once I was satisfied that I'd made good progress, I would move on to the second stage:

2) Convey: Almost every single expert agreed that when it came to proposals, marriage or any important part of a relationship, communication was key. Miles already knew I wanted to get married, which was great, so all I had to do in this stage was take it one step further by hinting about the type of proposal I'd like.

I had to make the engagement process easy for him. Several experts said that often men *wanted* to propose, but were worried about not choosing the right ring, so that made them nervous about taking the leap. That was probably why Miles hadn't asked me to marry him in Paris.

It made sense. There were a billion different types of engagement rings to choose from. If I didn't tell Miles which ones I liked, how would he know? Poor guy must be feeling overwhelmed. I thought I'd hinted at the kind of style I liked before, but I'd probably been too subtle.

I knew Miles. He was a perfectionist. Before making big decisions, he liked to research all the options thoroughly. I remembered when he was buying a coffee machine, he'd spent hours looking at reviews, comparing the pros and cons of the different options. So if he had to start researching rings from scratch, with no guidance on what I'd like, it would take him ages. This was why me helping him would be the perfect solution.

The same went for the proposal. I needed to give him some ideas about exactly what I'd like so he didn't have to get stressed out trying to guess what to do or how to make our engagement extra special. Miles wasn't a mind reader. He wasn't to know that getting down on bended knee at the top of the Eiffel Tower was what I was hoping for.

But I wouldn't make that mistake again.

Yep. Miles would be much more relaxed about popping the question if he had ideas for both a ring and the type of proposal that I'd love.

Great! That was the communication side of things sorted.

And finally…

3) Conclude: Now I'd like to hope that the Convince and Convey stages combined would definitely be enough to secure a proposal, but like Roxy mentioned, time wasn't on my side, so I needed to have a deadline in mind.

Having a fixed timeline with the Six Months to Love challenge I'd followed last time had been effective, so it made sense to put some kind of time limit on this plan too.

I didn't like to think of it as being an ultimatum. I hated that idea. Although I knew from looking at some forums earlier that some women used them and they sometimes worked out, I didn't feel comfortable doing that. It felt a bit like blackmail. *Marry me or else our relationship gets it…* I didn't want that. But at the same time, I couldn't wait around forever.

Granted, I hadn't waited an eternity. Some people might think I was crazy for being worried about not getting a proposal after two years when loads of couples were together for five or ten years before getting hitched. That'd be fine if we were in our twenties. But I was thirty-six. Like it or not, my biological clock was ticking, and as old-fashioned as it sounded, I wanted to be married before I had kids. For us to be a family with the same surname.

I'd done the calculations. If most wedding venues got booked up a year in advance, even if Miles proposed to me tomorrow, by the time the wedding was organised, I'd be thirty-seven. If he took several months before popping the question, I'd be fast approaching thirty-eight.

If we tried for a baby straight away, by the time I gave birth, at best, I'd be thirty-eight or, most likely, thirty-nine. And ideally, I'd love at least two kids. I'd prefer to have a two-year age gap between them, you know, to give my body a bit of a rest and to get used to motherhood. So if I did that, I'd be in my forties when our second child arrived. Of course, it would hopefully still be possible then, but now that I had found the future father of my children, why hang around? I wanted to get married and start a family ASAP.

I loved Miles with all my heart. I really did. He was a good guy. More than good. Great. *Amazing*. And I knew he'd said he still wanted to marry me and I really wanted to believe him, but I was on a schedule here.

As sensitive and caring as Miles was, he didn't have to worry about the ticking biological clock. He was thirty-nine now, and as a man, it wouldn't matter whether he got married at forty or fifty. So there was less of an urgency.

I didn't want to push him to propose, but at the same time, I couldn't keep holding on. I *had* to have some kind of date in mind. It was the end of October now, so I had to think about what was reasonable. Christmas?

Actually, I wondered if that was what Miles had had in mind when he'd said 'soon'. A Christmas proposal would be pretty wonderful. And it was one of the most popular times of the year to get engaged.

He could propose on Christmas Day when we visited his parents. Maybe he would put the ring in a cracker or under the tree. *That would be so cool.*

Or maybe Miles was planning a proposal at Hyde Park Winter Wonderland? I cast my mind back to when we'd gone to the annual festive fayre last December. We'd had so much fun going on the brightly lit fairground rides, walking around the quaint Christmas markets holding hands, drinking mulled wine and stuffing our faces with sugary donuts. It was such a magical night.

Or he could be waiting for it to snow. I could just picture the scene. Miles looking up at me, holding the ring box as the snowflakes fell on his face. *So romantic.*

Then again, now that I thought about it, I couldn't remember the last time it had snowed at Christmas in London…

Aha! So that could mean he was planning a trip to Lapland instead. Miles would dress up as Father Christmas, I'd sit on his knee, he'd ask me if I'd been naughty or nice, wink, wink, then he'd whip out a ring.

Oooh! Just thinking about it got me excited. We could take photos next to the reindeer too. It would be *brilliant.*

Christmas wasn't too much longer. If waiting ten more weeks would mean I'd get my perfect festive proposal, then I guessed I could manage to hold on a bit longer…

Just.

Oh, what the hell. Miles was the love of my life, so I supposed I could give him until New Year's Day. That would also be a good time. We'd probably go and watch the fireworks by the River Thames like we had before, and just as the clock struck twelve, he could ask if I wanted to be his wife. *Amazing.*

The New Year gave him eleven weeks. That was *more* than generous. That was almost a fifteen-month extension on the year we'd originally agreed on. Plus, by that time it would be around four months since we'd last discussed marriage, which should more than cover the definition of *soon.*

Yep. Rather than seeing it as an ultimatum, which would be too pushy and mean I'd have to tell him directly to *propose or else*, this would be more of a *reasonable deadline*—a realistic goal. It should give Miles plenty of time to plan the perfect proposal. Especially with all the help I'd be giving by steering him in the right direction with the ring.

He'd have multiple opportunities. Christmas, the New Year and I was sure we'd have at least one more romantic getaway. That would be *three* ideal chances. I'd put everything on a plate for him. All Miles had to do was turn up and say those five little words: *Alex, will you marry me?*

And if he didn't?

My heart sank just thinking about it. Although I didn't want to imagine that scenario, I had to consider it.

The reality was, I had no choice.

If Miles didn't propose by New Year's Day, as much as I hated to say it, we'd have to have a serious conversation about our future…

CHAPTER TEN

I took the chicken out of the oven and rested it on top of the stove. It looked and smelt heavenly.

The Convince stage had begun.

Tonight I was cooking Miles a very special dish. Some might call it old-fashioned, but I reckoned the saying was true: the way to a man's heart is through his stomach. Yep, as far as I was concerned, there was nothing wrong with making a nice meal for someone you loved. Especially if you were trying to show them how wonderful your lives could be if you were together. *Permanently…*

The chicken needed to rest for ten minutes, so I opened a bottle of wine.

After the timer sounded, I carved the chicken, then poured the juices from the roasting pan on top before garnishing it with fresh herbs and lemon slices. Apparently this stage was super important, so I made sure I followed the instructions to the letter to maximise the chances of everything working.

'Dinner's ready!' I cried out, bringing the dish through to the dining room.

Miles was about to sit down, then realised he'd left the lights on in the hallway and bedroom. Probably in the bathroom too, knowing him, but I couldn't see that far. Of course I'd noticed, but there was no way I was going to nag him about it. Tonight needed to be perfect.

Miles returned and I shared the food out on his plate.

'This looks incredible, thanks. You didn't have to go to all this trouble.'

'No worries!' I gushed. 'I *love* cooking for you!'

Especially when I know that this poultry has magical powers...

You see, this wasn't just any roast chicken. It was an *Engagement Chicken.*

I'd come across the story and recipe purely by chance. When I was doing my research, I'd noticed a notification on my phone. At first I'd thought it was another post from Karen, so was going to try not to look, but it turned out it was one of the bridal blogs I'd just started following. They'd posted a story with a link to an article all about it.

I'd never heard of Engagement Chicken before, but legend had it that in the 1980s a *Glamour* magazine fashion editor had given the recipe to her assistant to cook for her boyfriend, and a month later, he'd proposed. This had led to other colleagues trying out the recipe, and several more had got engaged. Then when *Glamour* had published the recipe, more than seventy women had written to the magazine about their success stories after whipping up the dish.

And it wasn't just in the eighties that this happened.

Apparently, Prince Harry proposed to Meghan after they cooked up a roast chicken.

Now, I wasn't born yesterday. Obviously, I knew that their relationships had to be pretty solid in the first place and their other halves must have had other non-poultry-related reasons for proposing. But it was worth a shot, right? It fitted perfectly with the Convince stage of my plan, and I had nothing to lose by trying.

So I'd hot-footed it to the supermarket, picked up a whole chicken, three lemons, rosemary, thyme and sage sprigs and some flat parsley, raced home again and started preparing it.

It had come out well. Looked quite similar to the photo in the article. Crispy and juicy. The scent of the lemon and thyme smelt divine too. This could be it. This tasty bird could quite literally be my meal ticket. I could be just one chicken dinner away from Miles popping the question. Whoop!

'So how was your day yesterday and tennis earlier?' I asked. Miles had been knackered when he'd got home last night so had showered and gone to bed whilst I stayed up working on my plan. Then today he'd gone to the gym in the morning before meeting Todd in the afternoon, so we hadn't had a chance to catch up.

'Gym and tennis were great today. Last night was a messy one. I was fine, but we found Leon, one of the male nurses, asleep on the toilet.'

'Blimey. He must have had a lot to drink.'

'Way too much. Anyway, yesterday was a good day at work.'

It was hard for Miles to go into details. Because of patient confidentiality, he couldn't talk about the ins and outs of what happened like most people did. But a good day usually meant the children he'd seen were making progress.

'Glad to hear that, darling.'

'Oh my God!' Miles gushed. 'This is seriously the best roast chicken I've ever tasted. It is *so* good.'

Yay!

This was already going well.

'Glad you're enjoying it.'

'I really am. Anyway, how about you? How was work yesterday? That photo you sent of Scooby in the morning was sweet.' He poured some more gravy over the chicken. 'I showed it to some patients. They couldn't believe you work with a smiling dog.'

'Yeah, he's such a cutie.' I regularly sent Miles photos of the siblings. Miles adored animals as much as I did, plus I knew the pics helped to cheer up his patients. After all, who didn't love looking at adorable dogs? 'I also finalised the details for the Hero Dog of the Year competition, so I'm going to launch the campaign on Monday.'

'Excellent!'

'And Karen is engaged…' Well, *of course* I had to tell him. I studied Miles' face to see his reaction.

'Really?' He raised an eyebrow. 'That's nice. To the TV actor guy?'

'No, she broke up with him ages ago.'

'The screenwriter?'

'The screenwriter?' I frowned, racking my brain trying to remember when she'd dated one. *Oh yeah.* It was two boyfriends before last. Think she went out with him for about a month before she got swept off her feet with the set designer, then the hotshot producer. 'Not that one. She's engaged to the film director.'

'Director?' Now it was Miles' turn to frown. 'When did she start dating him?'

'About five or six weeks ago.'

'Six weeks?' Miles' eyes bulged from their sockets. 'And they're engaged? Already? That's fast!'

Tell me about it.

'Yeah… she said he didn't want to wait around. He knew she was a catch and wanted to prove how devoted he was to her by putting a ring on it before someone else took her off the market…'

Hint, hint. I knew I should have risen above it, but I couldn't help it.

As I recounted what Karen had said to me on the phone, I felt my voice wobble. It wasn't fair.

'It's a bit hasty if you ask me. Marriage is supposed to be something you do for the rest of your life. You need to be sure it's the right person. It's not something you jump into after just a few weeks.'

Part of me wondered if that was why Miles hadn't proposed yet. Because he still wasn't sure if I was *the one*. My stomach sank. That was why this plan was so important. If he had any doubts, it would help to convince him.

'Well, Karen said that when you know, you know…'

'I get what she means, but… anyway.' Miles shrugged his shoulders. 'Each to their own. I wish them all the best.'

Was that all he had to say? No comment on when *we'd* get engaged? The night was still young, though. I had more tools in my arsenal. It was time for the next part of the plan…

'What do you think of the roast potatoes?'

'They're delicious, lovely and crispy. *Everything* is delicious.' Miles licked his lips and my heart did a little happy dance.

Mission accomplished.

'I tried out something I remembered your mum mentioning. After you boil them, you shake them around in the pot so they're rough around the edges, which helps to make them extra crispy.'

'Mum does know how to make a good roast potato. And yours are just as tasty.'

'Thanks! Speaking of your mum—well, your parents—it's been a while since we've visited. Maybe we should take a trip to see them. They're always saying we should go round more often.'

It was true that his mum and dad *did* ask us to come and see them more regularly. They lived in Kent, and although it was only just over an hour away, we tended to only visit for big occasions. You know, Christmas, Easter, birthdays, that kind of thing. But maybe it was time to change that. Unlike my own parents, I actually enjoyed spending time with them.

Full disclosure. That wasn't the only reason I wanted us to visit. The truth was, I needed their help. I needed them to encourage Miles to propose and convince him that I was wife material. They were the people whose opinion Miles valued and trusted the most in the world. So if they were to give him their blessing and a little nudge, he'd definitely ask me to marry him.

His mum, Mary, in particular was sure to be on board. She was always gushing about how happy she was that we'd found each other, so if I said the right thing to her, I was sure she'd get the hint and be happy to help move things along. I also remembered reading in one of those articles that mothers-in-law were the best people to encourage their sons to pull their fingers out.

I felt a little icky and manipulative about doing this, but it was for *us*. For the greater good. He'd get to see his parents, which would make them all happy, and I'd be one step closer to my proposal which would make me happy. It was a win-win. Killing two birds with one stone.

'You read my mind. I was just thinking it had been a while since we'd seen them. Great idea. In fact, why don't we go next weekend? Mum will be so happy.'

'Brilliant!'

It was only day one of the Convince phase and I was already feeling more positive. Miles had devoured the Engagement Chicken and we'd arranged to visit his parents, so they could help persuade him to put a ring on it. This was fantastic progress.

Like that Hannibal guy used to say in *The A-Team*, the '80s TV show my brother was obsessed with: 'I love it when a plan comes together…'

CHAPTER ELEVEN

'Doing anything fun this weekend?' asked Jada. She got up and came to sit on the sofa by my desk, where Purdey was snuggled up on a blanket.

I quickly saved an image of a gorgeous engagement ring I'd spotted on Instagram to my collection.

Given that the Convince part of my plan was in full swing, I thought I'd get a head start on preparing for the Convey phase. So this week I'd been dedicating my lunch hours to looking through some new potential ring options to add to what I already had in my folders before making a final shortlist. That way, when it came to dropping hints, I'd have a much clearer idea in my mind about what I would like.

Doing research also helped to ease the sinking feeling I got whenever I saw one of Karen's increasingly frequent Instagram posts, which of course were all focused on her engagement. Each one felt like a stab in the heart and reminded me of how I was being left behind.

As much as it hurt, I couldn't mute or unfollow her.

That would be rude, so I had to engage, which wasn't easy. But knowing that I now had a solid plan gave me hope. It made me feel better about things. Like I was taking action and controlling my destiny.

'Miles is out tonight with his friends from work,' I said, turning away from the screen to face Jada, 'so I'm going to treat myself to the last two episodes of *Say I Do*.'

Miles had invited me to join him, but the bridal experts online (the sensible ones) recommended giving a man his space and not being too clingy, so I thought it was better to let him have his male bonding time. Plus I was excited about seeing the climax of the series. 'I've been trying to save the episodes, but it's just too addictive. Have you watched it yet?'

'No.' Jada shook her head. 'I haven't.'

'You *must*! Even if you're not into bridal stuff, it's *brilliant*. It's so emotional the way the guys surprise their partners with proposals and the news that they'll be getting married in a matter of just days. I bet you can't watch one episode without laughing and crying happy tears.'

That was so true. All the couples had been through some sort of hardship or grief or faced challenging times, so when they surprised their other halves with the news that they'd organised a spontaneous dream wedding, it was hard not to get emotional. I always had a box of tissues beside me.

'Wow, you're really into it, aren't you?' Jada said.

I definitely was. I used to dip in and out of my favourite bridal shows, maybe watching one or two episodes a week, but now I'd started my plan, I'd been more committed to watching an episode every evening if I had time after preparing dinner. It was good research.

'Yep! And the guys in the show, Gabriele, Thai and Jeremiah, they're *amazing*. I wish they were my best friends. I'd love to meet them and get some tips for planning my wedding!' My mind drifted to a happy place as I pictured the amazing dress, venue and food they'd source. 'Yeah, so anyway, I'll be watching that, and if I get time, afterwards, I might squeeze in an episode of *My Fantasy Wedding* or *Say Yes to the Dress*. I love seeing them try on different gowns until they find *the one*.'

'Any plans that *don't* involve bingeing on bridal shows?' Jada raised her eyebrow.

'Actually, yeah. Tomorrow I'll be playing tennis with Miles.' I sat up straighter in my chair.

'Tennis? That's cool. I didn't know you played.'

'I don't. I just thought it would be nice for us to do something together.'

It kind of all happened by chance. When Miles came home on Wednesday night, he was a little bit sad because Todd had messaged to say he couldn't make tennis on Saturday. I hated to see him down and knew how much he looked forward to his weekly matches, so before I knew it, I found myself rubbing his shoulders and volunteering my services.

I hadn't played in decades, but after the offer to help had flown out of my mouth, I began to mull over the idea. And the more I thought about it, the more it seemed like a good decision. I remembered the phrase I'd read when doing research for my plan: *the couple who play together stay together*. Doing more shared activities was another thing that was recommended to help speed up a proposal.

Miles and I already did a fair amount of couple stuff. Weekend breaks once a month and going out for dinner.

Miles watched romcoms with me every Sunday afternoon, so just as he made an effort, I thought it would be nice to take more of an interest in his hobbies too. Even though I was pretty sure I'd hate it, if it made Miles happy it would be worth it. Plus it'd fit neatly with the Convince part of the plan, which was definitely a bonus. *Win-win.*

'That's good. It's nice to make an effort to do things together when you're a couple. Keeps things fresh. I used to love going…' Jada bowed her head and her voice trailed off. Was she about to tell me something about a past relationship?

Even though we talked openly about most things, she'd never spoken about her love life. Pretty sure she was single, but I had no idea about her dating history. I was certain she'd open up when she was ready. Jada took a deep breath. 'I don't have anything special planned this weekend. Might cycle around Clapham Common or go for a run. I'll see how I feel.'

'Sometimes those are the best weekends,' I said quickly to reassure her that I wasn't going to probe her about her past or current relationship status. 'The relaxed ones. Playing it by ear.'

'Yeah.' She strained a smile. 'So are you any good at tennis?'

'I doubt it! I haven't played since I was at school. I was okay back then, but definitely nothing to write home about.'

'I'm sure you'll be great.'

'Thanks for the vote of confidence,' I said, wondering if maybe I should watch a few YouTube videos now to refresh my memory and get some tips. Then again, I only had ten minutes left of my lunch break and there were still a few more ring websites I wanted to check out. I'd figure out the tennis stuff tomorrow when I was on the court.

'You're welcome. If in doubt, just channel your inner Serena Williams or something.'

'Ha! If only!' I chuckled. 'I'll give it a go. Either way, I'll tell you all about it on Monday.'

CHAPTER TWELVE

'Would you like to do a little warm-up first or get straight into it?' said Miles, twirling his tennis racket around in his hand.

We were at the indoor tennis court about to play our first match together. I wasn't looking forward to the act itself, but no pain, no gain, right? I was sure it couldn't last more than a couple of hours and once it was all over, Miles would be happier and our relationship would be stronger.

I thought about Miles' question. Warming up would be the sensible thing to do, but it would only prolong the process. Plus, if we warmed up, I might get more nervous. It was probably better to just dive straight in. Hopefully once we started playing it would all come back to me. Yeah. I was sure it would be just like riding a bike.

'I should be fine, don't worry. Just pretend that I'm Todd.' I didn't want him to think I was some weak woman who couldn't hit a ball.

'If you're sure…' Miles raised an eyebrow.

I stood at the baseline, swinging from side to side like

the pro players always did whenever I watched Wimbledon to help me look like I knew what I was doing, then waited for Miles to serve.

As the ball hurtled towards me, I swung my racket enthusiastically and… missed.

'Sorry…' I winced. 'Just, you know, finding my groove.' I took a deep breath and resumed my position.

'Okay, we won't count that point.'

'No, no. It's fine. You won it fair and square.'

'If you insist…'

Miles served again. *Whoa*, that was fast. I *almost* touched the ball this time, but missed again.

Jeez. This was harder than I remembered.

'Don't worry. I'll get the next one! I think it's because I'm wearing leggings. There must be a reason why the female players wear skirts. Must help them move better around the court…' *Yeah. My outfit was totally the reason why I was so crap at hitting the ball…*

'Uh-huh…' Miles smirked. He served once more and again until he'd won the entire game without my racket so much as giving the ball a little tickle.

'Alex, darling, you know the point of the game is that you're supposed to actually *hit* the little round thing coming towards you?' He smiled.

'*Ha, bloody ha*. Very funny. I *know* that. I'm just getting started. Luring you into a false sense of security so you *think* I'm rubbish and then bam! I'll dazzle you with my amazing tennis skills.'

Chance would be a fine thing. I knew I'd be rusty, but didn't quite think I'd be *this* bad.

Miles served again. I lifted my racket in the air, but

nothing. The ball went flying past me. This was so embarrassing.

'Okay, this won't be much fun for you if you can't return my serve.' Miles walked around the net and towards me. 'Let's just call that game a little practice. Here, let me help you.'

Miles came behind me. I could feel the heat radiating from his body and smell his delicious woody scent. *Mmm.* Pretty hard to concentrate with him so close to me.

Come on, Alex. Focus.

'So, let me show you how to hold the racket properly.' Miles slid his hand over mine. 'Let's try the Continental Grip, which is good for serving, drop shots and volleys.' He held my racket out and turned the string area. 'Put your right hand out like you're shaking hands with the grip part of the racket…' Miles moved my hand this way and that around the grip until he was satisfied that I was holding it correctly. He told me what he was doing, but I'll be honest, I was still a little distracted. Feeling his hands on top of mine was doing all sorts of things to my body.

'Okay, thanks. I'll try it that way,' I said.

'That's the spirit!'

Miles stood in front of me and flashed his megawatt smile. It always made my stomach flip. Maybe it was the way it made his face beam and his big brown eyes sparkle. Or the way it showed off his soft, juicy lips… And he definitely knew how to rock a tennis outfit. The white shirt clung to his abs, and his long, muscular legs looked good in a pair of shorts. *Yum.*

'Actually, I don't think it's the leggings or my rubbish grip that are the problem.' I stepped towards him. 'I think I would perform *much* better if I had a nice, slow, long kiss…'

'Yeah?' He came closer, his lips now millimetres away from mine. 'That's a shame.' He smirked and started walking backwards towards his side of the court. 'No kisses until you actually start hitting the ball.'

'Such a tease!' I folded my arms.

'Me? Never! But, if you focus and win a few games, you never know, I might give you a lot more than a few kisses…' He winked.

'Oh, really?'

'Yes, *really*.'

Now *there's* an incentive.

I didn't know if it was Miles' mini tutorial or the promise of some bedroom (or maybe even changing room) action later, but suddenly I started hitting the ball. *Very useful for playing a tennis match.*

By the time we got to the second set, I'd even won a couple of points. Miles was still thrashing me and I probably looked ridiculous on the court, but at least I was trying.

'Now you're getting the hang of it, I might practice serving some aces,' said Miles.

'Um… okay…' I winced. *God help me.* I was already struggling with his normal serves. I didn't want Miles to have to dumb down his game too much for me, though, so I attempted to just suck it up and braced myself. Seconds later, as the ball whizzed past me at what seemed like five hundred miles an hour, I wished I hadn't agreed.

Especially when Miles served another ace. Then another.

I *had* to save the game. As he served the next shot, I

zoomed across the court as if my life depended on it and just managed to clip the edge of the ball before skidding, involuntarily doing the splits, then toppling over onto my side, legs akimbo.

'Shit!' Miles rushed over. 'You okay?'

'Not really. *Ouch!*' I groaned. 'I don't think I've had my legs open this wide since…'

'Since the time we decided to experiment and try out that Lustful Leg Kama Sutra position?'

'Yep…' God, that was *so* uncomfortable. It was supposed to be super stimulating and create some extra intense orgasms or something, but actually trying to lift my leg up and put it on Miles' shoulder whilst we were both standing face-to-face was no picnic. It didn't take long to realise I definitely wasn't flexible enough for that. Or for tennis, judging by my performance today.

Miles doubled over in a fit of giggles.

'Sorry! I just got a flashback of me trying to hoist your leg up and you screaming *don't split me!*'

'That wasn't my finest moment.' I couldn't help myself either and burst out laughing.

'Come on, Ms Gymnast. Let's get you back on two feet.' He lifted me up.

'Thanks.'

'Want to carry on?'

'Yeah…' Truthfully, I'd rather be curled up at home on the sofa, but as much as I hated it, I'd started, so I should at least try to finish.

'That's my lady.' Miles walked back to his side of the court. 'So the good news is you actually made contact with the ball again, which was a great start. The bad news is I still won the point!' He smirked.

'You're so competitive!'

'Well, you did say you wanted me to treat you as an equal and play just as I would with Todd, so…'

Why did I say that? In fact, right now I was also questioning my reasons for agreeing to this torture and humiliation in the first place.

The couple who play together get engaged and stay together, I reminded myself, adapting the saying to suit my needs.

Come on, Alex. You can do this.

After Miles won the game completely with aces, it was my turn to serve.

Time to try and turn things up a notch and channel my inner Serena Williams and Maria Sharapova.

As well as being unbelievably brilliant at tennis, they were also known for their shrieks, yelps and screams of enthusiasm on the court. So maybe if I grunted when I served, it would help me hit the ball better. I'd heard that grunting helped players feel more confident and in control. The fact that it might also put some of their opponents off had absolutely no influence on my decision whatsoever. *Honest.*

On the first attempt it didn't work, but on the second I actually started hitting the ball better. I won a point. Then another. *WTF.* I was getting better.

Come on, Alex, I said to myself, swinging my hips. I jumped up and down on the spot then served.

Yay! My first ace.

Shut the front door. I'd won a game!

'I won! I won!' I danced around the court. Granted it was only one game out of probably a dozen, but it was still an achievement.

'Yeah, you did. Unfairly!'

'What do you mean?' I crossed my arms, trying not to giggle. 'I won it fair and square!'

'*Yeah, right*. You were shamelessly distracting me with your grunting, jiggling your boobs and flashing your knickers!' Miles smiled.

'You like the grunting, do you?' I grinned.

'You know I do. I usually only get to hear that when we're in the bedroom.' He winked.

'Not just in the bedroom. Sometimes in the living room and bathroom too…'

'*Mmm*… I remember the bathroom. In Paris…' He licked his lips. 'Stop distracting me!' He laughed.

'Sorry!' *So not sorry.* He'd just told me his weakness. 'Anyway, I may be guilty of boob jiggling and grunting, but I'm not even wearing a skirt, so I'm not guilty of flashing my knickers.'

'Oh, *really*?' He glanced between my legs.

I looked down and *bollocks*. My leggings had ripped in the crotch area and I was flashing my pink knickers.

'That was an accident!' Must have happened when I'd skidded. Shit.

'Yeah, yeah, sure,' he chuckled. 'I believe you. Anyway, come on. Enough distractions. Let's get on with it. I've got a match to win.'

We continued to play and just when I thought I was finding my feet, there was a commotion by the door. I looked over to see a group of boys walking in and climbing the steps to the spectator area.

What?

Oh no.

Embarrassing myself in front of Miles was one thing. I

knew that when he teased me, it was just friendly banter. But attempting to play in front of strangers was a whole different kettle of fish.

'I didn't realise they let people watch when you've booked the court,' I whispered.

'Yeah, sometimes members finish practising early and come and see other people play. Todd and I normally don't mind. It pushes us to play better. Don't worry. I'm sure they're harmless.'

I took a deep breath and took my position. We hadn't been playing long before the giggling started. I could feel them glaring, and from the corner of my eye I saw them pointing. I tried to keep my cool, but it wasn't working.

'Nice knickers, love!' one of them shouted. Shit. I'd forgotten about that. What was it with me and flashing my underwear? First after leaving the loos at that meeting and now again here. Mortified.

'Hey!' snapped Miles, turning to face them. 'Come on, be nice, guys.'

Miles went over to his sport bag and pulled out a jumper.

'Here.' He walked towards me. 'Would wearing this around your waist make you feel more comfortable?'

'Thanks.' I took it from his hands. 'It might slow down my dazzling footwork, but at least it'll protect my modesty.' I wrapped it around me and tied a couple of knots so it wouldn't fall off.

Just when I thought I was finally getting somewhere, I found myself right back at square one. I could feel the boys staring at me. Watching every move and misstep. Although I managed to return a couple of Miles' serves, it wasn't long before I started missing the ball again.

They grew noisier and the more I heard them laughing, the worse I got. By the time it was my turn to serve, my confidence had crumbled.

I tried to block them out. I threw the ball up in the air and hit it, but it caught the net then landed on my side.

'You're supposed to serve it *over* the net, love!' They laughed.

'That's it!' Miles snapped. 'Hold on, Alex.' He stormed over to the guys. I couldn't hear exactly what he was saying, but he looked pretty pissed. Within seconds, they got up and left the court.

My hero.

'You okay?' He came and rubbed my shoulder.

'Yeah…'

'What did you say to them?'

'It doesn't matter. I've never seen them here before, but they were bad sportsmen. That's not the way to do things. It's not how the game is played. If you're watching, you're supposed to respect the players, not act like arseholes.'

'Thanks for sticking up for me.'

'You're my lady.' He wrapped his arm around me. 'I'm not going to just stand there while they take the piss. Look, we've had a good session and I really appreciate you coming. Can't have been easy for you. Should've seen me the first time I got back on the court after years of not playing. I was terrible! You've done pretty well, considering. What do you say we try again another day?'

'Okay.' I hung my head.

I wanted to be strong and carry on, but I was completely out of my comfort zone. I had been struggling before they'd started heckling me, and the truth was, I hadn't enjoyed this at all. Watching Wimbledon with a glass of Pimm's was cool, but actually playing myself wasn't fun. *What's to love about being humiliated?* I just hoped they hadn't filmed me or something. The last thing I wanted was to go viral for being the worst tennis player in the world.

There was no hiding from it. I was supposed to be convincing Miles that I was someone he could share his hobbies with. Showing him that I was wife material. But I had to face facts: today I hadn't done a very good job. *At all.* Looked like the plan was proving to be much more challenging than I'd hoped.

CHAPTER THIRTEEN

'Mary! Ron!' I said as they threw their arms around me.

Thanks to some amazing hugs and reassurance from Miles last night and after giving myself several pep talks, yesterday's embarrassing tennis debacle was behind me. And now that we'd just arrived at Miles' parents' house, I was filled with renewed optimism. Although the match hadn't gone to plan, I was sure that this stage of the Convince phase would be a success.

'Great to see you!' I rested my head on Mary's shoulder. She always smelt like the freshest, sweetest roses. So comforting.

'Likewise.' Ron flashed a big grin. Even though Miles wasn't his biological son, he still had the same wide smile that instantly put you at ease.

Bouncer, their adorable Labrador, left Miles' side and jumped up on me. Talk about a warm welcome. His family definitely knew how to make a girl feel special.

'How's it going, old man?' Miles patted Ron's back firmly, then rubbed his hand on his shiny bald head.

'Less of the *old*, thank you!' He chuckled, taking our bags and putting them in the hallway.

'You know I'm only kidding, Dad. You don't look a day over ninety-five!' Miles laughed.

'Excellent!' Ron grinned. 'Your mum's anti-ageing creams are working a treat on me, then! Come on, son.' He wrapped his arm around Miles' shoulder. 'Help me bring in some more wood for the fire.'

I loved this house. It was a cute country cottage with colourful flowers and wisteria growing outside. It looked like something out of a storybook. It was all warm and cosy and inside they had a proper fireplace. We needed it as the temperature had really dropped these past few days. Winter was well and truly here.

'I'm just finishing off a carrot cake,' said Mary. 'Fancy giving me a hand?'

'You had me at cake!' I smiled.

She linked her arm in mine and led me into the kitchen. Mary was petite like me. Maybe she was an inch or two taller—perhaps five foot five. She had short salt-and-pepper hair, and although she was probably in her early seventies, she still looked youthful. Smooth skin and plump cheeks.

'Oh wow!' My eyes fixated on the showstopper on the counter. Two large round slabs of carrot cake had been sandwiched together with a creamy filling. I felt my stomach doing a happy dance just looking at it. 'That looks delicious.'

'I know how much Miles loves carrot cake, so I thought I'd rustle one up for dessert. Lunch will be ready in half an hour, which means we have enough time to decorate it.'

The aroma of roast beef filled the room. This time my stomach rumbled. And not quietly either. Sounded like an earthquake had erupted. How embarrassing.

'Sounds like someone's hungry!' Mary chuckled.

'I think it's the excitement of sampling your delicious food.'

'You're too kind.' Mary blushed. 'So Miles tells me you've been quite the master chef lately. Whipping up Michelin star meals. Careful not to spoil him too much.'

'I'd hardly call my meals Michelin star,' I said, thinking of how it was typical of Miles to talk me up to his family. *So sweet.* Also a great sign that my efforts were having the desired effect. 'Just you know, good home cooking. Like I'm sure you always gave him.'

'He'd be so lucky! Thankfully, Miles was one of the least fussy eaters I've ever met. He was happy with fish fingers, peas and chips, sausage and mash. Anything I'd put in front of him, he'd practically lick the plate. I think, what with his past experiences, he was just thankful to have three square meals a day. And even after he'd been living with us for a few years, he still could never get over the fact that there was always food in the fridge or snacks in the cupboard.'

It always broke my heart when I heard about Miles' past. Before being adopted, he used to live with his mum, who was an alcoholic. She rarely did a regular food shop. Unless of course it was to buy her daily bottle of whisky. The free lunch he got at school was often all he ate for the whole day. Sometimes if he was 'lucky' and could find enough money lying around the house, he would go to the corner shop and buy a packet of crisps for dinner. No child should ever have to go through that. Thank God his teachers realised how badly he was being treated and got Social Services involved.

'He always talks about his childhood with you guys with such affection. He loved living here. Finally having a proper family life.'

'It was mutual. Ron and I waited so long to have a child. Miles was such a blessing. Even as a teenager, he didn't give us any trouble. Like everyone, he had his habits, for example leaving the lights on.'

'Yep!' I chuckled. 'I can confirm he hasn't grown out of that one!'

'I can imagine! I always said to Ron if anyone within a ten-mile radius was lost, they'd soon find their way to our home. It was always lit up brighter than a lighthouse. Apart from Miles' attempts to give Blackpool Illuminations a run for its money and send your electricity bills through the roof, how's it going with the living together? You two still getting on well?'

This was my chance. Mary and I didn't often get much time to chat alone together. With the boys outside collecting wood for the fire and out of earshot, this would be the perfect opportunity to sow the wedding seeds.

'It's going great, actually. Brilliant. I love living with Miles. I'd happily spend the rest of my life with him…'

I left my words hanging in the air, hoping that Mary would catch my drift.

'Ooh!' Her eyes widened. 'Maybe I need to start looking for a new hat…'

'I hope so! I'd marry Miles tomorrow. I'm just waiting for him to ask…'

'I'm sure he will, darling. *Soon.* He's seen how happy me and his dad have been and always said he'd love a life like ours. I mean, Ron and I aren't perfect, of course. We've had our ups and downs just like any couple, but we've had some wonderful times together. The day we got married was one of the best days of my life.'

'Ah, I bet!' I imagined her and Ron saying their vows at the altar, then pictured myself in a church with our closest friends and family surrounding us as I enthusiastically said those two magical words: *I do.* 'If Miles and I could have even a fraction of your happiness, we'd be lucky. I'm so excited to start our lives together. Properly as a married couple. I'd love it to happen quickly.'

'I'm sure it will.'

'I mean, we'll probably go on another lovely weekend away somewhere soon, so that would be ideal.' Must remember to look up some locations and talk to Miles about booking somewhere ASAP.

'Sounds lovely, dear.'

'Christmas would also be fantastic. Surrounded by you and Ron: two of the most important people in Miles' life. And Bouncer of course. I mean, how cool would it be to start the New Year planning a wedding?'

'That would be *very* exciting!'

Yes! Sounded like Mary was sold on the idea.

'Any chance of a cuppa?' said Ron as he and Miles entered the kitchen. Their timing was pretty spot-on. I reckoned I'd done just enough seed-sowing for Mary to bring up the marriage subject once we all sat down. We hadn't been here long, but already things were starting to come together.

During lunch, Ron and Mary filled us in on their recent

trip to Scotland. They said they'd visited a castle and mentioned how magical it was because as they were leaving, a wedding was taking place and they got to watch a bit of the proceedings.

Nice work, Mary, I thought to myself, sitting up straighter in my chair. *This was it.* She'd listened to what I'd said earlier and had now found a way to steer the conversation onto marriage so that she could fight my corner and tell Miles to get a move on. God bless supportive mothers-in-law.

'That must have been amazing,' I said, giving the conversation some extra weight. 'What woman wouldn't want to get married in a castle?'

'It really was lovely,' said Mary. *Here we go. Any minute now she's going to turn to Miles and give him a nudge*. I composed myself, ready to act all natural when she asked him when he was planning to pop the question.

'Poor lad was freezing in his kilt, though!' said Ron.

'I could see his teeth chattering in between smiling for the photos. I think he was wearing the kilt in a traditional way if you know what I mean…' Mary smiled.

'Lucky he wasn't caught by a gust of wind,' said Ron. 'I'm sure the guests didn't want an eyeful of his meat and veg!'

The whole table burst into laughter. That would have been one to leave out of the wedding photo album, I thought to myself as I imagined the horror of the guests if they'd been flashed. Wouldn't mind seeing Miles in a kilt with nothing underneath, though…

'So then we went back to the hotel and had a lovely afternoon tea. The scones were so delicious, I was tempted to ask the chef for the recipe…'

Hold up.

Why was Mary now talking about scones? That wasn't in the script. Not that we had a script formalised or anything, but what did afternoon tea have to do with asking Miles why he hadn't asked me the all-important question yet?

Focus, Mary. Focus.

'It was a lovely day. Rained a lot for the rest of our time there, but it was still a good trip.' Ron smiled.

'It was. Always nice to have a change of scenery, isn't it, love?'

'I agree,' I jumped in. 'Miles and I *love* our little getaways. We'll probably go on a romantic weekend soon,' I added, trying to steer the conversation back on course.'

'Yes, you mentioned that earlier,' said Mary softly. 'You two are becoming quite the jet-setters. Just back from Paris and now who knows which fancy city is next on the holiday list. It's nice to see you enjoying your time together.'

Phew. *And we're back on track.*

'We really are.' I smiled. 'And this is just the beginning.' I placed my hand on Miles' affectionately.

'Sure is.' Miles kissed me on the cheek. 'This woman has been so amazing. Playing tennis with me, cooking the most amazing food, running me baths. Honestly. Life just couldn't get better. I'm a very lucky man.'

Excellent. The plan is working.

'Awww.' I blushed. 'And I'm a lucky woman.'

Over to you, Mary.

'Ah. Look at these two lovebirds, Ron. It's so great to see you both so settled and happy. Now,' said Mary. 'Who's for dessert?'

Um, what?

Earth to Mary? What are you doing? That was the perfect opportunity to talk to Miles. Dessert can wait. Didn't you hear what he said? Help me out, won't you? Pretty please.

'It's a big fat yes to a large slab of carrot cake from me.' Miles smiled.

'Same,' added Ron.

'That's my boys!' Mary got up from the table.

'Alex?'

'Yes,' I said quickly, still wondering why she hadn't given Miles a proposal nudge. 'Of course. Wouldn't miss it for the world. Would you like some help?'

'That would be super, thanks!'

There was still a chance for me to salvage this. I followed her into the kitchen.

Mary took four plates out of the cupboard and put them on the counter before reaching in the drawer for a knife.

'That wedding you were talking about earlier sounded amazing!'

'Well, we didn't get to see much of it, but what we saw looked pretty spectacular.'

'I've always dreamt of getting married in a castle. I'd imagine it's like feeling like a princess for the day.'

'I certainly felt like a princess when Ron and I got wed.'

'Yeah. For a minute there I thought you were going to mention our wedding—I mean, ask Miles about us getting engaged…,' I said, thinking that would be the most subtle way to phrase it.

'Oh goodness, no!' said Mary.

Huh?

That wasn't the reaction I was hoping for. I thought she was on board. That she wanted us to get hitched. The shock in Mary's voice made it sound like it was the worst idea ever. And there I was thinking that she thought Miles and I would be perfect together.

'I'd never interfere with Miles' life in that way. I remember my best friend's mum was always meddling in her children's lives. Pushing them to do this and that. To go to college, to get a job, to get married, to have kids. She was always on their backs. I remember how much it used to get Hilda down. So I always vowed if I had children of my own, I'd be supportive of the decisions they made but not push them into doing anything. If Miles asks for guidance, then of course I'd be happy to give it. Otherwise, the path he chooses in life, what he decides to do and when, is entirely up to him.'

Dammit.

Trust me to choose probably the only mother in England who didn't want to see her son married off quickly.

I didn't see that one coming at all. It had completely derailed my plan.

I had to admit, though, that was a good mindset to have. Mary knew that Miles would listen to her, but she held back and just let him be a man by caring and trusting him to do what he thought was best. Kind of refreshing. Didn't bode well for the plan, though.

I could always try and ask to see their own wedding photos or something to lead them back on the subject later, or maybe ask to watch their wedding video. I was sure they must have one somewhere. That would definitely pull on Miles' heartstrings and help him to visualise us exchanging vows. But given what Mary had said, it didn't seem likely to work, and I'd pushed as far as I could for one day. Didn't want her to cotton on to what I was doing and think I was some saddo wannabe bride.

No. Admittedly, this was another setback. Today hadn't worked out as I'd hoped. But I wasn't going to let it deter me.

In fact, maybe it wasn't a complete failure after all? Mary hadn't suggested that Miles put a ring on it, but Miles on the other hand *definitely* seemed convinced that I was wife material. He said himself how lucky he was. How much he appreciated my cooking and me playing tennis with him. And that was the point. So actually, if I thought about it, I'd achieved exactly what I'd set out to. *Yes!* The Convince phase was a success. Which meant it was time to move on to the next stage: sowing my *dream proposal* seeds. I was so excited I could burst!

CHAPTER FOURTEEN

Almost ready.

I took a quick peek in the oven. One of Miles' favourite dishes should have finished cooking in about fifteen minutes, the table was set and he would be home any second now.

I'd made a Beef Wellington, which I'd serve with mash potato and veg. Today marked the start of phase two: Convey. Although I'd already convinced Miles I was wife material and this stage was all about subtly letting him know the kind of proposal I'd like, I couldn't exactly stop the whole Nigella routine, so I'd whipped up this special meal.

The thing was, though, I had to be careful with all this cooking stuff. When we were at Miles' parents' and he said that life couldn't be better for us, at first I was chuffed. After all, it showed that the Convince stage was working and I was making him happy, which was the goal. But at the same time, I didn't want to lull him into complacency.

Everything I was doing was designed to encourage

Miles to want to take our relationship to the next level—not just make him think things were perfect exactly how they were. If Roxy knew about my plan, I could imagine her saying that right now, not only was I giving Miles the milk for free, I was giving him the whole dairy section of the supermarket.

That was why this second stage was more important than ever. I needed to keep Miles focused on the ultimate objective: getting married.

The good news was I had something great planned. After lunch, I thought it would be nice for us to relax and watch some romcoms, which was one of our favourite things to do together on a Sunday afternoon. But we wouldn't be watching just *any* films. I'd picked out three very specific ones for a special romantic movie marathon. All of them contained the sweetest proposals, so they'd be ideal for hint dropping. It would be perfect.

'I'm home!' shouted Miles as he came through the door.

'I'm in the kitchen!'

I heard Miles walking down the hallway, then he came up behind me and wrapped his arms around my waist.

'Mmm… hello darling.' I spun around and kissed him on the lips. They were so soft and juicy. I loved them.

'Hello to you too,' he said before gently slipping his delicious tongue inside my mouth and flicking it against mine.

Maybe we should start with dessert instead, I thought to myself as Miles' firm body pressed against me…

No, no. There'd be time for *that* later. After the films. I had to stick to the plan.

'So…' I broke away slowly. 'Lunch is in the oven.'

'Great! It smells amazing.'

'It's your favourite: Beef Wellington. Home-made.' Apart from the puff pastry, obviously. I hadn't completely lost my marbles.

'Oh wow, thanks! You really do spoil me.'

'Ah, it's nothing.' I shrugged my shoulders, like I hadn't spent nearly two hours preparing it.

'Smoked salmon, avocado and pain au chocolat for breakfast the other week, that incredible roast chicken, those tasty home-made prawn and lemongrass fishcakes a few days ago, the delicious lasagne and now Beef Wellington for lunch? You've really been going to town with these meals lately.' He smiled, patting his stomach. He had nothing to worry about on that front. His six-pack would give a *Men's Health* cover model a run for their money. 'A man could get used to all these fancy meals.' He smirked.

Marry me and you could have this every day.

Then again, I wasn't sure I could keep this calibre of cooking up all the time, but I'd try. Maybe once or twice a week was more realistic…

'Well, you know, I just *love* cooking for you.' I stroked his cheek. It was true. Yes, it was time-consuming, but when I was single, I still had to cook for myself every day, so it wasn't that different. It was nicer being able to share your food with someone special rather than sitting alone at the dining table. It made me happy to see Miles enjoying my cooking.

'Thanks. I just want you to know that I appreciate it.' He took my hands in his. 'You don't have to do all this every day, though. I'd be just as happy with something quick like pasta and sauce from a jar, sausage and mash or a pre-prepared supermarket meal or something. I don't want you spending loads of time slaving away in the kitchen just for me.' Miles' face creased with concern. 'We're partners. A team. We should share the cooking.'

'Don't worry.' I smiled, gently squeezing his hands. 'It's not just for you. It's for us. We were eating way too many takeaways and ready meals before. Having a nice home-cooked meal is important.'

'Okay, but this week I'm definitely making something special for you. No arguments. Right, I'm going to have a quick shower. Back soon.'

Miles was one of the cleanest people I knew. He showered at least twice a day. Sometimes more. It wasn't just about wanting to be fresh in the morning or washing after commuting home on the tube. He explained it came from his childhood. When he lived with his biological mum, she was always drunk and rarely washed his school uniform. Because it wasn't exactly fragrant, the kids used to tease him. That had haunted Miles for years. He didn't have to worry about that anymore, though. He always smelt so woody and fresh.

It wasn't long before Miles returned and we got stuck into lunch.

'This is absolutely delicious.' Miles licked his lips as he polished off another mouthful of beef.

'Thanks! Glad you like it. So,' I said, gearing up for the first official Convey conversation, 'I was flicking through my diary earlier and I realised that it's already been three weeks since we went to Paris. Time flies, doesn't it?'

'It does. The other day I went into the supermarket by the hospital and they were already selling mince pies and big tins of Quality Street. Can't believe Christmas is two months away.'

I can. And although I was confident it *could* happen, it was best not to just rely on Miles popping the question then or at New Year's either. Putting all of my eggs in one basket was too risky.

'Exactly!' I was so tempted to add something about us getting older and not hanging around to do important things like get married and have kids, but that would have been too much. I had to sow the seeds gently. Do this the smart way, by dropping *subtle* hints. *Here goes the next part of the plan...* 'And it dawned on me that although I mentioned it when we went to see your parents, we haven't actually arranged our next weekend break yet.'

That had become our thing. Miles and I usually went somewhere every month. Sometimes a staycation, sometimes abroad. Before we got together, I never used to travel a lot. Mainly because I found doing the solo trip thing a bit lonely. It was definitely much nicer having someone to go away with now, though. This year we'd been to several places, including the Cotswolds, Devon, Prague, Lisbon and of course, Paris…

'That's true. I suppose with Christmas coming up, we might get busy. You know with parties and celebrations and sometimes they hike the prices up around this time. We can wait if you want. Go somewhere in the New Year or early February before the Valentine's rush?'

'No!' I said a little too loudly. 'I mean, no need for us to wait. I'm sure there's loads of deals on and I haven't got anything in the diary yet for the first weekend in December, so it'll be fine.'

'Okay. Might be best to wait until a few days before

we go to book something, though, in case stuff comes up at work, but it does sound cool.'

So far so good...

'I was thinking of somewhere romantic… somewhere special, with a nice setting and nice monuments and buildings with beautiful views. How about we go to Rome?'

'That sounds cool. I'm sure we can find somewhere to eat a delicious lasagne like the one you cooked the other day too,' he said, piling another mouthful of pastry and beef onto his fork. He was really enjoying it. 'I've heard the food there is amazing.'

Well, I was sure it was, but if all went to plan, we wouldn't be going for the food…

'We can visit romantic places—you know, like the Trevi Fountain, or maybe the Spanish Steps?'

I'd done my research. Whilst the Beef Wellington was in the oven, I'd googled *romantic hotels in Rome*. Then I'd decided it was better to work backwards. So I'd started looking for romantic places to propose in Rome first before searching for nearby hotels.

There were some great suggestions. The Spanish Steps were popular for weddings. I'd seen loads of lovely photos. There was one in particular of a bride with her beautiful train resting on the steps and her husband gazing into her eyes. Gorgeous.

The Trevi Fountain was another tip. The article recommended visiting at sunrise so it wouldn't be crowded and then you could capture the sunlight. *So romantic*.

Villa Borghese seemed like a contender too. We could rent a boat to row on the picturesque lake. *Oooh*. I had so many ideas. Now that Miles was on board, I'd start making preparations straight away.

'We definitely can't go to Rome without seeing the Vatican and the Colosseum,' Miles added, completely oblivious to my mention of proposal landmarks. As iconic as those attractions were, that wasn't really where I'd dreamt about getting engaged. But it was Miles' trip too, so we could work that into the schedule.

'Of course. We can find time to go there afterwards.'

'Afterwards?'

Oops.

'Yeah, after we've… yeah. We can go there.'

It was all settled. We were going to Rome. Visiting somewhere romantic would make it so much easier for Miles to propose. I'd widened the pool of opportunities. The more options Miles had, the more likely a proposal was to happen.

'Great. I am absolutely stuffed!' Miles put his knife and fork together on the plate. 'So what do you fancy doing now?'

'Well…' My stomach flipped with excitement knowing it was time for the second Convey activity. 'I thought you could help me settle a debate I was reading about today.'

'Oh?' Miles frowned. 'What's that, then?'

'So it was a poll about the film with the most romantic proposal of all time.' I pulled up the article on my phone to show him. I couldn't believe my luck when I'd stumbled on it earlier. It gave my plan extra weight, so it didn't seem like some random idea I'd just cooked up. 'Remember how on our first date we challenged each other to name our top romcoms?'

'Of course I do. I asked you to name one, then I agreed to increase it to your top five and then you cheated by giving me ten!'

'I didn't cheat!' I folded my arms in mock protest. 'Anyway, as I was saying, we always used to have our little debates about our favourite romcom actors and actresses and other stuff. So, this afternoon, I thought we could decide on the best film proposal. What do you think?'

'Could do...'

Yes! I cheered in my head. He was up for it.

'Great! In my mind, it's a toss-up between *Leap Year* and *Pride & Prejudice.* Oooh, and then of course, there's the one with Colin Firth and the Portuguese housekeeper in *Love Actually.*'

'I kind of remember them, but not vividly...' Miles frowned again.

'Don't worry!' I jumped up and switched on the TV. 'We can watch them and then decide.'

'What? All three of them? *Today*?' Miles' eyes widened.

'Yeah! It'll be a romantic movie marathon. We've got *loads* of time.' Admittedly, we didn't usually watch three romcoms in a row, but it would be fine. It would help him feel even more romantic. Get him firmly in the marriage zone, which is exactly what I needed.

'Okay, then.' Miles nodded. 'Set it up and I'll get the popcorn and a blanket.'

'Already done!' I picked up the remote and clicked on *Leap Year.* All I had to do when he came back in the living room was press play.

I wasn't sure about including this film at first. Didn't want him to think that I was planning on waiting for a leap year to propose. Or that I was considering proposing at all. Like I'd said to Roxy, I preferred the tradition of the man getting down on one knee. But the proposal in this film was so sweet and it had some important elements I wanted to communicate.

It wasn't just about the act of proposing, it was the *way* the man did it. Where he proposed, what he said and how he said it.

As much as I'd love Miles to pop the question, I'd prefer if he didn't just do it in front of the sofa. The amount of thought and effort that went into the proposal said a lot about his commitment and intentions. Ideally, I'd love it to be just like in a romcom. Super cool and romantic. That was the dream. And these films should hopefully give him lots of inspiration…

'So…' I paused the film at the engagement scene and turned to face Miles. 'One of the things I *love* about the *setting* of this proposal is that it's really romantic.' Hopefully Miles would put two and two together and make the connection between me describing my ideal engagement backdrop now and when I mentioned the romantic setting of Rome earlier. 'I mean, who wouldn't want to get engaged on top of a cliff with an amazing ocean view? It's gorgeous!'

'Uh-huh,' said Miles. 'But aren't you afraid of heights?'

'Well, yeah, sometimes, but…' Maybe I hadn't thought this one through completely. 'I mean, maybe not the cliff itself, but you know, the setting. It's beautiful. Don't you think?'

'Looks a bit windy if you ask me. And dangerous.'

That was true, actually. One gust of wind and they both could have been swept away. *Hmm…* not exactly a happily ever after.

'Yeah, okay, so maybe not a cliff, but tall buildings are okay. Tall buildings with, you know, walls, or barriers or things to stop you falling to your death.'

'That's always helpful.' Miles nodded.

'You know, *romantic* buildings like the Empire State Building or the Eiffel Tower…'

Just because he'd missed his chance last time we went to Paris didn't mean we couldn't go again.

'Right…'

'But like I said, it's not just the building that's important. It's also the *setting*. The backdrop. So in this film you've got views of the ocean. With the Eiffel Tower, it's views of Paris. It's all very romantic.'

'Yeah… so, shall we carry on watching the film?' said Miles.

'Yes! Of course. It's near the end now. Let's take a look at the kind of *words* Declan uses in his proposal too.'

This was going *great*. Setting and location had been successfully communicated. *Check*.

As soon as *Leap Year* finished and Miles came back from the loo, I loaded up the Keira Knightley version of *Pride & Prejudice*. This was more romance than romcom, but it didn't matter. It was all about the proposal. I snuggled up closer to Miles, wrapping the blanket around our legs and resting my head on his shoulder.

When it got to *the scene*, I paused the film again.

'So…' I switched on the light. Now it was early evening it was quite dark, and it was important for Miles to see my facial expressions and how excited I was about how the onscreen couples got engaged. 'I just adore the proposal in this film.' I grinned.

'What, the one by Mr Collins, where he promises her

he won't complain about her rubbish inheritance when they get married and then when she says no, he tells her he'll just keep asking anyway because he knows women play hard to get?' Miles deadpanned.

'No! Not that one. That was awful! I mean Mr Darcy's *second* proposal. Look.' I pointed to the screen. 'Here's another example of what I was saying about the importance of the setting. In this film, there's another beautiful backdrop. As you can see, they're in the fields, surrounded by nature...'

'But I thought you said earlier that you liked buildings. Tall and romantic, wasn't it? There are no buildings in this scene.'

'Well, no, there aren't, but... obviously skyscrapers hadn't been invented in the 1800s or whenever this was set. It's, well,' I stuttered. '*Iconic* buildings are great. They're ideal. That would be my preference, I mean, personally. But the important thing here is... well, what we should focus on is the beautiful sunrise behind them. *See?*' I clicked the fast-forward, then rewind buttons to find the perfect part of the scene to try and highlight what I meant. 'Now imagine a proposal on top of a beautiful building like the Eiffel Tower with a setting like that behind it.'

'Right...,' said Miles. 'Is the Eiffel Tower even open at sunrise?' He rested his finger on his chin.

'Um, not sure. But it could be sun*set*. That's nice too.'

'Uh-huh...'

'And what's *also* good about this film is the *language* Mr Darcy uses in the proposal. It makes it extra romantic.'

'What, speaking English like they did two hundred years ago?'

'Well, not *exactly* like that, but the *sentiment*. The

emotion. Where he talks about her bewitching him and how much he loves her and doesn't want to be without her.'

'Hmm. Shall we carry on watching it, then?'

'Okay!'

Another check to add to the list. I was so glad I'd conveyed the importance of the words in a proposal to him too.

After this, all we'd have to do was watch *Love Actually*, where I'd show him the scene with the big gesture Colin Firth makes when he proposes to the housekeeper he's fallen in love with in front of her family and the whole restaurant. Then Miles would be in no doubt about the kind of thing I liked.

It had only been two weeks since I'd made my plan and it was already going well. After three doses of romantic movie magic, Miles would be buzzing with ideas. Planning the romantic setting and words he'd use to make our engagement special.

Yep. If I kept this up, the proposal of my dreams would definitely be on the cards imminently. I could just *feel* it…

CHAPTER FIFTEEN

'Someone's happy this morning!' said Jada.

I caught myself humming 'Marry You' by Bruno Mars. Lady Gaga jumped off Jada's lap, barked and then ran out of the room.

Charming. I thought I was in tune, but clearly she disagreed. And to think I was about to compliment her on her pretty bubble-gum pink doggy jumper.

'Yep!' A grin bigger than the Joker's spread across my face.

'Did you get some *sweet, sweet lovin'* or something?'

'No…' I blushed.

'What, then?'

'Let's just say that Operation Proposal is in full effect!'

'Operation Proposal?'

'Yep. The plan I've created to make Miles propose quickly. Hopefully there'll be a ring on this finger *very* soon!' I gushed, sitting down at my desk with my coffee.

'Oh *really*?' Jada rested her finger on her chin. 'Tell me more about this plan…'

I paused. After blabbing to the whole world about how I thought I'd be getting engaged before and falling flat on my face, it probably wasn't wise to make the same mistake again. It would be much safer to just spill the beans once he'd proposed.

Screw it. I hadn't had a chance to explain it to Stacey yet, and I was bursting to share my progress with someone. Plus Jada seemed supportive, and she had said the other day that we're supposed to be a happy family.

I started by explaining that I was currently working on the Convey element, which was essentially all about communicating my proposal hopes.

'That sounds healthy.' She nodded. 'Communication is important in a relationship. Especially when it's something as serious as marriage.'

I was so glad she agreed. Well, at least I *thought* she did. For some reason, the more I explained about the Convey stage and that it was about hinting rather than saying outright what I'd like, because that would spoil the essence of how a proposal should be, the more she started to frown.

'Right…'

'So that's stage two. I've already completed stage one: Convince. There were a few hiccups, but I achieved what I'd set out to.' I filled her in on the cooking, elaborated on the tennis match and our recent visit to Miles' parents.

'*Sweet Jesus*,' said Jada.

'Sounds really promising, doesn't it!' I grinned before taking a sip of coffee.

'*Er, no!*' Her eyes bulged. 'It's a *disaster*! What fool told you this would be a good idea?'

Oh…

'Fool? What do you mean?' I frowned. 'This advice came straight from the experts' mouths. I got loads of tips online.'

'*Lord God.*' She shook her head. 'In an article called "How to scare away your boyfriend, forever"? It's a *terrible* plan.'

That was a bit much. I'd spent hours working on it. Sifting through the rubbish advice and cherry-picking the best bits. Jada didn't have to be so sceptical. She was starting to sound like my real family now and that wasn't a good thing.

'It isn't terrible. It's actually working!'

'Yeah?' Jada raised her eyebrow.

'Take yesterday. We watched three films that I'd handpicked because they all had perfect proposals so that we could settle a debate on which one was the best.' In the end, Miles had said he couldn't decide, so I'd said it was probably a tie between *Leap Year* and *Pride & Prejudice*.

'Miles sat through *three* romantic films?' Horror spread across her face. 'The man deserves a medal, a sainthood or something.' I wasn't surprised by Jada's reaction. Although she didn't mind some romcoms, she was more of a thriller, sci-fi or documentary fan.

'We watch romcoms every Sunday. Anyway, as I was saying, when it got to the engagement scene, I paused the film to explain which elements I liked—you know, in terms of the setting, location, the words, that kind of thing.'

'Jesus! I still don't get it, though. So that proves your plan is working, how exactly?'

'The plan is working because now Miles knows. I

conveyed my desires, so now he knows the kind of proposal I'd like.'

Jada put her head in her hands.

'No, Alex!' She shook her head again like a disappointed parent. 'Just *no*. Girl, please tell me you didn't actually say and do all those things…?'

You didn't need to be a rocket scientist to see that Jada was *not* a fan of the plan. I hadn't even got to the Conclude bit yet. Hmm… maybe I wouldn't mention that part right now…

What did Jada know anyway? Yeah, she was a couple of years older than me, so maybe she'd had more life experience, but that didn't necessarily mean she knew more about matters of the heart.

Although she'd told me about her family and her hobbies, like how much she enjoyed cooking, cycling and running, Jada still hadn't spoken about her relationships. I knew she wasn't married, though, because a couple of years ago she'd moved out of her own place and back to her grandad's house, which was where she was raised.

She hadn't been through what I had, so she wouldn't be able to understand how frustrating it was waiting for a proposal and why I had to take action. And although I spoke a lot about him, Jada didn't know Miles like I did.

'Miles is a perfectionist,' I said, thinking I needed to explain why I was pursuing the plan. 'When he does something, he likes to research it thoroughly. If I leave him to work out what I like by himself, it'll take him ages, so I'm just making things easier. Anyway, I don't know why you're judging me for taking control of my life and being proactive. What happened to giving support and encouragement like families are supposed to do? How can you not see that this is a *good* thing? I'm not waiting around for things to happen. I'm taking positive action.'

She sighed, ran her hands through her braids, then reached for a hairband to tie them up into a bun like she was preparing to have a serious conversation.

'It might not feel like it, but telling you that this plan is rubbish *is* being supportive. I'm trying to stop you from making what could be one of the biggest mistakes of your life.'

Talk about dramatic. This plan was going to transform my relationship. Positively. It was the way to get my happily ever after.

'I really don't see how this can be a mistake,' I huffed. 'I could have been all demanding, pushy and clingy, but I'm not. I'm being extra nice to Miles. I'm trying to take action, but doing it very gently. Why can't you see that?'

Jada exhaled loudly like a frustrated parent counting to ten in their head before they lost it with their kids.

'It'd be much better if you just waited and were patient.'

'Been there, done that.'

'I know you're convinced that you're being subtle, but you're not. Do you think that Miles likes being told what to do? How to propose and what colour boxer shorts you want him to wear when he does?'

'You're being ridiculous! I didn't tell him what to wear!' I rolled my eyes.

'You think Miles likes being lectured in the middle of a film about what city he needs to propose in?'

'I didn't *lecture* him… I was *conveying*. Helping to make his life easier by letting him know what I like.'

'Hmmm, but I wonder if he'll see it that way. Look, I

don't know Miles, but like I said, we're family now, so from one sister to another, I'm saying, please be careful. You're becoming obsessed by this whole engagement thing.'

'I'm not obsessed!'

'Oh, so spending most of your lunch hour looking at wedding blogs, reading wedding magazines or pinning pictures of dresses on Pinterest isn't being obsessive? *Hmm-mmm.* If you say so.'

What, was she spying on me now? I mean, yeah, I had been looking at a lot more bridal stuff these past couple of weeks during my breaks, but that wasn't being *obsessive*, it was just being *passionate* about something.

I was *researching.* Being prepared. Even though I'd learned a lot about events at uni and in my last job, I knew that planning a fairy-tale wedding was no picnic. The famous saying was true: *proper planning prevents piss-poor performance.* So if I put in the hours and the effort now, when Miles *did* propose, it would make the wedding organisation process a million times easier.

And I'd been enjoying the preparation. I loved reading my wedding magazines. I'd already found some great suppliers from them and I adored the real-life wedding features. Hearing about how other couples met, their engagement and magical wedding days was so cool.

'It's research.' I folded my arms. 'That's where I find lots of inspiration for my wedding planner folder. How am I supposed to organise the perfect wedding if I don't have everything mapped out in advance?'

'Whoa, whoa, whoa, *whoa*! Now hold up! You have a wedding planning folder? *Already*? Even though your man hasn't proposed yet?'

'Of course!' *Jeez*. Now I definitely knew Jada had never been engaged. Everyone on Instagram or in the bridal and engagement articles I'd read had one.

One lady even had a sparkly bridal trunk at the bottom of her bed where she collected things for her wedding day. She had a box of different earrings she'd been collecting, different blue things for the 'something blue', all the wedding magazines she'd saved since she was a little girl, old wedding favours, wedding DVDs… you name it. If it was bridal-related, it went in the bridal treasure trunk. She didn't let the fact that she didn't have a boyfriend stop her. She was convinced finding her Mr Right was just around the corner and she wanted to be ready for him when he arrived.

It also reminded me of Charlotte in *Sex in The City*. I remembered an episode in the first season where she had a 'wish box' with photos and cutouts of the kind of husband she'd like, her dream home, that kind of thing. Lots of women did it.

'I have virtual folders. Y'know, where I save stuff from social media, but I also have a huge proper old-school folder. I cut out pictures from magazines, and since I started my plan, I've been updating it every evening. Well, not *every* evening. Sometimes I watch an episode or two of *My Fantasy Wedding* instead.'

'This is worse than I thought,' Jada sighed. 'Seriously. Look, I know it must be hard with that Karen girl ramming her engagement down your throat every five seconds, but don't let her situation turn you into some marriage-obsessed maniac.'

'I'm not!' I protested again, feeling insulted. Yeah, dealing with Karen's constant posts was challenging, but if anything, it had motivated me to take action instead of continuing to be so passive. Rather than wallowing in self-pity, I'd taken a difficult situation and turned it into something positive.

'It's your life and I can't tell you what to do, but if I were you, I'd think about packing that folder away. At least until you actually get engaged. And maybe cut back on the *research* and that *My Fantasy Wedding* show you're always talking about. It's messing with your head.

'But...,' I attempted to object, but Jada was on a roll and I couldn't get a word in edgeways.

'And as for your plan, *oh boy*... there's not enough hours in the day to explain all the problems with that one and I need to wee. But all I'm saying is, you're a good person and I'm sure Miles is too. He seems to really love you, so just trust that he'll propose when he's ready, because if you keep this Convey and Convince foolishness up for much longer, you'll risk driving him away and losing everything.' Jada got up from her seat and headed to the bathroom.

Ouch.

That was a bit dramatic.

I liked Jada, but I disagreed with her opinion of my plan and me being some sort of bridezilla waiting to hatch. Talk about exaggerating.

I mean, yeah. I had been spending a lot more time on my folder, watching bridal shows and scrolling through Instagram accounts lately, but no more than the average soon-to-be bride. It was a perfectly normal thing to do. Plus, Miles had been working late a lot more recently, which meant that even after preparing dinner, I still had an hour to kill. So focusing on bridal stuff kept me busy until he came home and we spent quality time together.

No. I knew Jada meant well, but I wasn't going to let her opinions derail me. As she'd rightly said earlier, this was my life, so I didn't need to do what she recommended.

I was making good progress, so it didn't make sense to stop now. Operation Proposal was still well and truly on.

CHAPTER SIXTEEN

The entries for our Hero Dog of the Year competition were coming in thick and fast. They were all so heartwarming.

Today I'd read about two dogs who'd chased away a fox that tried to grab a three-year-old girl whilst she was playing in her family's garden. Then I got a bit emotional hearing about a gorgeous golden retriever therapy dog called Max who visited a children's hospital with his handler to help seriously ill kids. So adorable.

I also loved the story of a little beagle called Gordon. The owner, Hayley, said that he was like medicine for the family. Whenever anyone was ill, he wouldn't leave them. She said when she was bed-bound for a week, even though he was a playful dog who usually loved being outside, he came and stayed with her for the whole time. The family had to convince Gordon to leave her bedside to eat and drink because he was so loyal, he just wanted to be there and keep her company until she felt better. It really melted my heart. Animals never ceased to amaze me. We were going to have a hard job choosing a winner.

Just as I was about to log off, a post popped up from Karen. It was a photo of her and a group of very pretty people raising champagne glasses and smiling.

Best. Night. EVER. Had so much fun at my engagement party!

#Bridetobe #InstaBride #EngagementParty #Celebrity-Wedding #Champagne #LALife #Actresslife

'What the…?' I shouted.

'What's up?' Jada frowned. 'What happened?'

'She had an engagement party last night!'

'Who? Karen, your bougie, diva LA friend?'

'Yeah, my best friend. She's not really a diva…' Karen kind of was, but I couldn't exactly admit to that.

'She can't be your best friend either. Not if she's thrown an engagement party and not even told you about it.'

I couldn't argue with that. There had to be some mistake. Maybe she'd sent me a message about it on WhatsApp and I'd missed it. Or she could have DM'd me on Instagram.

I quickly looked through my messages then checked my voicemail and texts. Nothing.

'There must have been a mix-up…' Or maybe because she knew I wouldn't be able to make it, she didn't think it was worth mentioning. I would've still liked to have known, though. To wish her well, or if she had time, I could've video-called just to say hi and be part of it, even from afar.

'Maybe…' Jada raised her eyebrow. I knew she wasn't impressed. That made two of us.

Another barrage of images popped up. As well as loads of posed photos of Karen with different guests, there were pictures of the venue too, which was very plush. It actually looked more like a wedding than an engagement party. There were long tables, which had been decorated to the nines with fancy settings and flowers, lots of gold-and-white balloons and a giant cake. All that must have cost a bomb. And that couldn't have been something that was organised overnight. Which meant she'd had enough time to mention it to me if she'd wanted to.

'I need chocolate.' I opened my desk drawer and rummaged around, looking for my snack supply. I had a few healthy cereal bars but also a little chocolate stash for the afternoons when I needed a hit of sugar to perk me up. Or for stressful situations, like when I'd just discovered my best friend had thrown an engagement party without even telling me. 'Fancy a Snickers?' I held out a bar for Jada.

'*Show us your knickers! Show us your knickers!*'

Oh dear. I forgot about him…

'Language, Mr Chilli!' I said to the parrot perched by the filing cabinet in the corner, which was where he liked to hang out sometimes.

According to Goldie, poor Mr Chilli was raised by a pervert. He saw and heard all sorts of things in the bedroom where his owner used to keep him, so his vocabulary was a bit saucy, hence the name.

Because he grew up mimicking what he heard around

him, when his owner decided he didn't want him anymore, unsurprisingly there weren't many people who wanted to have a potty-mouth parrot in their home, so Goldie had rescued him just over a month ago.

'Show us your knickers!' he chirped again.

'Stop!' I said.

'Not a good word for him, Alex…,' warned Jada.

'*Stop! Don't stop! Ooh. Don't stop!*' repeated Mr Chilli.

Dammit. You had to be so careful when he was around. Certain words, particularly ones that rhymed with something bedroom-related could trigger him. *Snickers* clearly rhymed with *knickers*, and *don't stop…* well, I could only imagine what *that* reminded him of.

We tried to encourage Mr Chilli to hang out in one of the many other rooms, but he ended up in the office at least once a day, and of course, there was no way Goldie would put him a cage. All animals were allowed to roam, or in his case, fly freely here.

As much as I loved him, it was tricky having him around, especially when we were talking to customers. Luckily, now it was quiet.

'I'll take him down to Goldie.' Jada held out her arm and Mr Chilli flew onto it. Sometimes Goldie was the only one who could calm Mr Chilli down when he went on one of his X-rated rants. She just had a way with all of the animals. It was like she was some sort of magical healer. She just had to say a few words to them and they were instantly soothed.

I bit into my chocolate bar and checked the clock. It was home time. If it had just gone five-thirty here, it'd be 9.30

a.m. in LA. Anyway, it wasn't as if Karen was sleeping. If she was posting, that meant she was wide awake. Chocolate was cool, but the effects would only be temporary. To avoid this going round and round in my head and ruining my evening, I needed to give Karen a call and find out what happened.

'Hey, honey!' Karen answered after three rings in a voice that sounded almost American. Where had her South London accent gone? 'I was gonna call you later.'

'How are you?'

'I am literally *dying*! I have the hangover from hell.'

'Looked like you had fun last night…' I was gritting my teeth so much I wasn't sure the words would come out, but somehow they did.

'Yay! You saw my posts! I have *so* much content to upload. I really should get an assistant to do this all for me, but y'know. Want to stay grounded.'

'Yeah…' *Grounded* wasn't exactly a word I'd use to describe Karen's behaviour lately. 'So, you didn't tell me you were having an engagement party?' I tried to keep my voice bright and breezy, but really I was pissed.

'Didn't I?' Karen paused. 'Oops. *My bad.* It's just been crazy busy lately. We had it at this super-exclusive hotel. The owner is a friend of Chuck's, so he did us a favour. The party was so lit! It was *ah-mazing*!'

'Wish I'd known about it.'

'Yeah, sorry, hon. But there'll still be tonnes more opportunities to celebrate. The bridal shower, the hen party and then the weddings.'

Wow. She really was going all out.

Hold on. Did she say *weddings*? As in, plural?

'Weddings?'

'Uh-huh. Oh God!' She gasped. 'Didn't I tell you about that either? Duh! Engagement brain!'

What the hell was engagement brain? I'd heard of baby brain, but as far as I knew, proposals didn't affect your ability to remember to tell your best friend important things.

'No, you didn't.'

'Well, we're having *two* weddings!'

She was having a laugh. Surely? One wedding was a big enough event to organise, never mind two.

'Funny!' I chuckled.

'What is?' Her voice turned serious.

Oh…

She wasn't joking.

Who the hell had two weddings? Did Posh and Becks? Did Meghan and Harry? Nope.

I remembered that Joe Jonas married Sophie Turner in Las Vegas and then in the South of France. But that was for legal reasons. Plus, Sophie played Sansa Stark in *Game of Thrones* for goodness' sake. She was actually famous. I'd expect proper celebs like her to have two ceremonies, but Karen?

Here I was desperate to have *one* chance to walk down the bloody aisle and she was having two. *Jesus.*

'Nothing… sorry. Jada was just showing me something funny. Two weddings! Great!'

'Yeah! Isn't it fab-u-lous? We thought we'd have one in London, which will be like a little warm-up—you know, a practice run for the main event. And then we'll have a *huge* one in LA! You'll be there, won't you?'

Two weddings. That was going to be expensive. Not just for Karen, but for me to attend. When I'd checked the flights to LA, they were pretty pricey. And unless I could stay at her place, there were the hotel costs to think about, not to mention the nights out, and I was sure Karen wouldn't want to do anything on the cheap.

And she'd mentioned a bridal shower *and* a hen party? Blimey. I was still saving up for my own wedding, so going to four big events wouldn't be easy. I'd probably have to sell a kidney to afford it all. But I'd known Karen for decades. I couldn't *not* go.

'You're my best friend! *Of course* I'll come to your weddings!' I sounded upbeat and enthusiastic. This was good. I was being a nice, supportive friend. Not an ounce of jealousy in sight. 'I'll come to *all* of them. London, LA, *wherever*! Just tell me the date and location and I'll be there. I'd do *anything* for my bestie!' On the bright side, because she hadn't invited me to her engagement party, I'd saved on going over for that at least.

'Awww, honey! That's so sweet!' Karen gushed. 'I'm going to lock down the date for the London wedding first. We're thinking sometime in March, so I'll keep you posted, okay?'

March?

'Wow, that's fast!'

'No point hanging around! We want to be married ASAP. When you know, you know. What's the point in waiting? I've got some exciting projects in the pipeline, and if I'm shooting, it'll be hard to get time off from set, so March works for us for the first one.'

'Oh, cool, I see. Okay.'

I'd done enough research to know that good weddings took time to plan, so I had no idea how she was going to make that happen. But knowing Karen, she'd persuaded

Chuck to hire the best wedding planner money could buy, so they'd be able to pull it off.

When I got married, I was going to take my time to plan things. Properly. Working in sales and event management for fifteen years had taught me that organisation was key. The last thing I would want was to be stressed with doing everything in just a few months. We'd need a year. Ten months minimum. Karen was crazy to rush everything.

'Anyway, hon, I better run. I've got *two* weddings to plan! First I need to finish uploading images from last night. Then Chuck and I are off for lunch at one of the venues on our shortlist. Getting the London wedding sorted should be easy, but we *so* need to nail down the date for the LA wedding. Everyone's asking about it. It's going to be the wedding of the year, I can just feel it. Oh! Where are my manners? How about you? When's your wedding? Has Miles put a ring on it yet?'

Like a knife to my heart...

If she'd stabbed me it would probably be less painful than asking that dreaded question.

'N-no,' I stuttered. 'Not yet... he will, though. Soon...'

'*Awww, hon.* You *poor* thing,' Karen said like she was consoling a small child. 'It'll happen for you. Just hang in there. You'll find someone to love you properly one day. Actually, they'll be tonnes of hot bachelors at my weddings. Anyway, don't forget to like and comment on my posts. And repost. I want as many people as possible over there to know about my engagement. It could go viral. I've always fancied being on *Lorraine* or *The Graham Norton Show*! Kisses!'

She hung up.

'Aaargghh!' I groaned.

Hang in there.

You'll find someone to love you properly one day.

I knew she was my best friend and I understood that this was a really exciting time for her, but sometimes Karen really pushed my buttons.

'What's madam done now?' Jada crossed her arms as she walked back to her desk. 'Apart from letting you find out about her party on social media?'

I didn't even know where to start.

The fact that she didn't even seem that bothered about forgetting to tell me? Or the multiple weddings, which she'd only mentioned because I'd just called her? Otherwise, who knew when I would have heard about it.

Oh. Let's not forget patronising me about Miles not proposing yet and casually suggesting I trade him in for another guy, like he was some deadbeat, rather than the man I was in love with.

And as for appearing on *Graham Norton*, as much as I supported Karen's acting career and admired her ambition, somehow I didn't think that me sharing some photos of her engagement party was suddenly going to propel her to the top of Graham's guest wish list.

'She thought she'd told me, but she's suffering from *engagement brain* at the moment, so it slipped her mind.'

'She's suffering from what now? Engagement brain? That's foolishness.'

'And she's having two weddings…'

'*Please*. Who *is* this woman? Who even has two weddings? I don't even think Queen Beyoncé and Jay-Z did and they're legit celebrities.'

'Each to their own, I suppose,' I said diplomatically. I

didn't want to sound like I was bitching about my friend. I mean, because Karen was in LA, maybe having a ceremony in London would make sense. It meant that those who couldn't afford to travel to the States would still get to celebrate with her. But it wasn't even like she had loads of family and friends in London anyway.

'And please don't tell me she asked about Miles proposing again?'

'She did…'

Sensing my stress, Bonnie jumped up on my lap. Maybe stroking her fur was what I needed right now.

'That girl is toxic. A friend should support you and lift you up, not make you vex. Okay, if they see you doing something that's gonna mash up your life, then yeah. It's time for some tough love'—Jada was obviously referring to her thoughts on my plan—'but twisting the knife in because she's got engaged and you haven't yet is just messed up. That's some playground, *Mean Girls* shit.'

Jada wasn't wrong. But Karen was one of my oldest friends. No, she wasn't perfect, but we'd known each other for ages. And she was obviously so caught up in the excitement of being engaged that she wanted that happiness for me too. If she met Miles in person, she'd understand that he *was* my Mr Right.

Maybe it was her strange way of looking out for me. Karen was probably just as frustrated as I was that he hadn't proposed yet. She just didn't have a very good way of expressing herself. That was all.

'It's just her way.' I continued stroking Bonnie, and she purred with appreciation. Having her here on my lap was helping. I started to feel calmer. 'Karen's not the most tactful person, but I'm sure she didn't mean any harm.'

'If you say so. Anyway, you know her better than I do, and I'm sure she must have some good points.'

'Yeah,' I replied, scanning my brain to think of them. Karen was good fun. She was ambitious. She always went for what she wanted in life. I admired her determination. *See?* Lots of good qualities. I was sure I could list a load more if I had time, but I needed to get home. 'She does. Well, little lady'—I picked up Bonnie and put her down on the sofa beside my desk—'I'm going now, so I'll leave you to keep Jada company.'

'Hopefully, if I can get this market analysis stuff done, I won't be far behind you.'

As well as managing all aspects of the accounts, ordering supplies and basically running the company so that Goldie could focus on taking care of the animals, Jada was also working on the business plan for the new hotel site. When she explained what was involved and all the customer, market and competition analysis plus the financial projections she had to do, it made my head explode. It didn't faze her, though. Jada was one of the smartest women I knew.

'Good luck with that! What are you doing afterwards? Going running tonight?'

'No. I'm cooking for Grandad.' She often did that. Jada was always looking out for him. She'd even moved in to keep him company after her grandma had passed away.

Jada had always been really close to both of them. Jada's mum had had her when she was a teenager, so her grandparents had pretty much raised her. Not because her mother wasn't committed to doing it herself. The grandparents knew that Jada's mum had always wanted to become a successful lawyer. The dad hadn't stuck around, and they hadn't wanted their daughter to give up on her dreams. So they'd helped take care of Jada whilst her mother went to uni and then law school to help provide a better life for them all.

Sounded like their support had paid off. Jada's mum was now a successful judge, living in Atlanta and happily married. And even though they were miles away, they still kept in touch. Jada was very proud of her.

'What are you cooking?'

'Curried chicken and rice. I normally don't make it during the week, but Grandad said he felt like it, so I thought I'd treat him. I'll bring in some tomorrow if you want.'

'Does Michael Bublé like Christmas? Yes, please!' I loved when Jada brought in her cooking.

'Cool. I'll bring an extra container for you.'

'Looking forward to it already.' My stomach rumbled in anticipation. 'See you tomorrow.'

CHAPTER SEVENTEEN

I *don't get it.*

What was wrong with everyone?

It was Saturday morning and I was having coffee at a little café in Clapham with Stacey, and just like Jada, she wasn't a fan of my plan.

I'd explained it all to her, including Conclude, the deadline part, and she'd just kept shaking her head and going on about being patient. *Again.*

What happened to being a strong woman and taking control? It was the twenty-first century for God's sake. If I wasn't going to propose to Miles, at least I could try and drive the proposal forward rather than just sitting on my hands and doing nothing. Right?

'I know you won't want to hear this, but it all sounds a bit desperate… trying to get his mum to make him propose, all the elaborate meals you've been cooking. Is that really why you want Miles to propose? Because his mum told him to be a good boy and do it already? Or because he's being led by his stomach? Come on, Alex. And as for the ultimatum, that won't end well.'

'It's not an ultimatum. It's a deadline.'

'Call it whatever you want. And I'm not sure you've thought it through properly. I mean, how will he meet the deadline if he doesn't even know it exists?'

I explained that I *had* thought it through. The deadline was something I'd put in place as a goal. An objective to work towards that should fit within what Miles had told me.

Setting D-Day for two months' time should definitely cover his description of 'soon'. Obviously I couldn't tell Miles about the date explicitly, because I'd like him to propose because he *wanted* to. I needed to be sure that he wanted to be with me forever, and the only way I'd know that was if he asked me to marry him. That would prove he was fully committed.

'Right…' Stacey raised her eyebrow. 'If you say so. Look, Miles is a good man. I don't think he needs a deadline or ultimatum. Especially one he knows nothing about. He's not a mind reader. If it was anyone else, then maybe you'd have a reason to worry, but he's trustworthy. If he tells you he'll do it soon, believe him.'

It was so hard trying to explain my strategy to people. I'd just have to continue alone, without updating Stacey or Jada on my progress. Yes, some things hadn't quite gone according to plan, but on the whole, it had been working well and I had a few other ideas to try. I still had faith in my methods. Hopefully the Engagement Chicken would work its magic soon too. Stacey and Jada would both be eating their words when Miles proposed in Rome.

'Anyway, enough about me,' I said, switching the

subject. 'What have you been up to? You said you had something exciting to tell me. Are you leaving M&E? Have you got a new job?'

A massive grin spread across Stacey's face.

'You could say that… at least I will have a *very* important new role in approximately five months' time.'

'Five months? That's a long time to wait before starting a new job.'

Unless…

As Stacey beamed and started stroking her stomach, the penny began to drop…

'You're going to be an auntie!' Stacey gushed. 'I'm pregnant!'

As those last two words fell from her mouth, a mixture of emotions flooded my body. First it was like a firework had been set off inside of me. I was excited. I knew how much she and Bobby had wanted to start a family, so this was great news for them. But then as the firework began to fizzle out, I felt a rush of sadness for myself. Selfish, I know, but I couldn't help it.

Here was yet another friend, moving on with their life, their relationship progressing, whilst I was being left behind.

It felt like everyone I knew was getting engaged or married or having babies. They were the 100 m sprinters racing through the finish line of personal successes, whereas I was stuck at the starting block. Watching them from afar as they celebrated their victories, preparing to stand on the podium, whilst my achievements put me smack bang in last place.

I hated feeling this way. I didn't want to be that person who didn't like seeing other people being happy or doing well. That wasn't me. I loved Stacey. She was a wonderful friend. I wanted the best for her. She and Bobby deserved this happiness. I had to get over my own issues and insecurities about the lack of progress in my relationship, push my feelings to one side and celebrate this great milestone with her.

'Oh my God! That is *AMAZING* news!' I threw my arms around her. 'You and Bobby are going to be the best parents ever! You're going to ace being a mum. I'm so happy for you!' I genuinely believed every word.

'Thanks! We still can't quite believe it. We wanted to wait a bit before telling anyone, you know, just in case, but we're so excited!'

'I can imagine!' I said, pushing through my emotions. 'So have you thought about names, or how long you'll work for before going on maternity leave? Tell me everything!'

I sat there listening to Stacey talk all about her plans. They didn't mind whether it was a boy or a girl as long as it was healthy; she'd probably work until she was six or seven months and then take early maternity leave. She and Bobby had been saving up for it. Then she wanted to take at least two years off from work to enjoy those special moments with their baby. They were even thinking of moving out a bit further afield, outside of London, so that they could bring up their child in the best environment.

As I tried to take it all in, my head was spinning faster than a ballerina doing a pirouette.

Stacey was having a baby.

It was great that they had savings and that Bobby made enough for them to live off his earnings rather than her rushing back to work like most mums had to. They'd really thought it through. Planned how to give their child the best possible start in life. I'd love to be able to do that too one day.

Stacey was pregnant.

And she might be moving away soon too, so I probably wouldn't get to see her that often.

I could feel the tears building, but I couldn't let them fall. This was Stacey's moment. And God, I'd never seen her so happy. She looked like a child that had just been told that they'd be spending the whole summer on an all-expenses-paid trip to Disneyland. She was ecstatic. There was no way I was going to ruin this for her.

'This baby is going to be the luckiest in the world! Hold all those thoughts for a sec, please. I'm bursting for the loo, but I'll be right back. And when I am, you'll have to tell me about what your parents said when they heard the news!'

I put on my bravest smile and got up from the table and made it to the toilet just in time before the tears began to stream down my face.

God. Get it together, Alex.

If you're going to cry every time one of your friends gets engaged or pregnant, you better invest in some Kleenex shares right now.

I guessed this was the reality of being in your thirties. Truth be told, it had started in my late twenties. People getting hitched or knocked up. Settling down. Adulting. Properly.

It had affected me before. Of course it had. But for some reason, it was really hitting so much harder now. Was it because I felt like I was so close to joining the engaged or married club, but hadn't quite got my membership application approved yet? I had the man I'd always dreamed about meeting, but I was falling at the final hurdle.

Or maybe it was an age thing, because I was so conscious that time was running out?

Either way, I had to get a grip. Pull myself together and woman up. The engagement would happen. So would the wedding and then the babies. I still had Miles. And at least we still had our weekend away. In four weeks' time, I would finally be speeding towards the finishing line. Just like Karen, I'd be newly engaged. I just had to keep putting my hopes and dreams out there. Keep communicating with the universe.

Stacey herself always believed that if you put things out there, they would happen. She'd proved that with her relationship with Bobby, their marriage and now their baby. I should do the same.

If I manifested my desires and of course continued with the plan, it would happen. In Rome.

Yes.

I wiped my tears away, took a deep breath and stood straighter.

I was going to be okay.

The perfect proposal I'd dreamt about for years was only one month and one plane ride away.

Our trip couldn't come fast enough.

CHAPTER EIGHTEEN

'Do you mind if I use your laptop whilst you're in the shower?' I asked Miles as I plonked myself down on the sofa.

'Sure, go for it.' He touched the trackpad, entered his password, then passed it to me.

'Thanks.' As he left the room, my heart started thumping.

I'd been to-ing and fro-ing about this idea since I'd got home from work earlier. Weighing up whether it was okay. But the more I thought about it, the more I decided it was harmless. It wasn't as if I was hiding the fact that I was using Miles' laptop. It was no biggie. I did it all the time. The screen was larger than my tablet. Sometimes he borrowed my iPad too. What I was about to do was totally above board. Most importantly, it was helpful.

Our trip to Rome was only a few weeks away, and if Miles was going to propose, I knew he'd prefer to do it with a ring. He was a perfectionist. But of course, how would he know what ring to buy unless I conveyed what I liked, right?

So, tonight I thought I'd do a little digital hinting. I was going to look up my top three favourite rings online, then the internet would take care of the rest.

How?

Well, the internet monitors us. When we go on social media or visit websites, they track our activity, then start sending us adverts for things they think we'll like. Which meant, if I started looking at jewellers and engagement rings, you could bet your bottom dollar that pretty soon, Miles would start getting ads for them. See? Nice and subtle.

Some people even reckoned that the internet listened to us. I'd always dismissed it as a conspiracy theory, but then one day, when I was working at my old job, Stacey and I were chatting with our receptionist, Kandi, who'd agreed to go camping for the first time with her new boyfriend. They had a long drive ahead of them and she was worried about how she'd answer the call of nature if they were somewhere remote and Stacey suggested she buy a female urination device. A funnel type thing you can use to wee on the move. Not literally whilst you're moving obviously, just, you know, when you're out and about with no toilet nearby. Kind of the equivalent of a man peeing in a bottle.

We'd all laughed about it and thought we'd better get back to work before Steve started breathing down our necks. I'd completely forgotten about it until two days later, when I was scrolling through social media and an ad popped up advertising, yep, you guessed it, female urination devices.

I mean, come on. What were the chances? I'd never

even thought about their existence until that conversation and I definitely hadn't searched for them online. It was completely random. So how else did they know to advertise it to me? *Hmmm…* something felt fishy.

Anyway, I had no idea if it was just a freaky coincidence or not, but I thought I may as well put both theories to the test.

First, I looked up the ring that was right at the top of my wish list. It had three beautiful diamonds to represent our past, present and future. *Awww.* Next, I opened a fresh tab and searched for my second favourite before doing the same for the third. *Done.*

'I'm looking for a beautiful *engagement ring*. I'd *love* a beautiful *diamond ring* so I can get *engaged*, with an *engagement ring…*,' I chanted, loudly holding the laptop up to my mouth so it could hear me. I paused, to check the shower was still on so that Miles wouldn't suddenly walk in, then continued. 'Please, internet, show me lovely adverts for my *favourite diamond engagement rings* on this computer. Pretty please…'

I read the names of the jewellers, their website addresses and the specific ring names out loud three times. Just to be sure the internet robots or whoever the tracking spies were could take notes. Okay, I admit, I did feel like a bit of a plonker, but at least no one else knew what I was doing. Thankfully, it was just me and the internet, so no risk of Miles overhearing me, then calling the authorities to get me sectioned. Silly or not, it was worth a try, right? I had nothing to lose.

What with Karen's *two* weddings and Stacey announcing her pregnancy, I had to throw everything at securing this engagement. The clock was ticking so loudly

I felt like I was perched on top of Big Ben. The sooner Miles and I got engaged, the sooner we could get married. And the sooner Miles and I got married, the sooner we could start trying for a baby. I was doing this for both of us.

Ideally I would have preferred to have done this last month, to give Miles more time, but the jewellers I'd chosen all had shops in London and said if they didn't have the particular ring in store, they should be able to order it within a fortnight, so it should still be absolutely fine.

Maybe I'd just leave a tab open with my favourite ring, just to help make things easier for him…

There. I'd visited the websites and talked about engagement rings out loud. Another Convey activity completed. I breathed a sigh of relief. More good progress. I hadn't let Karen's digs or my disappointment about the fact that my personal life wasn't panning out as well as my friends' get me down. I'd stayed positive, shown initiative, and hopefully now, I was another step closer to getting a long-awaited ring on my finger.

CHAPTER NINETEEN

Time to post some pics. I tried to upload something on Instagram at least every other day.

Before I'd started, Goldie and Jada had both been too busy to set up social media pages, but I knew it would be important to help us get new customers. I usually put up cute photos of Scooby, Flapjack, Princess or Lady Gaga chilling in the living room, playing in the garden or sleeping on one of the comfy dog beds. If we had permission, I'd also post snaps of any new guests that were staying with us. I always tried to add a customer testimonial once a week too.

It was going well. We now had a few thousand followers and most importantly, when we asked new customers how they'd heard about us, a lot of them said it was from Instagram or Facebook.

My phone rang, and I glanced at the number flashing on the screen. It was Karen.

To what do I owe this pleasure?

These days it was usually me who messaged her. That

was what friends were supposed to do to see what was going on in each other's lives, rather than waiting to find out on social media.

Yesterday, thanks to her posts, I'd discovered that even though they hadn't confirmed the venue, they'd already started cake tasting. She'd put up a photo of Chuck feeding her a slice of extravagant sponge, captioned:

Time for cake tasting!

There was no way Karen ate that cake. I'd put money on her spitting it out as soon as the photo was taken. Since she'd moved to LA, she was more interested in green juicing and nibbling lettuce leaves, so I couldn't imagine her eating something with carbs or anything containing dairy.

Anyway, I doubted Karen was calling to check how I was, so it had to be something about her. Maybe she was pregnant too. Or perhaps she wanted to let me know that Chuck's *people* had *reached out* to Adele to ask her to sing at their wedding. With Karen, anything was possible.

'Hey,' I answered the call, bracing myself for what was to come.

'Hey, bestie!' she beamed.

Bestie? Karen *definitely* wanted something.

'How are you?' I asked before realising it wasn't necessary because she'd be giving me a full rundown imminently.

'I'm *ah-mazing*! Looks like we've got the venue shortlist for our LA wedding, so now I need to sort out London!'

'Great!' I sensed something else was coming…

'I need to really push forward with organising everything over there. So…'

'So…?' I already didn't like the sound of this.

'*So*, because you're my bestie and you're like *the* event planner extraordinaire, I mean, you've been doing events since you left uni and you're in London, I thought you could help organise my London wedding for me!'

Oh Jesus.

My stomach sank.

Help? I wondered how much help she was talking about. Of course, as painful as it'd be, I'd lend a hand, but Karen could be high-maintenance, and I didn't want to end up being lumbered with organising the whole thing. That would be a nightmare. I could guarantee it. There was no way our friendship could survive something like that.

Luckily Karen was still babbling away about why it was such a great idea, which gave me more time to think of a diplomatic response.

'And I thought it would be perfect too because that way you could be more involved. I know you felt left out of the engagement party and everything, so this could be your chance to *really* be part of the action. Plus, I know you've already done a tonne of research on weddings—you know, with that bridal folder thing you have—so you wouldn't even need to do much, because you've already done the groundwork. You're not going to need it anytime soon, so you might as well put it to good use now.'

Ouch.

If Karen had swung a wrecking ball at my stomach it would have hurt a lot less.

'Well, I—'

'Anyway,' Karen jumped in, 'I'm coming to London in two weeks, so if you could start by setting up some appointments at venues, wedding dress shops, you know, that kind of thing, that would be *fabulous*.'

She hadn't even waited to hear if I was happy to do it. She'd just assumed.

And she wanted me to use the research I'd done for my wedding to plan hers because I 'wasn't going to need it'?

Breathe…

Keep calm.

Karen was my oldest friend. I needed to put my own feelings to one side. Helping her was the right thing to do. She didn't have any sisters or many other friends over here so she needed me. I couldn't let her down.

Also, although as usual her delivery was completely insensitive, she was right—I wasn't using my research right now. I probably wouldn't need to do any visits for another month or two when Miles proposed, so it couldn't hurt for me to see some dresses and venues in person, in advance. When Miles did propose, if I'd already visited some of the places with Karen, it would save me time.

Yeah. Maybe it wasn't a bad idea after all. I could help Karen and indirectly help myself too.

I'd do it. I'd help Karen arrange the appointments. But I'd definitely need to draw the line at planning the whole wedding for her. That would be too much.

'Sure. I can help you set up some appointments…'

'You're a star!'

'And I'll help out where I can with the wedding planning…' Jada jumped out of her chair and mouthed *What?* 'I mean by helping you to set up appointments and stuff like that, but I won't be able to organise everything. I've got loads on with my new job, the competition we're running, and planning a wedding, even a small one, is pretty involved.'

'No worries, hon! I'll probably hire a celebrity wedding planner to do most of it anyway. They'll be used to dealing with stars and have lots of cool contacts. But you know, I don't want to put all my eggs in one basket and it's good to have someone there to do the groundwork, just in case. So, dress shopping and venues are the top priority, okay?'

'Yeah.' I closed my eyes, wondering what I'd let myself in for.

'*Awesome!*' Karen said in an American accent. 'I'll send you my flight details so you know when I'll arrive. If you could get cracking on the appointments ASAP and send me the details of what you've set up by tomorrow, that would be *ah-mazing*.'

'I don't know if I'll get time to do it by tomorrow…'

'Anyway, hon, I've gotta run. Can't wait to receive your updates!'

She hung up. Out of the corner of my eye I could see Jada shaking her head.

It had only been a couple of minutes since I'd agreed to help Karen out, and even though it would benefit me in some ways too, something already told me it was a decision I was going to regret…

CHAPTER TWENTY

The countdown was on. Only two weeks to go until Rome, and I couldn't wait.

Tonight I was going to let Miles know that it was all arranged. I'd booked the flights literally the day after he'd said he was up for going. They were a bargain, and I knew they'd only skyrocket the closer we got to the date of travel, so it made sense to snap them up straight away. The more money we saved on flights, the more we'd have to spend on celebratory champagne, a slap-up meal and the cost of the accommodation.

Somehow, I'd managed to hold out until two days ago to book the hotel. Normally I wasn't bothered about having all the bells and whistles, but when I'd seen the room on offer, I couldn't resist. It was grand, with beautiful paintings on the ceiling, and had a large four-poster bed. I'd never slept in one of them before. It was pretty pricey, hence why I was grateful to have saved on the flights, but what the hell. It was an important occasion. It wasn't every day that we went to Rome, and it wasn't every day that I was about to get engaged.

I know I'd thought it was going to happen in Paris and I was wrong, but things would be different this time.

For starters, I knew Miles must have seen the page of engagement rings I'd left open on his laptop, because when I'd had a brief look at his history a few days later (I wasn't snooping—it was the only thing I'd glanced at, for literally two seconds, I swear), he'd looked at a couple of pages on the jewellers' website. *Woohoo!*

Secondly, I'd got my wedding ring finger measured the day after I used his laptop and bought the cheapest ring I could find that fit. I wore it for a few days on the ring finger of my right hand, because apparently, it was a similar size to the one on the left, then I'd strategically put it out on my bedside table. Somewhere Miles could easily see it. How else would he know what size to order if he didn't have a ring to use as reference? It was another way to remove all obstacles from the process and make his life easier.

Anyway, it took a while for him to cotton on to the hint, but when I came back from doing my legs, bums and tums class at the gym one evening, the ring had been moved. Miles must have used a ruler to measure the diameter of it or something, which was great.

With the ring finally sorted and the location organised, he had everything he needed.

The hotel was also perfectly positioned. Right near the Spanish Steps and Trevi Fountain, which was another reason it was so expensive. It would be worth it, though, because if Miles wanted to propose at sunset or when it was much quieter, we wouldn't have to travel far or get up too early. Not that I was bothered about that though. I'd wake up at three a.m. if it meant I'd finally get my dream proposal.

So we were all set. I'd got the flight details and the hotel's web page all up and ready on my iPad, ready to show it to Miles when he came home. He'd be so happy and relieved. He often did a lot of the organisation of our weekends away. Miles had loads on at work lately, so it would be one less thing for him to do.

And here he was.

I heard the key go in the door and went out to the hallway to greet him.

'Hi, darling.' He strained a smile. That wasn't like Miles at all. He looked like he had the weight of the world on his shoulders.

'Everything okay?' I helped him out of his coat and hung it on the stand whilst he slipped off his shoes.

'Not really. Hard day at work.'

'Oh, baby.' I wrapped my arms around his waist and gave him a squeeze. 'So sorry to hear that. Can I get you something? A drink? Want me to set the bath for you?'

A hard day at work for Miles usually meant one of two things. Sometimes it was just a 'normal' hard day. You know, the ones that most people had. Just not getting everything done like you wanted to, or having too much to do and not enough time. But unlike most people, in Miles' job, a hard day could also mean losing a patient. A child. I still didn't know how he coped with that pain. It was unbearable just thinking about it. The thoughts swirling around your mind, wondering if there was more that you could have done to save them. Awful. Just awful.

Of course, there wasn't. Miles and his team were some

of the best paediatricians in the UK. But they were only human. And there was only so much even they could do.

Because of the whole patient confidentiality thing, Miles could never really talk about it in detail, so needing to bottle it up when he got home must have made it even harder.

But over time, I'd learnt how to try and help him manage the pain. Sometimes there was nothing I could do. I just needed to give him space. Leave him to be alone with his thoughts and wait for him to let me know when he was ready to have company. Other times, though, a long hug would help or a relaxing bath. Nothing could erase the gut-wrenching feelings of sadness and disappointment, but I always wanted to make sure I was there for him. Even if I could reduce the pain by one percent, it would be worth it.

'It's okay. I didn't lose a patient today, thank God,' said Miles. A wave of relief washed over me. 'Just got a lot on. We're so busy at the moment.'

'Sounds like a drink is in order, then, and maybe a foot rub?'

'Yes to the drink, but you know what I'm like with foot rubs. I want to love them, and when I sit down to have one I always wonder why I don't take you up on your offers to do it more often. But then as soon as you touch my feet, I end up giggling like a five-year-old. Not good for my male pride.'

I burst out laughing. It was true. Miles was so ticklish. One stroke of his soles and he'd be wriggling around like a hyperactive worm, begging me to stop. Foot rubs to Miles were like kryptonite to Superman. When he was in a particularly sensitive mood, he was like putty in my hands. If I was rubbing his tootsies he'd literally agree to do *anything* to get me to stop. Thinking about it, that would be the ideal time to ask him to propose, but that wouldn't be very romantic.

'That's exactly why you should have one. I'll get you laughing in five seconds flat. It's guaranteed to cheer you up. Come on! You know you want to. It's not good for my *female* pride to know that my technique is so rubbish that my boyfriend laughs at me every time I try.' I smirked.

'Well, I suppose I could give it another go… You can't improve if you don't have a chance to practice. I'll make that sacrifice. Just for you.'

'Excellent!' I kissed him on the lips. 'I'll try and do it firmer this time, so my fingers feel less like a load of feathers dancing on the bottom of your feet.'

'Sounds good. I could do with one or two laughs tonight as I've got some bad news.' My stomach sank as I wondered what it could be. Then again, once I told him about Rome, he'd be feeling much better.

'Oh no. What is it?'

'I'll tell you after we've had a drink,' said Miles.

'Okay. I have some good news, so hopefully that'll cancel out whatever bad stuff has happened.'

'Even better. You okay to fix the drinks whilst I have a quick shower?'

'Course! What do you fancy? Beer, wine or actually, how about some Prosecco?' Apart from an occasional G&T, Miles tended to avoid drinking any spirits, especially whisky or anything too strong. Another consequence of his childhood and seeing his mum off her head every day.

'Yeah, why not. I suppose I could make yet another

sacrifice tonight and force myself to drink a glass of chilled Prosecco,' Miles joked.

'Coming up!' I said enthusiastically. Prosecco would fit perfectly with the Rome announcement too. Help get us in the mood for our trip.

Whilst Miles was in the shower I got some nice peppermint foot cream, put it on the coffee table, laid a bath towel over the sofa, then went to the kitchen to pour two glasses of Prosecco.

'I'm ready to be tickled to death!' shouted Miles from the living room.

'You mean you're ready for your nice relaxing foot massage?' I walked into the room to see Miles grinning, dressed only in his boxer shorts, with his legs stretched out on the sofa.

Goddamn.

A Roman sculpture had nothing on him. His chiselled chest was still glistening from the body cream he'd slathered all over after having a shower, and his thighs looked more solid than a block of twenty-four-carat gold. And unlike so many of those statues, I could see the package in Miles boxer shorts was very generous. Right now it wasn't Miles' feet that I was interested in massaging…

'*Mmm-mmm*… I'm not sure if I want to honour my offer of a foot massage anymore.'

'What?' Miles covered his mouth in mock horror. 'After I've got myself all worked up for it? So cruel! You said you'd give me one!'

'I did.' I took a gulp of Prosecco, sat on the sofa beside him and stroked his chest. 'And I do want to *give you one*, but not a *foot* massage,' I added cheekily.

'Oh *really*?' Miles sat up and started running his fingers through my hair, slowly… fuck. I loved it when he did that. It was as if he'd activated every single nerve ending in my scalp. My body instantly began to spark. 'What did you have in mind, then?'

'Well… I was thinking of putting my hands elsewhere…' I slid my hands over his boxers.

'*Mmm*… well, I suppose I could make my *third* sacrifice for tonight and let you take advantage of me. On one condition…'

'What's that?' My mind was already imagining all the things I'd like to do to him.

'That you let me take advantage of *you* first.'

'Hmmm… that's a pretty big ask.' I raised my eyebrow, then leant towards him. 'But I can make an exception. Just for you…'

Miles' mouth collided with mine and our tongues flicked against each other's hungrily. He lifted my T-shirt over my head, gently pushed me back on the sofa and straddled me. Before I'd had a chance to catch my breath, he began tracing his tongue behind my ears.

Up. Then down.

Oh. So. Slowly.

The sensation of his warm, sweet breath on my skin felt divine.

Miles started nibbling my earlobes, then continued downwards towards my neck.

Oh God. He knew that was my weakness. It got me every time.

He kissed along my neck and all across my shoulders. *Jesus*. My body was now covered in goosebumps.

Miles unclipped my bra, tossed it on the floor then

brushed his fingers along the centre of my chest. My nipples hardened. I felt myself holding my breath, willing him to touch my boobs. But I knew he wasn't going to rush it. I'd have to wait a little longer…

Miles' fingertips continued down my stomach, up along my sides then across, gently skimming my breasts. I whimpered. I wanted him so badly. I could already feel the tingles and anticipation building between my legs. And his hands hadn't even reached down there yet.

God, his touch.

It was like Miles' fingers were made with some sort of orgasm-inducing magic. With him, sex wasn't just about getting straight down to business. Yeah, we sometimes enjoyed a quickie, but mostly, Miles liked to take his time. He enjoyed caressing me. *Savouring* me. He was a generous lover who cared as much about the appetizer as the main course.

Miles leant forward and started circling the outline of my breasts, teasing me repeatedly with his tongue.

'*Oh God…*,' I moaned, sliding my hand inside his boxers and stroking him. 'I want you…'

'Not yet…,' he whispered. Hearing his voice turned me on even more.

He began licking and sucking my nipples whilst he rolled down my knickers and leggings. His mouth then continued exploring my naked body, trailing down past my belly button, heading further south in between my legs until…

Ooh.

As his tongue flicked against my clit, it took every ounce of concentration for me not to lose my mind right there and then. My heart was racing so fast it felt like it could fly out of my chest at any moment. Miles always knew *exactly* where and how to touch me.

I groaned with pleasure, digging my nails in his back and grinding beneath him. He was driving me wild. I didn't want to come yet. And I knew I would if he continued.

'I want you,' I repeated. My chest was heaving rapidly and I was panting like I'd just run a 200 m sprint.

Miles lifted his head casually, licked his lips, then smirked.

'Ready to take advantage of me now, are you?' I could see the desire burning in his eyes.

'Yes!' I cried out, desperate to have him.

'If you insist…'

He didn't need to tell me twice. This time I pushed *him* back on the sofa and climbed on top.

I ran my tongue across his chest and down his abs. He tasted all woody, spicy and delicious. His scent was always so intoxicating.

Miles was still wearing his boxer shorts and it was time to remedy that. I peeled them down his firm thighs, and his solid rod sprang to attention. My pulse quickened. I couldn't wait to feel *all* of him.

As I eagerly took him in my hand, sliding up and down, I felt Miles grinding beneath me.

'Baby,' he moaned. 'Now is a *very* good time to take advantage…'

Got it.

As much as I wanted to continue touching him, Miles was telling me he was ready. I raised my hips and lowered myself down onto him.

Jesus.

That felt so *good.*

We rocked backwards and forwards. Slowly at first. Each thrust deep and sensuous. But as Miles started stroking my clit again, the intensity increased and I began to pick up the pace.

He sat up, still with his fingers working their magic between my legs, and began sucking my nipples. I squeezed my eyes shut. This was fucking amazing.

As I bounced up and down, running my hands over his body, Miles' thrusts became more intense and blood pumped furiously through my veins. Any minute now I was going to come. I didn't need to tell him not to stop. Our bodies were so in tune that he knew I was on the edge and exactly how to tip me over…

I held out for as long as I could, but the wave kept building and I was powerless to stop it. I let out a long, loud moan and threw my head back as what felt like a million fireworks exploded inside of me.

Ever the gentlemen, Miles waited until I'd finished, then released too.

Holy shit.

I collapsed on his chest. My head and the whole room were spinning.

What a way to start our weekend. Not too shabby for a Friday night.

'Worth the sacrifice?' I asked, my heart still pounding.

'*Definitely*,' Miles panted. 'Actually, this selflessness has made my soul feel so good that I'd be up for making these kinds of sacrifices as often as you'd like.'

'You're *so* kind…' I was still struggling to catch my breath. 'Maybe I should start calling you *Saint* Miller. You're just *so* giving.'

'I am.' He ran his fingers along my shoulders, down my side and across my bum.

His hands. Every time he touched me it was like electricity sparking.

'It's true. That orgasm you gave me was, just *wow*.' They always were. I meant what I said to Roxy the last time she was here. Sex with someone you loved was a million times better than some random hook-up. The feelings, the intensity, *everything* was off the scale. As corny as it sounded, making love was so hot.

'Same. Turns out I didn't need the foot massage to cheer me up.'

'Oh yeah,' I asked, stroking his glorious chest. 'What was your bad news?' Whatever it was, he'd surely get over it much faster now. Everything was always much better after we'd been intimate. It worked wonders for releasing any tension or stress. And that was before I shared the brilliant news about our romantic trip.

Just imagine. As if our imminent engagement wasn't exciting enough, the prospect of having two nights of hot sex like this in the fancy four-poster bed in our hotel room was the icing on the cake. I couldn't wait. I'm sure Miles would jump at the chance to *sacrifice* himself over and over and over again too…

'Well, you know we'd spoken before about maybe going to Rome in a couple of weeks?'

'Yeah…' My heart raced. I didn't like the use of the word *maybe* in this sentence.

'And I said we should wait until a few days before until we booked it?'

I sort of remembered him vaguely talking about that, but I think I was focused more on the *yes, I'd love to go to*

Rome part and maybe zoned out when he mentioned the finer details.

'Erm…'

'Well, I'm afraid we're going to have to hold off from making any reservations for the moment. Looks like I have to cover for Humphrey that Saturday, so we won't be able to go.'

I bolted up from Miles' chest.

You have got to be joking.

No.

My head must still be fuzzy from that orgasm. Maybe it was the Prosecco too. Miles couldn't have just said we weren't going to Rome the weekend after next. That our trip was cancelled.

Not the trip that I'd already planned where we were supposed to get engaged. Not the weekend away that I'd been excitedly counting down the days to more enthusiastically than a child gearing up for Christmas.

No.

There had to be some mistake.

'Did you just… so we're not going to…?' My stomach felt like it had plummeted a thousand feet as I realised what was happening.

'I'm so sorry.' Miles stroked my shoulder. 'I had a feeling this might happen. That's why I said we should wait to book anything. And thank God we held off. But don't worry. I'll make it up to you. And of course, we can go another time. Might not be before the end of this year, but like I suggested before, maybe we can go in late Jan or early Feb when things are a lot calmer. Okay?'

Okay?

No, it definitely was *not* okay.

This was our chance. His chance. A golden opportunity for Miles to pop the question.

The deadline for him to propose was 1st January. So going to Rome a month later wasn't going to work.

Fuck.

Half an hour ago everything had been great. No, not even. Ten minutes ago things had been peachy. We'd just had amazing sex and we had Rome to look forward to. Now that only left Christmas and New Year's Eve.

'Oh, darling.' Miles wrapped his arms around me. 'You're upset. So sorry. If I could get out of it, I would. But we'll go soon. I promise.'

Soon.

That was his favourite bloody word.

I couldn't speak. I was too worried I'd start screaming with frustration.

'I've just remembered!' Miles jumped up. 'You said you had some good news. I feel so bad about letting you down about Rome, so we both need cheering up. Why don't you tell me all about it…?'

CHAPTER TWENTY-ONE

It had been a long week.

Since that night with Miles dropping the bombshell about not going to Rome, I'd been a bit down. I hadn't touched my wedding planning folder. Not even once. Right now, it just felt like a waste of time.

I'd like to think that I was a realist. After that night, I'd realised that as much as I wanted it to, an engagement wasn't going to happen anytime soon. Miles was clearly snowed under at work and no amount of planning and hint dropping was going to change that. I reckoned that hoping for a Christmas proposal was my best chance, so there was no point in spending my evenings working myself up and getting excited before then.

Easier said than done, though. Especially with Karen's wedding preparations being rammed down my throat what felt like every two minutes. I was trying to be happy for her, but it was hard with her posting so often. Each joyful photo was a reminder of what I wanted but couldn't have. It wasn't good for my mental health. I didn't like the pangs of jealousy that struck my heart with every post I saw. So as well as putting my wedding folder to one side, I'd cut back on social media too.

Outside of posting stuff for the hotel, I'd made a point of only checking at lunchtime because I knew I'd be so busy at work, I wouldn't get a chance to wallow too much about the photos of venues, potential wedding dress options, and cake choices she showcased several times a day.

I'd tried not to let things get too weird with Miles. That night, he'd floored me by asking what my good news was. Of course, I couldn't admit that I'd got so carried away with wanting to get engaged that I'd gone ahead and organised the flights and booked the hotel. He'd clearly asked me to wait, so it wouldn't look good. What man would want to marry an obsessed woman who didn't listen?

After wracking my brain for a suitable answer, I'd said that we'd had some new bookings at the hotel, the competition was going well and that Goldie had hired a workman to start doing up her farmhouse, so that all being well, she could consider opening the new site maybe next summer. All of which was true.

Miles had thrown his arms around me, congratulated me on my progress in my new job and said how proud he was, which made me feel more guilty.

After dinner, I'd said our impromptu sofa session had worn me out so I was going to have an early night and read a book. I tried reading, but I couldn't focus, so I'd just gone to bed with Cuddles curled up beside me, feeling like such a fool for jumping the gun.

Just like I'd done after returning from Paris, the next

day I was faced with the embarrassment of cancelling things. Again.

I had to suck it up and lose the money on the flights. It would have cost more to try and change them, and although Miles had said we'd go at some point in the future, it wasn't like I had any idea when that would be. I'd lost the money on the hotel room. When I booked, there was a flexible option that allowed you to cancel for free up to forty-eight hours in advance, but it was more expensive. And of course I'd been so caught up in the excitement of booking that it hadn't even occurred to me that we wouldn't be going at all.

Very expensive lesson learned. Now this failed proposal embarrassment had happened to me twice, I couldn't make the same mistake again. I had to take a long, hard look at my behaviour. I couldn't keep letting my thoughts run away with me.

At the same time, though, my desires hadn't changed. I still wanted the perfect proposal and fairy-tale wedding and I still believed it would happen, but it was more likely when Miles was less stressed and had some time away from work. So I'd decided it made sense to put the plan on hold for a couple of weeks, then I'd pick things up again nearer Christmas.

I'd done the most important groundwork. Even though Rome had been cancelled, at least I'd convinced Miles I was wife material and he knew the kind of proposal and ring I would love. No doubt the internet was still serving him engagement-related adverts, and who knows, the Engagement Chicken's mystical powers could still be working their magic in the background.

Next time I started working on the plan, though, I'd be

more cautious. And less blinkered. No more booking weekend breaks without making absolutely sure it was the best time for both of us.

I needed to be calmer. Less obsessed. And not watching *My Fantasy Wedding*, focusing on my folder and scrolling through social media was definitely helping.

So was my job. Like Miles, things were pretty busy for me at work. It was good to have something else to focus on.

Tonight, I was off to see Audrey. Now that I wasn't occupying my evenings with wedding planning and Miles was often working late, I needed to find other fun things to fill my time. I hadn't seen her for ages, and when I'd lived next door, we used to always make a point of catching up regularly. So a visit was long overdue.

As I approached Audrey's house, I felt weird. I glanced at my front door. That used to be my home. Still hard to believe it'd been over a year since I'd moved in with Miles and put it up for rent. So far the tenant, a woman in her late twenties, had been good. She'd paid on time and Audrey said that generally she kept herself to herself.

It was so tempting to knock on the door and have a quick look around. See how she was looking after the place, but I didn't. I'd moved on. To a better life with Miles. Thinking about it, I'd had some pretty low times in that house. The Alex that had lived there was a different person to the one I was now. That Alex had been insecure in so many ways. She'd thought she had to look and dress a certain way. That the only way to keep a man was to sleep with him as quickly as possible. Thank God I'd seen the light and made changes.

I rang Audrey's bell. Within seconds, she'd opened the door.

'Good evening, Alex.' She smiled.

'Hey, Audrey!' I stepped into the hallway. 'Wow, I love your dress! You look stunning, as always.' She was wearing a bold red three-quarter-length wrap dress with an elegant gold necklace. It really complemented her striking silver bob. She could easily pass for at least a decade younger than her seventy-nine years.

'Why, thank you.' She ushered me into her living room. I glanced at the black-and-white wedding photo of Audrey and her husband hanging on the cute pink floral wallpaper. They made such a lovely couple. 'Just something I rustled up last week.'

'You made that?'

'Yes. You remember I told you I used to be a seamstress?'

'Yeah, that's right. In your twenties, wasn't it?' I remembered it ringing a bell. I sat down on the green-and-pink patterned sofa.

'That's correct. I continued on and off over the years. I haven't made many garments recently, but found myself with a few spare hours one afternoon and I needed a new dress for a function at the community hall last weekend, so I thought it would be the ideal opportunity. Everything in the shops these days just always seems so disappointing. Poor quality and often unoriginal. I didn't fancy what happened to dear Betty happening to me.'

'What happened to Betty?' I asked as she poured me a cup of tea and put out the plate of biscuits. Audrey always made sure she had a selection of digestives and custard creams laid out whenever I visited. If it was the weekend, she laid out jammy dodgers too as an extra treat.

'Well,' she sighed. 'It was rather awkward. Betty arrived at the function last month wearing the same outfit as Edna… she was most upset.'

'Really?' My eyes widened. Mainly because I'd assumed that at that age, women wouldn't give a toss about wearing the same outfit as someone else.

'Yes. She was concerned that it looked more flattering on Edna than her.' *Nightmare*. 'Anyhow, I find it is much easier to just make something myself. That way I can choose the fabric, style and of course avoid such issues.'

'Cool! So tell me about your function. Did you meet up with your friend Harold…?' I winked. I always found it fascinating hearing about Audrey's love life. You could have knocked me over with a feather when she'd come round to my place one day a couple of years ago when Roxy was visiting and casually mentioned that she still 'had relations' with a man from her bridge club.

'Harold? Oh goodness, no. He was getting a little dull. I've only got a few more years left on this earth. The last thing I want is to be bored to death. I need a little excitement. That's why I've taken quite a shine to Kirk…' A cheeky grin spread across Audrey's face. 'More tea?'

I see. I could tell from the glint in her eye that there was more to tell, but Audrey wasn't quite ready to divulge the details of her latest beau just yet. I wouldn't pry. I knew she'd tell me when the time was right.

Seemed like Audrey was enjoying herself, though. She was such an inspiration. She was living a full life. Always out at bridge club, or attending various functions at the community hall. She had a better social life than most people I knew in their thirties. Including me.

'I'm fine, thanks.' I took a bite of a custard cream.

'And you, dear?' She patted my knee. 'How are things with young Miles?'

I filled her in on what had been happening at work and with my personal life. After Jada's and Stacey's reactions, I didn't go into too much detail about my plan. I kept it general—you know, that I'd been doing more cooking, how terrible I was at tennis, seeing his parents, how disappointed I was about Paris and the cancelled trip to Rome because I was hoping that Miles would propose soon. I also told her Karen and Stacey's news.

I was always pretty open with Audrey. She was like a mother and grandmother figure rolled into one, which I really needed sometimes. It was helpful to get an opinion from someone who'd experienced more of life and could share their wisdom.

I didn't really speak to my own mum anymore. I got the odd text from her two or three times a year, probably to check I was still alive or to ease her conscience (then again, I wasn't entirely sure she had one), but that was it.

I blamed her for a lot of the issues I had with men and my lack of self-worth. Growing up, my brother and I always seemed like an inconvenience. Like we'd interrupted her enjoying herself.

Once she'd divorced Dad (after he ran off with his secretary and got her knocked up in true cliché style), Mum had gone on a man-rampage. She'd disappear in the evenings and leave us to fend for ourselves, then bring men back home and keep us up all night with her screams of ecstasy as they had very loud sex. And if that wasn't bad enough, she'd tell us how enjoyable it was the next morning. Not the kind of behaviour a child expected from their mother.

Then there were the constant digs: 'Don't wear trousers Alex or no man will want you.' Or, 'Women with short hair aren't attractive, Alex, you need to make your hair longer.' And, 'Why haven't you had sex yet, Alex? You're almost sixteen. It's time to become a woman!' *Ugh.* Her twisted views had screwed up my head for years.

Anyway, I was better off now without her. Audrey might not be blood, but she'd supported me more than my real so-called mother.

'Don't worry too much about the proposal not happening yet, dear. Things are different these days.' Audrey sipped her tea. 'As you know, I am a big advocate of marriage. I had many happy years with my Cecil, God rest his soul. But in this modern age, men and women can live happily together for years before they get wed. Some don't even tie the knot at all. Happiness comes in many forms. Keep an open mind. Whatever happens, I'm sure you and Miles will have a great life and he'll do right by you. He's a lovely chap.'

'He is,' I said.

'Now. Will you stay for supper or do you need to rush back for Miles? It's been so long since I've seen you and I'd love to hear more about your new job, Cuddles and your vibrant cousin Roxanne.'

'Yes,' I said. 'I'd love to. Miles will be just fine making his own dinner for one night.'

CHAPTER TWENTY-TWO

Karen had just texted to say she was five minutes away from the office, which probably meant half an hour. I couldn't leave until I'd sent an important email, so that should give me just enough time.

I still couldn't believe what had happened this morning. I'd opened my inbox to see that the night before, I'd had an email from Siobhan Reeves, one of the TV presenters of the *London Evening News*, and she'd agreed to be one of the judges for our competition. This was amazing!

I'd approached several local celebs, some through their agents if I could find their details, and others I'd direct messaged on Instagram or emailed. I wasn't expecting to hear back from them because they probably had people messaging them all the time, but I thought I had nothing to lose, so it was worth a shot. And she replied!

To be honest, I think it had a lot to do with me mentioning Roxy's friend Sophia. I think they'd known each other for years, so she'd put in a good word for the hotel, which meant Siobhan was expecting my message.

I was nervous about telling her that there was no money involved, but she was fine with it. She said she might even see if they could get it featured on their show. Could you imagine!? Goldie and Jada would be so chuffed. The local paper had already agreed to run a story on the winner. That kind of exposure could be major for the hotel.

So before I left today, I wanted to confirm the dates we had in mind. We'd close the competition next week, then I'd send her a shortlist. That should give me enough time to collate the votes from the other judges (Goldie, Jada and a couple of other animal experts I'd sourced) and get the trophies and the certificates made before Christmas, ready to announce the winner during the first week of January. I couldn't wait!

It was almost noon and I'd booked a half-day holiday so that I could go wedding dress shopping with Karen. Taking time off work wasn't ideal. I had so much to do with the competition, and since it was announced, we'd become a lot busier, which was great. I didn't really have a choice, though, because the bridal shop was booked up at weekends. The manager said coming on a Monday would be better because it'd be quieter, so we'd be able to try on a wider selection of dresses and have more of her time.

Yes. I'd said *we*. I may have mentioned that Karen and I were both brides-to-be. In my defence, it was the same woman I'd spoken to when I'd booked the appointment for the Monday after the weekend in Paris, so explaining that I hadn't actually got engaged would be awkward. Plus, if I was going to take time off to help Karen out, there was no harm in me doing a little bit of window-shopping for myself…

Me

Just finishing off some work, so best if you come up to the office. Won't be long. At least then you can meet some of the cute siblings!

Karen replied instantly.

Karen

Okay, hon. But I can't wait around too long. I want to try on as many dresses as possible.

Karen

Cute! Animals love me! Xxx

Me

Won't be long, promise.

Me

Cool! Xxx

'Karen's going to come up to the office.' I turned to Jada. 'I want to send this email before I go.' I'd got in just before eight a.m. so I could get a head start and leave earlier and Siobhan's email was a very happy surprise. She'd just replied to the message I'd fired off to her this morning, so I wanted to keep the momentum going.

'Oh *really*?' Jada raised her eyebrow. 'So I'll finally get to meet Madame Bougie in person… I'll have to check to see if we have a red carpet to lay down outside for her arrival.'

Jada really wasn't a fan.

'Karen's nice. *Honestly…*'

'We'll see…'

As predicted, half an hour later, the doorbell rang. I went downstairs to let Karen in.

'Hey!' I held my arms out. 'It's been so long!'

'Hey, bestie!' she gushed before giving me two cheek kisses, making a loud *mwah* sound with each one.

Karen was dressed in fitted white jeans, a white blouse with gold chains and a huge wide-brimmed tan hat, which almost caught me in the eye as she hugged me back. Despite the fact that it was November and pretty dull outside, Karen was wearing huge sunglasses with a big gold double-C Chanel logo at either side.

'Come in.' I ushered her inside. 'And here comes the welcoming committee.' Scooby came rushing towards the door. He stopped at Karen's feet, then started barking. That was strange. Normally he was so friendly. Flapjack followed and started growling. Even Lady Gaga, who'd raced into the hallway to find out what all the fuss was about, didn't seem impressed.

'Oooh, someone's grouchy!' said Karen.

'Flapjack's usually really happy. What's up, little one?' I bent down to stroke him. 'This is my friend Karen. She's come all the way from America. Los Angeles. Say hello!' He growled again and came and sat by my feet.

'This one looks more like my kind of girl.' Karen smiled at Lady Gaga. 'Loving the dress, cutie pie.' As always, Lady Gaga was dolled up to the nines, as if she was ready to step out onto some kind of doggie catwalk. Today she was sporting a pink-and-white polka dot dress. She glared at Karen, then spun around and darted back into the living room, like she had more interesting business to take care of.

'Anyway, I'm almost finished. Goldie, our owner, is on the phone, but come upstairs. My colleague Jada is dying to meet you.' That was true…

'Okay.' Karen slid her fancy handbag down her arm and started following me upstairs.

'Jada must have gone to the bathroom,' I said as I entered the empty office. 'She'll be back in a sec, though. Take a seat.' I pointed to the sofa and sat down at my desk.

'Erm, better not.' Karen wrinkled her nose. 'Don't want to get the dog or cat or whatever hairs on my Pradas.'

'Your Pradas?' I frowned.

'My jeans.'

'Oh, right. Here…' I pulled out a spare office chair. 'This should be pet-hair free.'

'It's okay.' She wrinkled her nose again. 'I'll stand. You won't be long, will you?' She glanced down at her diamond-encrusted watch. Definitely a million miles away from the Swatch watches we both wore as teenagers. 'It's just, time is ticking…'

Bit cheeky of her to keep banging on about time after being late, especially when I was taking half a day off today and a full day off tomorrow to look at venues. But that was what friends did to help each other out, I supposed.

'I'm almost done. We still have enough time to make our appointment.' I knew Karen was terrible with punctuality, so I'd factored in an extra hour as a contingency. I skimmed over my email one more time.

'So…!' Jada's voice boomed as she walked into the office. 'You must be Alex's mega-famous friend, Karen!'

Oh God.

Jada was clearly taking the piss. And she'd bought Mr Chilli with her, which could only mean trouble.

'Oh, well…' Karen blushed. 'I don't know about *mega* famous, but you know, I *do* have *lots* of fans. In fact, my fan base is growing every day. Alex, did I tell you, I'm up to fifty thousand followers on Insta?'

'No, you didn't…'

'*Wow!*' gushed Jada. 'A real celebrity in our office. We are *hashtag blessed*! I'm Jada, by the way. If I'd known you were coming, I would have made more of an effort so that we could take a selfie together! Such a pleasure to meet you.' Jada put out her hand.

'Likewise.' Karen gave Jada a limp handshake. 'And it's okay. You don't look that bad. We can still take a selfie together if you like. Anything for my fans.'

Seriously, Karen?

Sometimes she really was her own worst enemy. It was hard to keep insisting to everyone that she was nice when she said stuff like that.

Jada plastered a fake grin on her face to disguise her gritted teeth. I had a feeling she hadn't finished with Karen yet.

'Alex has told me *so* much about you!'

'All good, I hope!'

Jada paused, then let out a fake laugh, which I knew meant *You really don't want me to answer that*, but Karen probably thought Jada just found her hilarious. She *did*, but not in the way Karen would like…

'Alex, do you have a Snickers bar in your drawer? I'm craving chocolate. I'd love a *Snickers*…'

Uh-oh. Everyone knew that Snickers was one of Mr Chilli's triggers. Everyone except Karen, of course.

Suddenly Mr Chilli perked up. Jada turned him to face Karen.

'Show us your knickers!' He flapped enthusiastically. 'Show us your knickers!'

Karen gasped.

'Did he just…?' She stepped back in horror.

'You're normally such a *cutie*! Must be a *glitch*,' Jada said.

Oh no…

Cutie and *glitch* also weren't good.

'That's a big booty! Oooh, you dirty little bitch!'

'Mr Chilli!' I shouted. 'Sorry about this, Karen. He has a bit of a potty mouth sometimes. He doesn't mean it.'

This was a first. Karen was speechless. She was stood against the wall with her mouth open. Jada, on the other hand, was smirking, doing her best not to break out into a fit of giggles.

'You dirty little bitch!' he said again.

'Okay, Mr Chilli.' Jada stroked him as she approached the door. 'We better get you back to your room. 'Can't have you insulting our *celebrity guest*…'

'What a vulgar little shit!' said Karen. That was a bit harsh.

'He's sweet, really. He's not like that all the time.'

'*Whatever.* Can I use your restroom?' *Restroom?* She really was turning American.

'Course. Turn right and the bathroom's at the end of the hallway.'

Just as Karen left, Jada returned.

'You're *so* bad!' I shook my head.

'What?' Jada shrugged her shoulders. 'No idea what you're talking about…' She smirked.

'You brought him in here deliberately.'

'Might have done… Little Miss Bougie deserved it. She's even more stuck up than I thought. And a rubbish friend. I don't like how she treats you.'

'She's okay,' I said weakly. It was hard to stick up for Karen after she'd breezed in here like she was a bigger star than J-Lo, Taylor Swift and Oprah put together. Even the siblings didn't take to her. 'And isn't it a bit wicked to encourage Mr Chilli to swear? I thought Goldie was trying to wean him off the bad language.'

'I texted her when you told me her highness was visiting, and after telling her all about how she's always making you feel bad about the proposal, Goldie said we're family, so we need to stick up for each other, and a few strong words from Mr Chilli wouldn't hurt. And that was before Miss LA told me I "didn't look that bad" and called me a fan. *Girl, please*. It's not a wedding dress that woman needs. It's a reality check.'

Karen came back in the room.

'Ready to go?' She adjusted her hat and sunglasses.

'Yep.' I pressed send on my email. *Done*. 'Shouldn't take long to get there on the tube.'

'The *tube*?' Karen frowned. 'No way. I can't be seen on public transport. Can't you just order a cab?'

An Uber would cost three times as much.

'Sweet Jesus,' I heard Jada mutter.

'Okay,' I said, thinking I needed to get Karen out of here before she made herself look even worse. I supposed this was a special occasion and if we split the cost, it wouldn't be too bad. I opened the app. 'Let's go.' Luckily there was a driver just a few minutes away. 'See you, Jada.'

'Laters,' she replied. 'And good luck, Alex! You're going to need it.'

CHAPTER TWENTY-THREE

Crazy that there was traffic at this time of day. The tube definitely would have been a lot quicker. As the cab crawled along at a snail's pace, I saw that there were roadworks ahead. That explained it.

I was hoping we could get a bite to eat before we went to the bridal store, but there wouldn't be time to do that now. I had an apple in my bag and a packet of crisps. Looked like that would have to tide me over for now.

I was really excited to finally be going to the Forever Bridal Boutique. It had always been at the top of my list of places to visit for my dress. My folder was filled with gowns that I'd spotted in their shop. They'd been featured on so many TV shows and had a brilliant reputation. I'd spent ages researching different stores, but theirs always came out on top. It was a hit with both brides and the media, so I was sure we'd find something Karen liked.

I'd already seen a dress for myself which I was sure was *the one*. Hopefully they'd have it in stock and I could try it on later. Just the thought of sliding into it gave me goosebumps.

But today wasn't about me. It was all about finding Karen's perfect gown, so I needed to focus. At least whilst we were sitting in traffic, she could run me through what she was looking for. Every time I'd asked, she'd been vague and rushed me off the phone, saying she didn't have time to go into it. I'd texted her last week to ask her to bring some screenshots or pictures with her. Now we were alone she could show me everything.

'So, did you bring a scrapbook or some pictures of the type of dress you're looking for?'

'No need. I'll know it when I see it.'

What?

She had to be joking.

A wedding dress was probably the most expensive piece of clothing a woman would buy in her life. I even felt bad referring to it as a *piece of clothing*. It was much more than that. A wedding dress was precious. It was what everyone would be waiting to see. It *had* to be perfect. You couldn't just wing it. Or rock up to the store without a basic idea of what you wanted. There was far too much choice. It would be too overwhelming.

I cast my mind back to when I'd first started my folder and researched dresses. I'd been overwhelmed by what seemed like the millions of options available. First there was the style of the neckline. Sweetheart, portrait, scoop, one-shoulder… it was like learning another language.

Then there was the *silhouette*. The dress consultant at the store would need to know what style Karen wanted. She couldn't just turn up and say 'show me your dresses'. We'd be there until Christmas 2051. Karen needed to know whether she wanted a mermaid, trumpet, ball gown, A-line or one of the many other options.

I knew exactly what I wanted. A big princess ball gown with a sweetheart neckline was my dream dress.

Yes, please.

Like the top of a heart, the sweetheart neckline would accentuate my boobs tastefully and help me look taller. And having a ball gown silhouette was definitely a no-brainer. With that on, I could glide down the aisle like a princess. It had everything I wanted. It was classic but bold. It would make a statement. It was perfect.

'We can't go into the store without having some idea of what you want. Don't worry. We still have time. Let's start with the neckline. How would you like the top of the dress to look?' I started scrolling through some photos on Instagram. That was better than diving into my folder because all my images were sweetheart. 'How about this? It's a nice scoop.'

'No way!' Karen snapped. 'I'm going to be the centre of attention, so I need the wow factor. Especially if the paps are going to be there. I need to make an impact. You know, like when Liz Hurley wore *that* dress?'

'What kind of dress did she wear when she got married?'

'No, silly! Not her *wedding* dress. The Versace one that she wore when she went to the *Four Weddings and a Funeral* premiere with Hugh Grant in the nineties.'

I scanned my brain trying to think of what she was talking about. I wasn't clued up on all these designer brands that Karen seemed to love. I was more of a Zara or Top Shop kind of girl. Oh yeah… I think I remembered what she meant.

'Do you mean the black dress with the big gold safety pins down the side?'

'Yes!' Karen rolled her eyes. 'Something like *that* will hit the front pages. *That's* what gets column inches. You know, like when Sinitta just wore a few palm leaves as an outfit at the *X Factor* Judges' Houses with Simon Cowell?'

'Yeah…,' I said, casting my mind back. 'But what's that got to do with your wedding dress? Are you saying you want to walk down the aisle covered in leaves or a skimpy piece of material held together with a few pins?' I frowned.

'Of course not! But I need something that will have the wow factor. Y'know?'

'Er, okay…' I wondered if she'd been drinking. Sounded like Karen wanted something that definitely wasn't conventional. The brief seemed like it would be much bigger than I could handle on my own. The consultants at the store, on the other hand, probably came across strange requests like Karen's all of the time, so they'd know how to deal with it.

We hadn't even arrived at the store yet and I could already tell this afternoon was going to be interesting…

'Welcome!' said Nancy.

'Thanks!' I gushed as I stepped into the store. It was exactly like the photos I'd seen in the magazines. Plush white carpets, a table with a huge pretty pink-and-white floral centrepiece and, of course, rows of stunning wedding dresses on either side.

'Congratulations on your engagements,' she beamed.

'Thank you!' Karen gushed, putting out her left hand so that Nancy could get a good look at her giant diamond engagement ring.

'Stunning!' Nancy replied.

I shuffled awkwardly, hiding my hands behind my back. It hadn't occurred to me when I'd said we were both brides-to-be that there would be a ring inspection.

'I-I'm…'

'She's still waiting for—'

'My ring to come back from the jewellers!' I jumped in. I hoped Karen wasn't going to drop me in it, but I couldn't be sure.

'So, tell me, ladies. What kind of dresses are you interested in seeing today?'

'Well, I need something with drama. Impact. The wow factor. Something fitting for a person like me. I'm an actress, you see. I live and work in LA. My fiancé is a top Hollywood director. I've just flown in to see what London has to offer. I'm having two weddings. One here and one back home. I'll probably go for a Vera Wang gown for my LA wedding, but I'm open to suggestions for the London dress.'

'Right, I see.' Nancy nodded. 'So do you have an idea of the kind of neckline or silhouette you'd like?'

'Like I said, something with *drama*. Something sexy. Like you'd see on a red carpet.'

What was she on about? People didn't wear wedding dresses on the bloody red carpet.

'Sexy, you say? So perhaps something that emphasises the cleavage, tastefully of course?' Nancy pulled out a dress with a sweetheart neckline. 'Something like this?'

'Hell no! Looks like something my mum would wear.

Or a nun. But you're right. Something that shows off my tits. My ex paid good money for these boobs. Got to make the most of them.'

That was true. Most women would be offended by their boyfriend getting them a boob job for their birthday. Not Karen. She thought it was the best present ever. Said that he was so considerate because he knew it would help her get more work. I was pretty sure that wasn't his motivation. If Miles ever offered me one, I'd tell him to get lost, but each to their own. It was her body, so if it made Karen feel better, then more power to her.

'How about something like this, then?' Nancy pulled out a dress with a plunging neckline. *Wowsers.* Well, it was certainly attention-grabbing. With Karen's boobs, that would leave nothing to the imagination.

'Bingo! Now we're talking. The cleavage bit, though. I don't like the bottom of the dress or those horrible lacy sleeves. Looks like they've been torn off my grandma's curtains.'

Ouch. She had a point about the lace sleeves, but I probably would have put it more delicately than that.

'Let me have a look myself.' Karen started going through the selection of dresses on the rack. 'No. Too plain. Too mumsy. Nope. Too old-fashioned. OMG, no! Reminds me of a toilet roll dolly! *Gross!*'

Nancy and I glared at each other.

'I think I have an idea of what you're looking for. Something with a plunging neckline, and silhouette-wise, perhaps a mermaid style. A fishtail design will emphasise your curves and show off your amazing figure.'

'Exactly.' Karen beamed. 'Now you're getting it. *Well done.*'

'Glad to hear we're on the same page.' Nancy brushed off Karen's condescending tone. 'And what's your budget?'

'Don't worry about the money.' Karen waved her finger. 'It just has to be right.'

Oh, how nice it must be to be able to say those words.

Despite how she made it seem, Karen didn't come from money. We'd both gone to a state school and led pretty modest lives. Then she'd met some loaded guy when she was working on the perfume counter at Selfridges in her early twenties and was smitten.

He'd wined and dined her. Showered her with expensive gifts. Even though they only dated for a couple of months, she was hooked. After a taste of what she considered to be *the good life*, it was hard for her to date 'normal' guys from South London. She started hanging out at fancy bars and clubs, wearing posh clothes and acting differently.

The rich boyfriends kept coming. And because her new so-called friends were loaded and famous, Karen thought there was no way she could be seen working as a 'lowly sales assistant' when she was dating a footballer or actor or pop star. It would be bad for their image. So she gave up her job.

When her actor boyfriend said he could hook her up with a small part on an indie film he was working on, Karen jumped at the chance. That was when she caught the acting bug. Even though she didn't make the final cut and only ever had very small parts after that, she was determined to be the next Jennifer Lawrence. So a couple of years ago, she upped sticks and headed to LA.

As far as I knew, the jobs she'd had so far didn't pay

much, so I never understood where she got this endless supply of money. I didn't want to assume it came solely from her boyfriends, but… anyway. It was none of my business. If Karen could afford to buy a dress for five or ten thousand pounds, then good for her.

Nancy returned from the stock room with the first selection of dresses. She pulled back the pretty pink velvet curtain and took the gowns into the plush dressing room where Karen was already inside waiting. Then Nancy remembered another gown she had, so went to get it.

'I'll be back in a moment to help you on with the first dress. Please just take a look at them on the rail in the meantime.'

Nancy disappeared into the stockroom door. A few minutes later I heard a high-pitched scream. It was Karen.

Shit. I jumped off the comfy pink velvet sofa and raced into the dressing room. I hoped she was okay.

I yanked back the curtain, expecting to see her in a heap on the floor after twisting her ankle and falling over or something. But instead she was on a chair, in one of the dresses, clutching her chest. Pretty sure Nancy had told her to wait before trying anything on.

Maybe Karen had seen the price tag and almost fainted. That was what happened when you told a saleswoman that money was no object. The dress didn't look too blingy, though. And how much would it have to be to bring on such an extreme reaction. Ten grand? Twenty? The mind boggled.

'What happened? Are you okay?'

'No!' Karen shouted. I could hear Nancy's footsteps as she ran towards the room.

'Everything alright?' Nancy seconded.

'This dress…' She fanned herself as she gasped for breath. 'I tried it on and it fits!'

'That's a good thing, isn't it?' I frowned.

'No! It isn't! It… the label says this dress is a size ten and I am absolutely *not* a size ten! Like I told you earlier, Nancy, I'm a UK size eight! How is this possible? I've been busting my arse in the gym for the last three weeks and have followed the green plant diet religiously. Your stupid parrot was right, Alex. To be a size ten, I must have a giant bottom! I'm going to be a fat bride!' Karen started sobbing like a baby.

She cannot be serious.

How the hell could a size ten be considered fat? What did that make me and the majority of women in the world? She was being ridiculous.

'Please don't worry,' said Nancy calmly. 'A wedding gown is often one or two sizes higher than the size you wear in your everyday clothes.'

'Really?' Karen wiped her eyes and perked up.

'Yes. And remember, no one but us will know the number, so you don't need to worry. It can be our little secret.' Nancy smiled. She handled that well. Anyone else would have given Karen a slap across the face to bring her to her senses. God knows I was tempted to.

'Okay, then.' Karen's shoulders relaxed and she jumped up from the chair. 'That's a relief.'

'Now. Shall I help you try on another dress?'

~

We were now on dress number seven and I was starting to lose the will to live. On the plus side, Nancy's assistant had very generously kept me topped up with Prosecco, which was helping to numb the pain of sitting through Karen's dress tantrums significantly.

Each dress was either too boring, not wow enough, too long, too frumpy… I'd lost count of the adjectives she'd used, but none of them were positive. Except for the dress with a plunge neckline that was almost as low as Karen's belly button. I thought it was a bit too much, but it was the closest Karen had come to liking something.

I told Karen I needed to pop out and get some food. All the alcohol on an empty stomach wasn't a good idea. I'd asked her if she wanted something, but she said she would wait until she left and find somewhere to buy a freshly pressed green juice. I grabbed a sandwich and picked up some carrot sticks for Karen, just in case. I know she was convinced that she needed to diet to look good in her dress, but it couldn't be healthy skipping lunch like that. A few bits of veg was hardly enough to sustain her. But at least it was something.

I stepped back in the store, feeling a bit more energised, and looked at my watch. We'd been here for hours and I hadn't even looked at a single dress for myself.

Karen was busy rifling through the next selection of gowns Nancy had pulled out, so I had time.

I scrolled through the rack. So many choices and I knew this was only a fraction of the stock they had. Just as I was about to sit down, I spotted it.

The dress.

My dress.

It was the one I'd seen online and loved. I'd screen-grabbed it and saved it on Instagram. I'd adored it so much

I'd even printed out a colour copy at my old job when my boss went out for lunch.

I'd admired it so many times in my wedding planning folder and on my phone. And now here it was. In real life. In all its glory.

It was an ivory ball gown, with a sweetheart neckline. The beautiful full, voluminous modern ball skirt featured a scattering of 3D floral motifs, which were accentuated with tiny translucent silver sequins. It looked like it had been handmade by fairies or angels. It was magical.

'Seen something you like?' asked Nancy.

'Yeah. I've loved this dress for ages.' I pulled out my phone to show her my folder.

'So you like the ball gown style?' she asked.

'Love it! I've always wanted to get married in a big princess gown with a sweetheart neckline. This dress is perfect.' It would look amazing with a tiara too.

'Interesting…,' Nancy said. 'Well, you're welcome to try it on if you like?'

'Oh, I couldn't…' I said, thinking I was here for Karen. She was engaged and I wasn't. When I'd made the booking, and in the taxi, I'd said to myself that I'd like to try something on. But now that I was here, I felt silly pretending that I was actually getting married when Miles hadn't proposed yet.

Then again, why not? After a whole afternoon helping Karen, I deserved to try on my dream dress.

'Don't worry about your friend. She's on an important call. To her agent or something. Come on.' She smiled, plucking the dress from the rail.

I couldn't get in that changing room quick enough. This was my moment. I'd dreamt about this for so long.

As Nancy slipped it off the hanger, I felt my heart beating faster. I was so excited. I was glad I'd worn my good underwear. I'd also bought some heels to wear to give me a better feel of how the dress might look.

I stepped into the dress, then closed my eyes as Nancy zipped it up and fiddled at the back, pulling it in and clipping it to try get it to fit as best as possible. I was sure that when I ordered it and got the alterations done, it would fit me like a glove.

I didn't want to open my eyes until I knew that everything was in place. This would be the big reveal. I felt like I was on *Say Yes to the Dress*. But Nancy wouldn't even need to ask me if I did, because I knew I would give this gown a big thumbs-up. It was going to be perfect.

'You can open your eyes now,' said Nancy.

She didn't need to tell me twice. I opened my eyes, excited to see my reflection in the grand mirror.

Oh.

I glared at myself once. Twice. Then a third time. And I felt…

Nothing.

Shit.

I didn't get it. This was *the dress*. But somehow, it didn't feel like it was.

Don't get me wrong. It was nice. Pretty. I particularly loved the flowers on the design, but it wasn't me. It didn't suit me. Which made no sense. It had the neckline and silhouette I loved. I didn't feel the butterflies, though. My heart sank.

'So? What do you think?' Nancy asked.

'Erm…' I paused. 'I thought I'd love it, but I'm not

sure. Maybe it just needs to grow on me. Could I try it with a tiara, please?'

'Of course!'

Nancy swiftly returned with a tiara. I slid it onto my head. It looked pretty, but something still wasn't right.

'Would you mind taking a few photos from different angles?' I remembered reading that was important.

'No problem.' Nancy snapped away, then handed me back my phone. I scrolled through the photos. No. Something was off. I didn't feel like a bride. Even with the tiara on, I didn't feel like a princess.

Maybe it was because I knew that right now I was a fraud. I wasn't really engaged. Once I was, I might have a different glow or hold myself better.

'Alex, a dress shouldn't have to grow on you. Your gut will tell you when a gown is right. Would you like to try on some more dresses? I know you've got your heart set on a ball gown style, but I see you in something more minimal. Something sophisticated and chic. Like a slip dress.'

'Oh no! That will be far too plain. I only intend to get married once, so I want something more dramatic. This will be my big day, so I want to look like a princess.'

'It's up to you.' Nancy held her hand up. 'But remember, when you're choosing a dress, even if you think you have a clear vision of what you want, it's always good to try different styles. I've had so many brides fall in love with a silhouette they never even thought they'd wear. You never know. Picking a wild card might surprise you…'

I knew Nancy was trying to be helpful, but a slip dress was little more than a glorified nightdress. Simple was fine for some occasions, but not for my wedding. I needed something wow. Not Karen's cleavage-flashing, in-your-face level of wow, but you know. Something with more impact. A ball gown ticked all of those boxes.

'A little help in here, please!' shouted Karen.

'Sounds like you're needed!' I raised my eyebrow.

Nancy left and I followed behind her. Might as well get Karen's opinion on my dress. Don't know why, though. She was sure to hate it.

'How's it going?' said Nancy.

Karen was standing in a mermaid dress so tight that it looked like it would split if she moved or even breathed. That definitely wouldn't be comfortable to wear all day. Karen wouldn't be able to sit down or eat. Then again, seeing as she'd refused the carrot sticks I'd offered her earlier, eating at her wedding probably wasn't a priority.

'What's *that* dress?' Karen's eyes popped out as she saw me. 'I didn't realise you were trying anything on.'

'Well, yeah. It's kind of a dress I've had my eye on for ages. It was my dream dress, so I thought I'd try it on. I'm not sure about—'

'I love it!'

She does?

'Really?' I wasn't expecting Karen to be so enthusiastic. It was good to know she could be supportive. I knew she wanted the best for me and was rooting for Miles to propose.

'Yes! That will look great on me. Why didn't you show me that one?' she barked at Nancy.

No way. She wouldn't. This had to be a joke…

'Um, because it didn't fit your brief.' Nancy frowned, clearly as shocked as I was that Karen was considering my dress for herself. 'You said sexy, plunging, something to show off your curves, so…'

'Whatever.' Karen waved her finger. 'Let me try it on. I can have it as a backup dress. Or now that I think about it, I should have *two* wedding dresses for London. That one can be the dress I wear for the reception. It's probably cheap, isn't it, so even if I don't get to wear it on the day, it won't matter.'

'But…' I opened my mouth and tried to find the words. I was speechless. How could Karen even think about buying it for herself? I just told her it was my dream dress. Yeah, now I'd tried it on, it didn't feel right, but she didn't know that. I'd only said I wasn't sure. But I could have been referring to anything. The price, for example.

Karen had been pushing my buttons a lot lately, but this was some next-level shit. I'd gone out of my way to help her. Then the one time I decided to try on a dress for myself, she had to make it all about her. Like she always did.

I remembered when we were younger, her Saturday job, first car, boyfriends and clothes always had to be 'better' than everyone else's. Back then, I'd brushed it off as her just being competitive, but now she had really taken the piss.

I felt like telling her to stuff the dress up her backside and walking out of here right now. I was already wondering if it was too late to cancel the venue visits I'd set up for her tomorrow.

In fact, it wasn't just the visits I wanted to cancel.

With the way Karen had been acting, maybe it was time I cancelled our so-called friendship too.

CHAPTER TWENTY-FOUR

I stepped through my front door, kicked off my boots, took off my coat, then went and flopped onto the sofa. I definitely should be given a medal for my patience. I'd bit my tongue so many times during these past two days with Karen I was surprised I could still speak.

Yesterday, after Karen had asked me to take off *my dress* so that she could try it on, we'd stayed in the store for another hour and a half. Even now, I wasn't sure how I managed to do it without slapping her or storming out.

Karen tried on her favourite three dresses again and asked me to take dozens of photos of each one. I wouldn't consider myself a violent person, but I admit there were points where I wanted to take her phone and stamp on it. She'd made me so angry. By this point, Nancy and her assistant brought out another bottle of Prosecco, as if to help calm my nerves, but I didn't trust myself. I was probably only one glass away from telling Karen exactly what I thought of her. I didn't want to create a scene, so I decided to take the higher ground and just stew in silence.

In the end, Karen told Nancy that she'd be in touch this week to confirm whether she would buy one (or two) dresses. *Grrr.*

Thankfully, just before we left, Karen got a call from a 'contact' who invited her out for drinks in Chelsea, so I didn't have to spend any more time with her. When I got back, I was seething. Miles could tell I was in a bad mood and asked why. I couldn't tell him the full extent of how I felt, because it would probably freak him out. Could you imagine the conversation?

Yeah, so I'm pissed off because even though we're not even engaged (which by the way, I'm also very upset about), today I tried on my dream wedding dress. You know, the one I've had my eye on for months? The one that's in the giant wedding planning folder that you know nothing about that I've been working on for years, even before I met you, and Karen said she wanted to try it on and buy it.

Something told me that wouldn't go down well. So I just had to keep it simple and say that I'd been wedding dress shopping with Karen and she was super demanding.

As frustrated as I was, I decided it might also be a good opportunity to drop another little hint. I told Miles that there were lots of beautiful dresses there that I liked, that Nancy was lovely and that when I left, I told her that I hoped I'd see her again *very soon*.

And the result of my hinting?

Miles just changed the subject, asked if I preferred peas or broccoli with the dinner he'd cooked, then started scooping some food into Cuddles' bowl.

Great.

Anyway, this morning Karen and I had met up at 10 a.m. at the first venue. A fancy hotel in London that she'd insisted on seeing. As usual, she was half an hour late, so I'd asked the wedding planner most of the questions. The interior was stunning with huge crystal chandeliers and big pillars, but you definitely paid for it. The cost per head was a few hundred pounds. Yikes.

Next we'd visited a museum right in the heart of London. It had an eighteenth-century interior, antique furniture, a grand marble fireplace and a sweeping staircase. Not really my style, but it was popular for weddings and was one of the few venues in the area that you could hire exclusively.

I saved visiting my dream venue until last. After Karen hijacked my dress yesterday, on the way there, I started to regret adding it to the list.

I'd always wanted to get married in a castle, but the ones I liked the most were in Scotland, and I wanted to make sure it was as easy as possible for people to get there.

I knew weddings were already expensive to attend. There was the cost of the gift and maybe a new outfit. So I didn't want guests to have to think about spending hundreds of pounds getting there, paying for accommodation, etc. That was why most of the venues in my folder were just outside London. In Surrey or Hertfordshire. Which in theory was supposed to make the hire costs more affordable than big central London prices.

Rather than a castle, Haverly Court was a palace, so I could still feel like I was a princess, getting her fairy-tale wedding.

It was only about forty minutes from London Waterloo. Karen agreed to take the train as long as she went first class, which suited me fine as I told her I'd stick to standard, which meant that, thankfully, we didn't have to sit together.

When we arrived, I was blown away. As well as the palace itself, which had amazing historic architecture and pretty stone archways, Haverly Court also had stunning gardens. They would make a beautiful backdrop for the wedding photos.

There was the Grand Hall too, which could be used for the reception. I could just imagine myself gliding across the dance floor in my big ball gown dress like Cinderella.

It was the perfect venue. Unlike yesterday, when my dream wedding dress hadn't lived up to my expectations, I fell in love with this place at first sight. I adored it and I'd get married there in a heartbeat. Except there were a few challenges…

Firstly, it was booked up for the next fourteen months on a Saturday. Over a year to wait and I wasn't even engaged yet. Gutted. I really wanted to get married at the weekend, so that people could enjoy themselves and not have to worry about work the next day.

The other sticking point was that they weren't keen on having animals on the grounds and I'd kind of imagined having the siblings there. There was no way Goldie couldn't attend, and it wouldn't feel right for her to come without them. They'd already become like family.

The third and most significant issue was predictably related to money. The cost had gone up since I'd last checked. And by a lot. Another few thousand pounds, and when I'd got a loose quote before, I thought they'd included VAT, but they hadn't.

Turned out that if I wanted to have my wedding in the palace, I'd be looking at close to twenty grand, minimum, and that didn't include food or extras. I had savings, so did Miles, and I was sure his parents would help. I reckoned even my so-called dad would give me some money. That was always his way of easing the guilt. But we would still struggle. It was *way* over what I'd budgeted for.

There were still loads of other expenses to consider, like the cost of the dress, the flowers, the cake, wedding rings, bridesmaids dresses, transport… I just couldn't see how we could afford it. Unless I spread it across some credit cards or got a loan or something? I was sure it would be worth it, though. I only planned on getting married once, and I'd dreamt about it for so long that I wanted it to be right.

Even though I knew it would be hard for me to afford unless I robbed a bank or won the lottery, when we were being shown around the grounds, I didn't want to let Karen know how badly I wanted this venue. Because I knew she'd swoop in and take it for herself. In hindsight, I shouldn't have added it to the list if I wasn't prepared for her to like it.

In the end, though, it was fine. Karen decided that a central London venue would be a better option because then the media, who according to her were going to flock in their droves, wouldn't have far to travel.

She said she wanted to go and see some other London hotels this week: think she mentioned the Ritz, the Ned and the Dorchester. I could only imagine how much they would cost. Chuck must be as loaded as J.J. Abrams or Steven Spielberg.

Karen asked if I could take a few more days off work to come with her, but after already taking a day and a half annual leave, I told her I couldn't. Plus, I couldn't trust myself not to end up screaming at her. Yep. It was better all round if Karen went by herself.

I got up from the sofa, headed into the spare room and took out my folder. First I flicked to the wedding dress section. There was the printout of the dress I tried on yesterday. It looked stunning. Perfect. I still didn't understand why it hadn't felt right when I'd tried it on. So strange.

I continued turning the pages. *God.* I hadn't realised quite how many cut-outs of dresses I'd accumulated over the years. There were loads. And this didn't even include the ones I had on my phone.

They were all princess ball gowns, but some of them looked really dated. Funny how my taste had evolved since I'd first started this folder in my twenties. At this rate, by the time Miles proposed, if he ever did, fashion and my favourite dresses might have changed several times over. This folder would probably end up being like some sort of time capsule. *Jeez.*

I jumped to the venue section. There was sure to be some more options in here. None of them would be as amazing as Haverly Court, though. I needed to find a way to get the money to book it. Oh, and of course, there was the small matter of actually getting a ring on my finger first…

I wasn't going to fret about it too much right now, though. I'd promised myself not to get carried away again and to try to put my plan-related hinting activities on hold until Christmas, but that didn't mean I wouldn't still be hoping, wishing and praying for my dream wedding.

After having a little taste of what trying on dresses and finding the right location could be like in real life, I wanted to get engaged more now than ever.

CHAPTER TWENTY-FIVE

I was trying not to get excited, but it was hard.

Tonight Miles was taking me out on a date but wouldn't tell me where, because he wanted it to be a surprise.

I'd asked him what the dress code was and he'd said smartish or smart casual would be fine. He was looking very dapper in a charcoal-grey polo neck jumper under a black blazer with matching trousers and shiny shoes, so I thought I'd up my game and put on a dress and some heels.

It felt like ages since we'd gone out for the evening. Both Miles and I had been working a lot, and by the time we'd both got home and had dinner, we'd pass out on the sofa. I hadn't looked at my wedding folder for almost two weeks. Not since the night I'd got home after the venue visits with Karen. And I couldn't remember the last time I'd watched any bridal TV shows.

Putting in the extra hours at work had been worth it, though. I'd now finished compiling the competition shortlist. I had no idea how the judges were going to pick a winner. All the entries were so good.

'Taxi's here,' said Miles. 'Ready?'

'Yep!' I slid into my heels. Normally I wore either my Chelsea boots or trainers to work, so being a few inches off the ground felt so weird. Hard to believe now that I used to live in stilettos. How times had changed.

'Actually…' Miles paused. 'Hold on a sec. I just need to let the driver know that I'm surprising you, so not to mention where we're going.'

Oh man. Miles was really building up my excitement and letting my imagination run wild. How was I supposed to keep my mind from picturing all sorts of romantic settings when he kept teasing me like that?

After getting the green light, I locked up, then joined him in the Uber. I was hoping looking at the driver's sat nav would give me some clues, but he'd clearly moved it so I couldn't see without straining my neck. I'd just have to try another way to find out where we were going…

'So, I was thinking…' I turned to face Miles. God, he looked sexy tonight. He'd just shaved and his skin looked so soft and smooth, I couldn't resist reaching out to stroke it. *Mmm. Just like silk.* 'You know like when you were a kid and your parents took you on a drive, sometimes they'd play a game of I spy?'

'Yeah…'

'Well, how about we play a little game of our own now? Not I spy, but something where I ask questions about where we're going and you answer with yes or no?'

'But that will ruin the surprise!'

'Come on! Don't be a spoilsport! *Please!*' I pleaded like a child asking their parents for extra sweets.

'Okay… but I reserve the right to end the game at any point.'

'You mean if I get too close to guessing?'

'Exactly. In fact'—Miles rested his finger on his chin—'I'll give you four guesses. No more.'

'Oh, what!'

'Take it or leave it…' He raised his eyebrow.

'Okay!' I said, determined to guess the location. 'So is it in London?' *Dammit.* That was a waste of a question. It must be, otherwise we would have packed an overnight bag. 'Actually, scrap that question.'

'No can do! I must accept your first question. And *yes*. It is in London.'

I wracked my brain thinking of where we could be going.

'Does it involve a tourist attraction or somewhere well known?'

'Technically that's two questions!'

'No, it isn't! I just said it in two different ways for clarity. Let me rephrase: Does it involve a tourist attraction?'

'It does.'

Ooh. Where could it be? The London Eye? Maybe he'd reserved a pod just for us. Or he might have taken the hint about going to the Shard or somewhere with a nice *setting…*

No, no, no.

I'd promised myself that tonight I wasn't going to get carried away with hoping for a proposal. I'd promised Jada too.

Thinking about it, I was very low-key about this evening. Normally I'd be messaging Stacey, Roxy and Karen, telling them that Miles and I were going out on a romantic date and that maybe tonight could be *the* night. But after so many disappointments, I'd decided to just try and go with the flow.

Admittedly, after Miles had messaged me yesterday to ask if I was up for him taking me out, I had popped out during my lunch break to get a manicure—y'know, just in case. Nothing wrong with wanting my fingers to look their best. But apart from that, I'd only mentioned it to Jada, which was major progress.

Only two more questions left. I had to use them wisely. *Let's see.* I could ask if it would involve champagne or a celebration. That would seem like I was fishing to know if he was going to propose, though, which of course, I absolutely wasn't…

I could ask if it involved a romantic setting, but seeing as it was a date and we were dressing up, that would surely be a given too.

Hmm. This was proving harder than I thought.

'Does it involve dinner?'

'It does.'

'So we're going to a restaurant, then?'

'And that's your four questions all used up!' Miles boomed as he mimicked the voice of an enthusiastic game show host.

'That wasn't a question! It was a statement!' I huffed.

'A deal's a deal!' He kissed me firmly on my lips. 'I have a genius idea about how to spend the rest of this car journey…'

'Yeah…?' I replied cautiously.

'How about you just sit back, relax and enjoy the surroundings and some conversation with your boyfriend and let me surprise you?' He smiled.

'Okay.' I rested my head on his shoulder. He was right. It felt good to be dressed up and go out. And even though I was dying to know where we were going, rather than trying to predict and guess everything, for once I was going to try not to overthink it and just see what happened. 'I can do that.'

As we drove through Clapham and then along the busy Vauxhall roads, my shoulders started to loosen a little. I saw a group of girls in short skirts and heels hobbling towards the tube station. A shiver ran down my spine. It was almost the middle of December. They must be freezing. They only had on little jackets, and here I was in a taxi and I'd still brought my winter coat. God, I was probably sounding like their mother.

We drove straight along the Albert Embankment, past the MI6 Secret Intelligence Services building. As we continued, Big Ben and the Houses of Parliament came into view and were lit up beautifully. Everything always looked so pretty at night in London.

'We're here,' announced the driver as we pulled up at Westminster Pier on the Thames.

'Great, thanks,' Miles said as he got out of the car, then rushed around to the other side to open my door.

'Such a gent!' I said. 'Thank you!' Miles took my hand and then led me across the road.

'And here we are,' he said, standing in front of a large glass boat. It looked very plush with huge picture frame windows. I bet the views would be spectacular. 'Tonight I thought I'd take you for dinner on the Thames. I know you had your heart set on Rome, but with everything going on at work, I didn't know when we'd have time to go and I wanted to try and make it up to you. So I thought we could have a little night out in our own city. Enjoy a lovely three-course meal whilst we take in the sights and listen to the live jazz band. What do you think?'

'I think I love you!' I threw my arms around him. 'Thank you!'

'You're welcome. But hold on…' He pulled back from me and frowned. 'You only *think* you love me? That's a bit of a blow. Hopefully you'll be more convinced by the end of the night…'

'You know what I mean!' I squeezed his arms. God, they always felt so good. So firm and…

Actually. Was that a hint? When he said I'd be more convinced by the end of the night, was he implying that something was going to happen? That he had something planned?

For crying out loud.

Stop it.

Tonight my mind needed to be an engagement- and proposal-free zone. I was not going to read something into everything Miles said or did. If he looked into my eyes for more than a few seconds or took my hand in his across the table, I would *not* think he was about to ask me to marry him.

I would not be looking for any bulges in his pockets for evidence of a ring box. I was just going to relax and enjoy the evening.

Yes. I. Was.

Well, I was going to give it a bloody good try…

'I'm just teasing,' Miles chuckled. 'You make it too easy sometimes! Shall we?' He stretched out his hand.

'Yes, please!'

As we stepped onto the boat, the waitress handed us

both a glass of bubbly, which went down a treat. We were shown to our table, which was covered with a crisp white tablecloth, and sat down on the fancy wooden and burgundy velvet chairs. Not too long after we'd had a drink and a little chat, we set sail.

The jazz band, who were positioned towards the front in the centre of the boat, started playing a song I recognised as 'Cry Me a River' by Justin Timberlake.

'They sound great!' I tapped my feet along to the beat.

'Yeah, the reviews for them were pretty flawless. Kind of what swung it for me. There were a few different types of cruises, but I thought this one sounded like the best. Dinner, views of London, beautiful jazz music and spending time with my gorgeous girlfriend—what could be better?'

'Awww. You're such a charmer!' I leant forward and kissed him.

'It's true.' He took my hands from across the table and squeezed them gently. 'I love you, Alex. So much.' He stared into my eyes, then reached into his pocket…

Oh God... Oh God... Oh God!

My heart started beating faster.

Miles pulled out a tissue, then held it up to his nose and sneezed.

Oh…

'Sorry,' he sniffed. 'There's a cold going around at work. Think I must have caught it.'

So much for not thinking about proposals.

That's the last time. I swear. At least until Christmas Day...

'Poor thing.' I winced. 'I'll make you some honey and lemon when we get home. Jada gave me a new cold-busting remedy I want to try out. And I love you too. Thank you again for tonight. I'm having a brilliant time.'

As we tucked into our starters (I'd opted for the tomato and basil soup and Miles had gone for the mushroom tart) and then our mains, the band played a range of jazz classics, pop tunes and of course some Christmas songs. Miles and I were glued to the window taking in the phenomenal views. We spotted so many iconic London landmarks as we sailed down the river. The London Eye, Tower Bridge and the striking skyscrapers of Canary Wharf, which shone brightly.

After we'd finished our melted chocolate pudding dessert, the band announced they were opening up the dance floor.

'So what do you reckon?' said Miles. 'Fancy a bit of cheek-to-cheek?'

'I thought you had two left feet.'

'Guilty as charged, but I'm up for giving it a go and embarrassing myself if you are.' He stood up and held out his hand. 'May I have this dance, *madame*?'

'Well, of course, kind sir,' I mocked in a posh voice. 'Although less of the *madame* if you don't mind. Makes me sound about a hundred and two.'

'No problem, *mademoiselle*,' he chuckled.

Miles led me onto the dance floor, which was already quite full. My eyes went straight to a couple in their fifties, who were sashaying and swaying. They looked like they were having the time of their lives.

Miles pulled me in close to him and I rested my cheek against his. He moved side to side in time to the beat.

'You told me you couldn't dance!' I gasped. 'I was expecting you to be stepping on my feet.'

'I do alright,' Miles said modestly, sliding his hand down my back. 'My parents used to play jazz a lot on Sunday evenings and have a little dance together around the living room, so I picked up a few moves.'

'Well, you're very good,' I said, loving the feeling of closeness between us.

'Why, thank you.' He moved his cheek away slowly and looked deeply into my eyes. 'You're not too bad yourself…' He leant forward and kissed me.

Swoon.

Kissing Miles was always amazing. The softness of his lips. The sweetness of his breath. The way his tongue gently flicked against mine. But somehow, right now it was even better. It was this evening. Everything about it. Our bodies being so close together. The music. The views. The mood. Being away from our daily routine. Spending quality time with the love of my life. It just made the kiss more intense. Right now, with Miles' mouth on mine, it felt like everything and everyone else in the room just melted away and it was just the two of us here, alone on the dance floor.

Except it wasn't.

The sensation of Miles' hard-on pressing against me and my urge to do something with it brought me swiftly back to reality. Miles realised at the same time too.

'Mmm.' He pulled away slowly. 'I'm getting a little bit *too* excited…'

'Me too. Thirty seconds longer and we would have put on a little show of our own…'

'Let's save that until later…' He pecked me again on the lips. 'There's something I need to do first.' Miles released his arms from around my waist, then glanced down between his legs. 'In a minute. Once I've cooled down…'

I burst out laughing as I caught sight of the bulge in his trousers, which definitely wasn't in the shape of a ring box. More like an aubergine…

'Tell me, Mr Miller.' I put my hand in front of his face as if it was a microphone. 'What are your thoughts on the state of the UK economy? Can you explain, step by step, how to fill in a tax return? And after that maybe we can discuss all the different shades of white paint? Do you prefer cream white, off white, white cotton, ultra white, bone white…?'

Miles yawned like he hadn't slept for days. That was exactly the reaction I knew he needed. He glanced downwards again.

'Worked like a charm. Boring questions are always guaranteed to kill my hard-on faster than you can say Viagra. *Thank you.* Back in a sec.'

I swayed to the song as Miles started walking across the dance floor. The couple I saw earlier were now slow dancing to 'You Are the Sunshine of My Life.' The man was gazing into her eyes like she was the only woman in the world for him. So sweet.

As I looked over, Miles was talking to someone in the band. Miles nodded. The man did the same, then Miles showed him something on his phone. They smiled at each other and then Miles stood beside him.

What was he up to?

Before I had time to think of what was happening, the song finished, the band stopped playing and the lead singer opened his mouth to speak.

'Ladies and gentlemen, are you having a fabulous evening?'

'Yes!' we all chorused.

'I can't hear you. I said, are you all having a fabulous evening?'

'Yes!' the audience repeated, louder this time. 'So tonight, ladies and gentlemen, we have a special request from Miles. How you doing, Miles?' He put the microphone in front of him.

'I'm good, thanks. Enjoying the music.' I still had no idea what was going on.

'Thanks, man. So Miles asked us to dedicate this next song to a very special lady in his life. Alex. How you doing, Alex?' I smiled and waved awkwardly.

Everyone was now staring at me and I felt really nervous. My mind was racing and my heart was pounding like a heavy bassline. If I hadn't sworn earlier this evening not to think about proposals, I might have started to believe that Miles was going to propose to me in front of all these people…

'I'm great. Thank you!'

'Looking beautiful tonight,' said the band guy. I blushed. 'So Miles had something he wanted to say…' He passed the mic back to him.

OMG.

OMG.

I held my breath, waiting for what was going to happen next.

'Alex, I just wanted to let you know how much I love you, baby. This song is dedicated to you.' Miles handed the mic to the singer.

'That's beautiful, Miles. Just beautiful. We better get

on and play this for you, Alex. Enjoy the rest of your evening, everyone.'

The band started playing 'All of Me' by John Legend. I loved this song and the meaning behind it. The lyrics were beautiful.

'I hope I didn't embarrass you.' Miles pulled me closer to him. 'I just felt like declaring to the world—well, all the people on this boat—how much you mean to me.'

I just wanted to melt.

In that moment, I was completely overcome with happiness.

'Thank you.' I took his head in my hands and kissed him. 'I love you, so, so much.'

I really did. With all my heart.

When the song finished, I exhaled. Miles wasn't proposing. And for once, I didn't mind, because somehow tonight it didn't matter. I could feel his love for me radiating like the sun on a blazing hot summer's day.

Miles and I must have danced for about five songs in a row. It felt so good. Funny in all the time we'd been together we'd never gone out dancing before. Partly because we'd both declared ourselves to be rubbish at it, but also when you thought about dancing, you tended to think of the two extremes. Well, I did anyway. Either a wild night clubbing, which I hadn't done in years, or ballroom dancing, and neither sounded that appealing to me. But tonight I was really enjoying it.

Roxy was a big fan of shaking her booty (and not just in the bedroom). She was addicted to *Strictly Come Dancing*. She'd be proud to see us out here. I'd definitely be up for doing more of this, but right now, I was bursting for the loo.

'Sorry. I have to press pause on our dance,' I said, reluctantly lifting my head up from Miles' shoulder. 'Got to go to the ladies'.'

'Me too. Not the ladies', obviously, I mean I was enjoying our dance so much I didn't want to break away.' Miles flashed his killer smile.

'What are we like?' I slapped my forehead, wondering if holding our wee for so long would do us any harm. 'Meet you back here in five?'

'Five minutes?' Miles laughed. 'Can't see that happening somehow. I know you. By the time you've queued up, been to the loo, washed your hands, powdered your nose and struck up a conversation with some random strangers, it'll be at least fifteen.'

He was right. I still had no idea how men could be in and out of the gents' in a few minutes, whereas for all the women I knew, going to the ladies' on a night out was a mission.

'You've got a point.' I smirked.

'Remember we're docking in half an hour, so try and be back before then so we can have one last dance.'

'I'll try…'

Whilst Miles sailed straight into the loos, there was a queue of three women in front of me. Not too bad, I supposed. I'd had worse.

The queue went pretty fast, and just as I was coming out of the toilet and walking towards the sinks, the woman I'd seen earlier on the dance floor came inside.

'Loved your dancing out there.' I smiled. 'You and your husband look like real pros.'

'Thanks!' She grinned. 'We've always loved dancing

together. Actually, I'll tell you a little secret,' she whispered. 'Arnie isn't my husband…'

'Oh, right, sorry,' I said, wondering if I'd put my foot in it. Was he her illicit lover or something? They had to be involved somehow. There was no way she could say he was her best mate or brother or something. Cringe.

'No need. I was just trying to make myself sound dramatic! He's not my bit on the side or my hubby. He's my partner,' she giggled. 'I'm Babs, by the way. You're Alex, right?'

'Well remembered!' I said, thinking about the band guy announcing my name.

'It's the name of one of my granddaughters, so not one I could forget!' She smiled. 'Arnie and I have been together thirty-two years, but we're not married. I mean, we might as well be, but not formally. We just never got round to it, that's all. Life just kind of got in the way. You know, raising four kids and all the tough stuff families go through.' She leant back against the sink and sighed.

'It's not easy, is it?' I dried my hands on the paper towel, thinking how hard it must have been bringing up four children. My mum had struggled with two.

'It isn't, but we've been together through thick and thin. Arnie nursed me through my illness.'

'I'm sorry,' I said. Babs shrugged her shoulders, which I hoped meant that she was now fully recovered.

'Thanks. Those were some dark days. He supported me through grief, loss… I could always count on Arnie. Then I was there for him when he was unemployed. Really knocked his confidence. Ah. Anyway. Look at me babbling on. Telling you my life story. Arnie is a diamond.

The best. We love going out dancing. It's always been our thing.'

'Well, it shows. My boyfriend and I were admiring your moves all night.'

'Oh, thank you.' She blushed. 'We do try. Who knows, maybe now the kids have moved out, we'll tie the knot one day. Or maybe we won't. He'd be keen to, but I don't mind either way. We're still committed to each other and madly in love, and that's the important thing.'

I guessed I couldn't argue with that.

Every day on social media I saw happy couples posing for the cameras and gushing in their captions about how much they loved each other. But even though we'd only been on this boat for a few hours and obviously I didn't know Babs and Arnie from Adam or what went on behind closed doors, to me, what they had seemed like real, authentic love. They genuinely seemed crazy about each other.

'Yeah, your Arnie looked smitten.'

'As did your young fella. Professing his love for you like that. I saw the way he looked at you too. He couldn't take his eyes off you. Keep hold of that one, Alex. Good men like him and my Arnie are hard to find.'

'I will.'

'Anyway, I better go to the loo quickly so I can get back out there and have a little boogie before we dock.' Babs started jigging up and down on the spot.

'Same. Nice talking with you. Enjoy the rest of your evening.'

'You too!' said Babs before darting into a cubicle and closing the door.

I came out of the ladies' almost floating. That was so

nice of her to say those things. I knew she was right. Miles was a keeper.

The way that he'd organised this wonderful evening for us. Planned everything. Thought about how he could make me happy. He was so caring, considerate, fun and sexy.

It was easy to say you loved someone. But Miles' actions really showed it. I believed him. Now more than ever. He'd said we would get engaged soon, and I was really convinced we would.

Miles wanted to spend the rest of his life with me. I felt it in my heart. A proposal was coming.

It was going to happen at some point during the Christmas holidays. And this time I felt sure that I wouldn't have to plot or plan or drop more hints.

I'd put in the groundwork, sown lots of seeds, and it was almost time for the harvest. All I had to do was wait a couple more weeks and leave it to happen naturally.

CHAPTER TWENTY-SIX

'My darlings!' said Goldie, holding out her arms like a welcoming mother.

Wow. This place was impressive.

It was the Saturday before Christmas and Jada and I had just arrived at the farmhouse Goldie had been doing up to use as a new site. She'd invited us here for our Christmas work party. Because she wanted all the siblings to be part of our celebrations, Goldie thought it would be better to have it at home. Made sense. I didn't know any restaurants that would be willing to take in half a dozen animals during lunch service.

The farmhouse was painted a colourful lemon shade outside. It had a lush green garden at the front and a white fence surrounding it.

'It's looking great!' Jada said as she stepped inside and admired the freshly painted pastel yellow walls and newly laid dark wooden flooring in the hallway, then followed Goldie into the kitchen. The unmistakable scent of roast turkey and stuffing filled the room. Yum. It was so kind of Goldie to make this for us, even though she was vegan.

'Thanks, sweetheart! The guy who's been fixing it up has done a grand job downstairs so far. Still got upstairs to sort out, the loft and a few things I'd like added to the garden, but hopefully it'll all be done by late spring, early summer.'

'That would be ideal. Gives us time to build up advance bookings and arrange some kind of launch party or something to build a buzz,' I said, unpacking the bottles of Prosecco and nibbles I'd brought along.

'Wonderful! Well, get yourselves sorted, darlings, and then I'll give you a tour of the rooms that have been spruced up. I hope there's some rum punch in there.' Goldie grinned as Jada started unloading her bag. Scooby barked in agreement.

'You know me. I always bring some to get the party started!' Jada placed a large bottle of bright red punch from her bag onto the table.

'If the punch is half as strong as it was last year, we'll all need a couple of days to sleep off the hangover.' Goldie chuckled and Scooby licked his lips. Always thinking about his belly, that one. Little did he know there was no way he'd be getting any.

'I tried to make it weak, but I could hear my grandma cussing me from her grave. It's her recipe and it didn't taste right with just a few capfuls. Grandad agreed, so I chucked in half a bottle of overproof Jamaican white rum.'

Half a bottle. *Jesus.* Didn't sound like it was going to be for the faint-hearted. Jada emptied the bottle into a punch bowl and unpacked a set of matching glasses. Little pieces of chopped fruit swam around the liquid, and the alcoholic scent filled the air. Yikes, that really *was* strong. I wouldn't be surprised if Roxy could smell the rum all the way from North London. My mouth watered. Couldn't wait to try that later.

'I'm sure it will be fab! Thanks, sweetheart. Our lunch will be ready in half an hour, so after the little tour, we can feed the siblings, then get stuck into that punch!'

'Cool!' Jada nodded.

We followed eagerly behind Goldie as she showed us the large living room, which had two comfy-looking red-and-blue checked sofas and matching armchairs, all with a generous supply of cushions. Purdey and Bonnie were curled up on one settee, and Princess and Flapjack (and a single pink sock) were curled up on another. A border terrier called Rover that came from a new client was also sitting in front of the fireplace.

Casanova was on the rug humping Lulu, the stuffed teddy bear, or giving her some 'sweet Christmas lovin'' as Jada preferred to call it.

Lady Gaga sprinted into the room. She was booked in to stay with Goldie until the New Year. She stood at my feet and barked. I picked her up and gave her a cuddle.

'Looking good as always, young lady. Very festive!'

She was wearing a Santa dress made from what looked like red velvet with a white trim. Could always rely on her to bring the glamour to the party. I put her down on the sofa with the others and followed Goldie back into the hallway.

Next she opened the door to a large dining room. Like the kitchen, living room and hallway, it had a rustic feel. There was wooden flooring, and on the freshly painted blush pink walls there were photos of the animals hanging up in pine frames, which was a nice touch.

Normally Goldie left the doors open so that the animals had full run of the house, but I could see why she'd made an exception today. Goldie had set the table beautifully with festive candles, gold cutlery, red-and-gold crackers and pretty napkins with snowmen and snowflakes on them. If Flapjack spotted this stuff, especially the napkins, he'd steal them in a heartbeat.

Goldie closed the door, then took us to a large conservatory. Thanks to the glass roof and windows, the room was flooded with natural light.

'I thought we could use this as a kind of playroom,' said Goldie.

'Good idea.' I could just imagine boxes filled with balls and toys for the siblings to amuse themselves with.

Suddenly, I caught sight of the garden.

Bloody hell.

Well, I say garden. It was more like a field.

'Impressive, right?' Jada said. I hadn't realised that my mouth was wide open.

'Is that all yours?' I knew Goldie had said this place had a lot of open space, but that couldn't all be part of the house, surely?

'Certainly is, sweetheart!' Goldie nodded.

'It looks amazing!' I gushed. 'I can see why you wanted to use this place as another site. It's perfect.'

Goldie opened the large doors and we stepped outside. Within seconds, Scooby, Lady Gaga and Flapjack and the others had darted past us and ran outside.

They were in their element. This was definitely a better environment. Watching them running around and playing happily in the fresh country air was great to see. I was sure that loads of customers would love to know their pets could stay somewhere like this whilst they were on holiday. I couldn't wait to start promoting this place.

Goldie had arranged a special Christmas lunch for the siblings in the kitchen. As well as a special three-bird feast which had turkey, duck, goose, cranberries and other veg, she'd ordered in loads of treats. So far I'd spotted pawsecco, reindeer and Santa-shaped chews, pet-friendly 'mince' pies and pupcakes for dessert. It didn't surprise me that she'd gone all out. Goldie's priority was always making sure they were happy. Scooby was in his element.

I took a few photos to add to our Instagram page. I was sure our followers would love to see the siblings' festive celebrations. That was the only time I went on Instagram these days. For work.

I'd been on my personal Instagram account a lot less. Partly because Karen had pissed me off so much when she was over that I didn't want to see her rubbing her engagement in my face anymore. It wasn't good for my mental health. So I'd switched off notifications and felt much better for it. Seeing as she claimed to have so many 'fans' now, I was sure she wouldn't miss my likes and comments. And I couldn't remember the last time I'd saved some images to my collections folder. Discovering that my dream wedding dress didn't suit me when I'd tried it on had kind of thrown me because I'd thought I was so sure.

At first, I'd told myself I'd start looking at dresses and stuff online again once I'd had a chance to take a step back and re-evaluate. Except it had been a few weeks now and I hadn't had the time and strangely not the inclination either. Weird, because I still wanted to get married. One hundred percent. I checked through the photos, then put my phone away.

Whilst the siblings tucked into their lunch, I put the crisps, nuts, sausage rolls, falafels and some mini vegan quiches onto some plates and Jada poured the punch into our glasses.

I reached into my bag and pulled out three Santa hats to get us in the festive mood. Couldn't let Lady Gaga have all the dressing-up fun.

'Nice!' Jada pulled out her hairband, sending her braids tumbling down past her shoulders, then put the hat on top. 'Love a Christmas hat. Thanks!'

'Cheers!' Goldie pulled on her hat and we raised our glasses. 'Merry Christmas, my darlings! Thank you for all your hard work this year. You ladies are diamonds.'

'Cheers!' I took my first gulp, then coughed as the liquid slid down my throat a little too easily. It had a kick to it, but I loved the sweet, fruity flavour. 'You weren't joking. That is strong, but very, very delicious. I hope you'll be carrying me home tonight?'

'I'm kind of a lightweight, so I was hoping *you'd* be carrying *me*, sis…' Jada laughed as she opened the dining room door.

'Don't worry, sweethearts! I'll be getting you a cab home.'

That was generous. I'd just planned on sharing an Uber with Jada later. Even though it felt like we were in the deep countryside, this place was only a ten-minute car ride from the station, and the train here only took around thirty minutes from Clapham Junction. I'd checked before I'd accepted the job because Goldie had told me from the beginning that she had plans to either open a second site or relocate. So as much as I wanted the role, I had to be sure I wouldn't be commuting for something crazy like four hours every day.

'We can just get an Uber,' Jada said.

'I won't hear of it. Anyway, grubs up!' Goldie carried the plate of freshly carved turkey as well as a nut roast, then put it down on the dining table. She was quickly followed by Scooby. He'd just eaten his own meal but, of course, couldn't resist coming to check out ours.

During dinner, Goldie told me more about her background. I knew she'd worked with animals for years, but seriously this woman was like Mrs Doolittle. She'd owned, fostered and rescued probably every type of dog known to man.

'I've had a few jobs.' Goldie shrugged her shoulders. Jada rolled her eyes.

'Don't listen to her. She's had more than a few. This animal whisperer has worked with animals for over forty years. Name any job working with them and Goldie's done it.'

'Not any job,' Goldie replied.

'Come on!' Jada protested. 'She's worked in zoos, animal charities, rescue centres, pet grooming salons, pet hotels, vets…'

'That's where you met, wasn't it?' I remembered Jada telling me that when I first joined the company.

'Yep. I met Goldie about fourteen years ago, when I was twenty-four and she was working at the local vet. I loved her personality. She was fun and you could just tell how passionate she was about animals. Dennis, my grandparents' dog, adored her, so when she left, I used to take him to Goldie's house.'

'Dennis was such a cutie.'

'He was. We miss him.'

'So how did you guys go into business together?' I remembered not long after I'd started, Jada had explained that she'd worked in the city and fancied a change. She'd started telling me the story, but the phone had rung and she hadn't got to finish it.

'Well, I was working at a big accountancy firm in the city, earning good money, but burnt out. I wanted something more rewarding and less stressful.'

'I hated seeing you like that. You always looked like you had the weight of the world on your shoulders, sweetheart.'

'Sometimes it felt like it.' Jada took a large glug of Prosecco. 'When Phil, Goldie's husband, passed and I went round to see her, as usual, Goldie wanted to find out how I was rather than worrying about herself. I told her I was stressed and she suggested I come and work with her.'

'Phil and I had always planned to open the hotel. We came up with the idea together. But then he went and died, so I decided to go ahead and do it in his memory. The hotel was our family home and he left me this farmhouse. He'd bought it for me as a surprise and was going to do it up and use it as a country hotel for dogs. Trouble was, I knew what to do with animals, but not with all the business side of things. I don't care about spreadsheets. I don't do this for the money. I'd do this for free if I could.'

'That's Goldie's strength and weakness,' Jada sighed. 'She's got a heart of gold. But that doesn't pay the bills. Anyway, she said we could build something together. I did the business plan and it seemed viable. My grandma was also sick at the time, and I was worried about not getting enough time to see her, so it seemed to make sense. Goldie was already getting bookings, but she didn't have time to take care of the financial side of things or deal with customers, so I stepped in and, well, you know the rest.'

It was nice to hear more of the story. I'd known the basics, but Goldie never really spoke much about her husband. Maybe it was still too painful, and I know she always liked to be upbeat.

We heard the door go.

'Hello?' Goldie called out.

'Oh, so sorry, Goldie. I didn't realise you had company.' A tall, handsome man was stood at the doorway. He had a full head of striking silver hair and a neatly trimmed beard. Sort of how I'd imagine David Beckham to look in his late fifties.

'Oh, hello, William, I didn't realise you wanted to work today. Sorry, where are my manners? William, this is Jada and Alex. These are the diamonds that work with me at the hotel. Jada and Alex, this is William. He's the man responsible for the fantastic work on the farmhouse.'

Within seconds, the siblings were crowding around William's feet. Bonnie was wrapping herself around his leg and Flapjack was jumping up, begging to be cuddled. Seemed like they already knew William and liked him too.

'Pleasure to meet you. Please, call me Willy. I always say to Goldie that William is so formal. Reminds me of when my dad used to tell me off,' he laughed.

'*Very* nice to meet you.' Jada was grinning widely.

'Anyway, I don't want to intrude. I can come back. Maybe tomorrow? To work?'

'Lovely, thank you.' Goldie smiled.

'Goodbye, all.' And with that, he was gone. As soon as the door shut, Jada clapped her hands with excitement.

'So… anything you'd like to tell us?' She winked.

'No…' Goldie blushed.

'Oh, please!' Jada rolled her eyes. 'He is *fine*! Don't tell me you haven't noticed. And I can tell from the way he looked at you that he likes you too.'

'He's here to get the hotel up and running. You know I don't have time for relationships. The siblings are all I need.'

'I think it would be nice for you to have a partner.'

'Sweetheart, I've already been married three times. I'm in no hurry to make it a fourth. I'm not Liz Taylor, you know. And anyway, apart from Phil, who was the best hubby a woman could ask for, my relationships have always gone down the drain, because they said I prioritised the animals over them.'

I didn't realise Goldie had been married three times. Looked like the alcohol was making her open up a little more.

'Seems like this guy likes animals, though. He could love them just as much as you. And anyway, it doesn't have to be serious. Maybe it might be good for you to enjoy a bit of *Willy* this Christmas!' Jada threw her head back laughing. Goldie and I then realised the double meaning and belly-laughed too.

This was fun. I felt like I was getting to know them better. Goldie had opened up about her love life, so maybe now we were talking about relationships, Jada would open up more about hers. Although she'd told me loads about her relationship with her mum and grandad, she still hadn't shared any details about her romantic history.

'What about you, Jada? Anyone special you'll be kissing under the mistletoe or any *willies* you'll be enjoying this Christmas?'

Suddenly, the laughter stopped.

Oops. Too far? Maybe I shouldn't have mentioned the willies bit. I blamed the rum punch.

'Who's for pudding?' Goldie jumped in. 'I've got mince pies and Christmas pud. Normal ones and vegan ones. And we can have it with vegan ice cream or custard. What do you fancy, ladies?'

Okay, then…

Clearly Jada definitely didn't fancy talking about her relationships and Goldie knew why.

I wondered what had happened. I didn't think Jada was dating anyone now, so it must have been something she'd gone through in the past. Whatever it was, judging from their reaction, that topic was under lock and key. And if they weren't willing to talk about it even after several glasses of rum punch and Prosecco had loosened everyone's tongues, then something told me it wasn't something that I was likely to find out about anytime soon. Which made me want to know even more…

CHAPTER TWENTY-SEVEN

Today was the day.

Christmas Day had arrived and we were on the sofa at Miles' parents', about to open the presents.

I'd already had a good scan of the gifts under the tree after breakfast, looking out for small jewellery boxes in particular. I couldn't see anything of that shape, but that didn't necessarily mean anything.

Miles could have put it in a bigger box. You know, like nesting dolls. Maybe one large box led to a medium one and then a smaller one until, *ta-da*: I reached the treasure and found an engagement ring tucked away inside.

There wouldn't be long to find out…

'Top up?' asked Ron, clutching the jug of Buck's Fizz that Mary had prepared earlier.

'Oh, go on, then!' I passed him my glass.

I enjoyed spending Christmas with Miles' parents. It felt like how it was supposed to be. Being in the company of people who loved each other, sitting around the tree, laughing and joking.

Christmas with my family was rarely like that. In the years that Mum and Dad were together, they'd always argue about something or other. Usually with Mum criticising Dad's choice of gift.

'Got your secretary to get this for me, did you?' she'd snarl, turning her nose up at the bottle of perfume. Or Dad would leave after we'd opened the presents to see 'a friend', which would put Mum in a foul mood. That either meant she couldn't be arsed to make Christmas lunch or, if she did, she'd end up burning it to a crisp because she was up in her room by herself. In the end, Nick and I took over the cooking. It was the only way we were sure to get something edible.

'So…' Mary dived under the tree, picking up the first present and looking at the gift tag. 'This one's for Miles, from Alex.'

'Ooh…' Miles took the rectangular gift box and shook it, trying to guess what was inside. There was no way he could, though. I was sure of it. He undid the ribbon excitedly, took off the lid and then burst out laughing as he pulled out a bright yellow shower sponge. 'You know me so well!' he chuckled.

Miles and I tended not to buy each other loads of expensive gifts. In my old job, I remembered so many of my colleagues stressing themselves out trying to find the perfect present. Splashing out on extravagant things for their other halves, as if somehow the bigger the present, the more it proved their love.

Rather than doing that, Miles and I agreed to just buy each other a few token gifts. You know—little things that didn't cost a lot but were sure to be appreciated—and then one main present. Nothing too crazy, though.

'Is he still showering several times a day and using sponges like they're going out of fashion?' Mary grinned.

'Yep!' I nodded.

'Nothing wrong with being clean!' Miles shrugged his shoulders. 'And at least they're recyclable.'

'Whatever floats your boat, son!' Ron slapped him on the back playfully.

'Anyway, who's turn is it now, Mum?' said Miles. The next few presents were ones that Ron and Mary had bought each other, then they opened the gift Miles and I had got for them: two show tickets to see *Dreamgirls* in the West End. They'd always wanted to go, but never got round to making a booking. Mary screamed with delight when she saw what was inside the envelope.

After that I opened one of Miles' gifts. It was a rectangular box. I shook it but didn't hear anything. I ripped the paper and then the packaging. It was a personalised glass that read:

Alex, save water, drink wine. Preferably rosé.

That was me all over. Nothing beat a cold glass of White Zinfandel. 'I love it!' I kissed him on the lips. 'Thank you.'

My second gift from Miles was a bottle of rosé—after all, he'd said, there was no point having the glass and nothing to fill it with. I'd definitely be opening that to enjoy at lunch with everyone.

Then it was time for our main gifts. Miles opened his first.

'Fuck!' Miles' eyes widened as he opened the envelope. 'Sorry, Mum, Dad.' He winced. 'This is brilliant! Thanks, darling!' He threw his arms around me.

I'd arranged two professional tennis lessons for him. I

definitely needed them more than he did, but he'd put them to much better use. I knew Miles was really passionate about the sport, and since he'd been playing with Todd every weekend, I thought he might like to take his game to the next level.

'Glad you like it.' I smiled.

'Does this mean we need to call Andy Murray and let him know there's a new tennis champ in town?' quipped Ron.

'If I were you, I'd send a memo to Djokovic, Nadal and Federer too. I'm sure after two lessons, I'll be ready to take them all on,' Miles laughed. 'In my dreams! More chance of me watching the Wimbledon Final from the royal box with Kate and Wills next summer. I'm not bothered, though. I just enjoy playing.'

He wasn't fooling me. Miles was competitive, and I knew he loved to win, so hopefully these lessons would give him the edge.

'Anyway, time for your *proper* present, Miss Adams…' He winked, then got up and went to the chest of drawers at the other end of the living room. 'I left it here for safekeeping. Didn't want you finding it before I was ready to give it to you…'

OMG.

Could it be?

It had to. What else would he be afraid of me finding?

He pulled out the box, returned to the sofa and placed it in my hands. I opened it to find…

Oh.

Well, this was great. Unexpected, but still great.

'Wow, thanks!' I looked down at the two tickets to Rome.

'I've cleared it with work this time, so we'll definitely be getting on that plane. I know how much you really wanted to go and I promised I'd make it up to you, so I wanted to keep my word.'

That was really sweet. I'd kind of thought that was why he'd taken me on the river cruise, but I wasn't complaining. I'd always wanted to go to Rome and was disappointed when we'd had to cancel.

I looked at the dates. Second weekend in March. That was almost three months away. It was fine. Even though I didn't get a ring under the tree this year, the day was still young. And there was still New Year's Eve. Miles had said *soon*. He wouldn't make me wait another quarter of a year for a proposal. Like he'd just said, he was a man who kept his word. It was one thing him agreeing that we'd commit to marriage in the first year and then me being relaxed about two years passing because we were living together, but stretching a proposal to March? Surely he wouldn't.

After all the present unwrapping, Miles and I took Bouncer for a walk and then came back and curled up together on the sofa whilst Mary and Ron busied themselves putting the finishing touches to lunch.

They'd insisted they didn't need our help with the meal, only with setting the table, which wouldn't take us long.

I scrolled through the TV, looking for something for us to watch in the meantime. It was mainly repeats. Different TV Christmas specials, *Home Alone*, the usual.

It was strange flicking through the channels of normal TV. Because most things I watched these days tended to be on Netflix or on catch-up, I'd forgotten how it felt to have to sit through three minutes of adverts.

'Oh yeah.' Miles sat up in his chair as an advert for a new family film came up. 'I keep meaning to ask, will you come to the cinema with me the Saturday after next? There's a film I really want to see. I've been waiting ages for it to come out.'

'What type of film?' I asked, already suspecting I knew the answer.

'Action,' Miles replied.

'Great!' I said sarcastically. 'Lots of guns, and shooting and two-hour car chase scenes,' I groaned.

'But there'll probably be some romance in it too, so maybe you'll like it.'

Yeah, right. Some weak damsel in distress who falls for the bad boy and then, when her love interest's enemies come and hunt them down, she trips over her own two feet as they run away and gets shot or some rubbish. *Sigh*. It was only fair, though. Miles watched lots of romcoms, so I didn't mind going to watch the occasional manly movie with him.

'Okay,' I said, scanning the TV guide. 'Ooh, *Love Actually* is on at three. What are the chances of us persuading your parents to watch that instead of the queen's speech?' Even though we'd only watched the film recently, I was definitely up for seeing it again.

'I'd say slim to zero. It's a Miller family tradition. Christmas lunch and then spending ten minutes with Liz.'

'Liz, eh?'

'Yep. She insisted I call her Lizzie, because Queen Elizabeth was way too formal, but I said Liz suited her better,' Miles chuckled.

'I agree. From this moment on, she will now be known as Queen Liz.'

'Perfect. Anyway, no time to sit here chatting. We'd better get cracking with setting the table.'

'Aye-aye, Captain.' I jumped up, did a mock salute and followed Miles into the dining room.

We made fast work of laying everything out nicely. As it was Christmas, we used Ron and Mary's best china plates, multiple crystal glasses for wine and champagne, fancy gold forks and some festive red serviettes decorated with cute little Christmas trees.

'And now for the crackers.' Miles handed me a tray with five homemade crackers. Miles and Mary made them every year. It was another one of their cute traditions. These weren't filled with silly plastic paper clips or throw-away gifts that you'd never use, though. They were always chosen with care by either Miles or Mary. He said they'd always sat and put them together every Christmas Eve since he was a child.

I picked them up individually and put one above each plate, including one for Bouncer. They were made from red crepe paper, with gold ribbon tied at each end.

'Ah, that one goes here,' said Miles, picking up one of the crackers that I'd put where Mary usually sat. 'That one's for you.' He smiled.

At this point I really wanted to hope that mine had a *you-know-what* inside, but after so many false starts, I knew better than to get too excited.

I was right not to. At the end of dinner, when we all pulled our crackers, my gift turned out to be a tube of my favourite lip gloss. I'd run out a few weeks ago but hadn't got round to ordering another one, so it was perfect timing. Miles must have noticed it in the bin and ordered one for me. Really thoughtful.

I was glad I'd lowered my expectations because I hated the way they had dominated my thoughts. Take the amazing gift of those tickets to Rome earlier. Rather than just enjoying the fantastic present and thinking of all the wonderful things we'd do on our trip, I was immediately preoccupied with the date and thinking how much later it was over the deadline, which was kind of a buzz kill.

There was now only a week until the Conclude stage. Miles had seven days to propose before I had to sit down and have a serious talk with him about our future.

With it being the Christmas holidays, realistically, there wasn't much more I could do on the hint-dropping front. So rather than spending the whole week constantly on my toes, holding my breath for that magical moment, I decided I was going to just try and relax. To trust him, the powers of the Engagement Chicken, internet ads and all the other things I'd set up during my plan and thrown out into the universe and just see what happened.

My dreams weren't over yet. There was still time. Miles seemed more relaxed, so if he was planning on proposing, I reckoned it was most likely to happen before he went back to work in the New Year.

For the sake of our relationship, I really hoped I was right…

CHAPTER TWENTY-EIGHT

This was it.

D-Day.

In approximately four minutes and twenty-eight seconds a New Year would begin. And my relationship with Miles would change. For better or for worse.

With every second that passed, I was reminded of the Conclude stage of the plan. Time was almost up. The deadline for Miles to propose was looming.

It hadn't happened yet, and something told me that it wasn't going to. I could feel it at the pit of my stomach. I wasn't going to get my engagement.

We were sitting on the sofa at home with the TV on, watching the live coverage of the scenes along the River Thames. Gearing up for the countdown and the annual fireworks display.

We had planned to be there, but the tickets had sold out. We could have still gone and found somewhere further away to catch a glimpse of the display, but after spending the day at Winter Wonderland, we were both pretty exhausted. So Miles suggested we chill at our place with some champagne instead and ring in the New Year together from the comfort of our own home, rather than standing outside in the cold.

Of course I'd said yes. I was still on autopilot. Disappointed yet again that nothing had happened. At Winter Wonderland, we'd gone on different rides, had a few glasses of mulled wine, and nothing. I'd tried not to get my hopes up, but it was easier said than done. I knew we were running out of time. Every opportunity I thought Miles would use to propose just sailed past us. *Poof.* Gone. Like a puff of smoke.

So when Miles suggested staying in, I didn't have the strength to argue. I felt like the wind had been knocked out of me. A small part of my mind, the hopeful part, which still believed in fairy tales and happily ever afters, thought there was still a chance. That maybe once the clock struck midnight and the countdown was over, Miles would jump off the sofa, drop down on one knee and ask me to marry him. Yeah, a sofa proposal wasn't what I'd dreamt of, but at this point, I'd take it. Maybe how he proposed didn't really matter after all. Maybe the setting wasn't important. Maybe it was the sentiment and the thought that counted.

But the realist in me didn't believe that it was going to happen. I just sensed it. For some reason, Miles didn't want to marry me. Despite what he'd said, marriage was one step too far.

Ten.

Nine.

Eight…

Miles passed me a glass of champagne and squeezed

my hand. I tried my best to hold back the tears that were building. I would not cry. I would not cry…

Seven.

Six.

Five…

'This is it, baby!' Miles grinned. 'The New Year is coming!'

Whoopee-bloody-doo. I growled in my head, my stomach sinking. Breathe. Breathe.

Four.

Three.

Two…

His last chance. Maybe. Just maybe…

One.

'Happy New Year!' Miles kissed me firmly on the lips, then threw his arms around me. 'Woohoo! Here's to a brilliant year.' He clinked his glass against mine as the spectators on the TV hugged each other and started singing 'Auld Lang Syne.' 'Oh shit, I left the party poppers in the kitchen. Let me go and grab them!'

Miles jumped up from the sofa and disappeared into the hallway. Just as he did, a tear rolled down my cheek. I wiped it away quickly.

So that's it, then. It didn't happen.

What now?

I knew I'd have to have a long talk with Miles about our future. But I didn't really know what I'd say and how far I was willing to take it. Just tell him how I feel? Demand we get married or else? Just the thought of it made me feel sick to the stomach.

When I'd made my plan a couple of months ago, as part of the Conclude stage I'd said that if a proposal didn't happen, I would have to evaluate our relationship. But I'd genuinely believed that it wouldn't have to come to that. I'd honestly thought Miles would have popped the question by then, so there wouldn't be any need.

I mean, we might not have had Rome, but we had Christmas and New Year's Eve. Both perfect proposal opportunities. We even had the cruise. When he'd gone up to the band, declared his love and dedicated a song to me, that would have been ideal too. So why hadn't he?

I had to face facts. Miles loved me, but not enough. He was committed to me, but not enough. I wasn't enough for him.

When we'd got together and he'd agreed to the marriage commitment, he'd hoped I would be wife material. Maybe he'd meant it when he said we'd get engaged *soon*, but then I'd done something to put him off and he'd changed his mind. Decided it was a bad idea. And he didn't know how to tell me. The extra effort I'd made during the Convince stage hadn't been enough.

Or *soon* might have just been his get out of jail card. A word he used to avoid the question and drag things out for as long as possible, so that eventually I got so tired of waiting and hoping that I just gave up altogether.

Well, I couldn't sit here, drinking champagne and setting off party poppers, toasting a New Year which had already got off to a shitty start. I was going to bed. I needed to get some sleep. I had to prepare myself for a difficult conversation later.

One that was sure to be the toughest and most heart-breaking conversations I'd ever had in my whole life.

CHAPTER TWENTY-NINE

'Everything okay?' Miles frowned.

I was in the kitchen, slamming the cupboard doors, searching for a bar of chocolate I'd hidden for emergencies.

It was New Year's Day and Miles had just told me he was going to the gym.

He was so casual when he said it. 'I'm just going to work out. Got to try and burn off all those donuts we ate at Winter Wonderland,' he'd chuckled.

Yeah. It's fine for you to laugh, I'd thought to myself. *Everything's just one big joke to you. Us. This relationship. Marriage. My feelings. We shouldn't have just been eating bloody donuts at Winter Wonderland. You should have been proposing. Like you promised you would. But don't worry about me. You go and enjoy your gym session whilst I sit here upset, fretting about the state of our relationship.*

Well, it was one thing him pissing off to the gym and leaving me here. But if I was going to sit at home alone for the next couple of hours, I at least needed some sodding chocolate to keep me company.

'It's just you went to bed straight after the countdown yesterday and you've seemed a bit off this morning, which isn't like you.' He stepped towards me, concern etched on his face. 'Are you feeling okay?'

This was the point where I should take a deep breath and walk away. I'd hardly slept a wink last night. Tossing and turning. Wondering what to do about our Conclude conversation. The words I would choose. My brain was still muddled. A million thoughts swirling around faster than a washing machine on a spin cycle.

Yep. I just needed to make my excuses and walk away. Then use the time that he was out to sit in silence and think carefully about my next move, so that I didn't say something I'd regret. It was for the best.

'No, actually,' I snapped. *Shit.* The words flew out of my mouth before I could stop them. 'It isn't…'

Whoa.

That was exactly what I *wasn't* supposed to say. But all was not lost. There was still time to pull it back. No real damage had been done. I hadn't finished my sentence. I could add a load of things to the end of it. Like, 'I've got a headache, arm ache, *any* ache.' Yeah, that would work.

Just whatever you do, said my subconscious, *do not tell him how you're really feeling. You're angry. Frustrated and upset. Now is not the time to express yourself. It'll come out all wrong. Just take a chill pill, go in the bathroom, sit on the loo and take deep breaths. Go for a walk, find somewhere and scream. Or go for a run around the block to burn off your frustrations. Do anything. Anything except let rip.*

'I'm tired!'

Yeah, that should do the trick. Although, as far as he's concerned you spent almost eleven hours in bed, but... semantics. Just semantics...

'Sick and tired of waiting,' I snapped. 'Waiting endlessly for you to propose!'

Uh-oh.

This is not going to end well. Pull it back, Alex.

Pull. It. The. Fuck. Back.

Miles froze on the spot, his eyes popping out of his head.

'I'm tired of hearing you say "soon, Alex". When is bloody *soon*? Paris? Nope. Rome. Oops, that got cancelled. Christmas? No. Already gone. New Year's Eve? *Sorry*. That was yesterday and look.' I waved my wedding finger in the air angrily. 'Still *nada*. Soon is beginning to feel like *forever*! You said to me. You *promised* me that you would commit to marriage within a year. I didn't push for that because we started living together then. But I did say I didn't want to be living together for years before we got engaged and now it's starting to look that way. Our second anniversary was months ago and it was another let-down. What happened to all that bullshit you said at your parents' the other day about always keeping your word?'

'But I do...'

'Bollocks!' I screamed, steam coming out of my ears.

'I will! I just need a bit more time, that's all.'

'*Time?*' I shouted. I could hear myself sounding like some crazed woman throwing a tantrum, but I couldn't help it. 'You've had enough time! I don't have *time* to waste. I've already wasted two years and three months!'

Miles stepped back and flinched like he was physically wounded.

'Is that what you think our relationship has been?' He lowered his voice. 'A *waste*?'

Maybe I could have phrased it better, but I was angry. It was like I'd been possessed. I had no control over the words spilling from my mouth. I had to get them out. I *had* to tell him how I felt. All that time spent wishing, hoping, researching and working on my wedding planning folder for nothing.

'Well, if we don't get married, then what's the point of this?' I threw my hands up in despair. 'What's it all for? What does it mean?'

'*Seriously?*' Miles' mouth fell open. He looked winded. Like an angry bull had just rammed into his stomach.

'Clearly you don't want to marry me. Otherwise you would have proposed already. And you haven't, so you don't. You love me, yeah, but not enough. You say you're committed, but not enough. You've got one foot in this relationship and the other foot hanging back, just in case. You're just stringing me along. But I'm not some weak woman who'll just put up with it. I won't be another Jolene,' I snapped. Miles frowned. 'I won't let two years of waiting turn into fifteen years. I'm leaving.'

What the hell?

Where did *that* come from?

Before I knew it, I'd already turned on my heels, gone into the bedroom, pulled out an overnight bag and started chucking clothes and toiletries into it.

Miles followed me quickly into the room.

'Come on, Alex.' He placed his hand on my shoulder. I

brushed it off angrily. 'Don't you think you're overreacting? Let's talk about this. *Calmly.*'

'What's there to talk about? We've spoken about it many times before. You made a promise and you broke it. You knew marriage was important to me. I laid everything out for you. Communicated. Let you know what kind of proposal and ring I'd like. Made it easy for you. But you've done nothing! Made zero effort to propose or follow through on what you said.'

'That's not true!' he shouted. Up until now Miles had been calm, but now he seemed frustrated. Pff. *Join the club, Miles. Welcome to my world.* 'I know you don't think I've been taking your feelings seriously and keeping my word, but if you could just hold on a bit longer, I—'

'No!' I scowled, pushing past him to get through the door. It was too late. I'd reached my limit. I couldn't listen to any more excuses. I didn't want to hear any more of his stalling tactics. I just needed to get out of here.

I threw my Chelsea boots in a plastic bag, then put on my trainers and coat.

'I'm going to stay at Roxy's. Enjoy the gym.' I slammed the door behind me.

There. I'd done it. I'd *conveyed.* Fully. Told Miles how I felt, and I'd *concluded.* It wasn't the way I'd planned the words to come out. In fact, for once in my life, I hadn't planned any of that at all. But at least now everything was out in the open.

Was our relationship over? Probably after that outburst. But at least I'd taken action. I couldn't live like that anymore. The constant waiting, wishing and hoping. It was better to be single than to spend my days, months and years in a relationship, always wondering if things were ever going to progress. Being in a state of constant limbo.

No.

It might hurt for a while, but I'd get over it. I'd start again. Find someone who wanted to be with me completely. Who wanted to commit to me. Properly.

I'd thought that someone was Miles. That he was my soul mate. That I'd found my Mr Right, but just goes to show that clearly I was wrong.

CHAPTER THIRTY

'You sure you don't want to come out?' said Roxy, applying another coat of red lipstick.

I was still crashing at her place. It was now Monday night and it had been two days since I'd walked out on Miles. If I was honest, it felt like it had been months.

Since moving in together, we'd never spent more than a day apart and I was really feeling it. Strange if I thought about it. Apart from Tony, who I'd dated for four months in my early thirties, I'd been single for most of my adult life and almost always slept on my own. Guys never stayed the night. And yet after spending a year living with Miles, I'd developed separation anxiety. The bed just felt so big and empty without him.

But I had to woman up. Stick to my guns. Do what those experts said and let him realise the error of his ways. He was wrong to lead me on like that. Making me think there was hope when there wasn't. It wasn't fair.

Miles had tried calling, but I hadn't answered. I needed to get my head straight. I hadn't just left him hanging, though. Even though he'd hurt me, I couldn't completely ignore him. As someone who'd been ghosted in the past by so many men, I knew how horrible it was to be blanked. So I'd texted to say that now *I* was the one who needed time. Miles said he would wait to hear from me.

He said he missed me. I did too, but I just didn't know where we could go from here. If he couldn't keep his word about getting married, how could I trust his word on other things in the future?

Although I thought we needed to spend time apart so that he could think about what he'd done, or *hadn't*, I didn't think that going out with Roxy tonight would be a good idea.

'Thanks for the invite, but I'll pass.' I tucked my knees under my chin on the sofa. A night in was a safer bet.

'It'll do you good. If you and Miles are really going to call it quits, don't sit around here wallowing. I've always said, the best way to get over one man is to get under another!' She cackled.

Ugh. Everything about Roxy's comment made me want to throw up. The thought of breaking up permanently with Miles and the idea of being with someone else was heart-wrenching. No. A one-night stand wasn't even an option.

'Miles wasn't some random guy that I dated for a few weeks. He was special. He *is* special.'

'Okay, so you're not ready to hook up with someone else yet. You need a few more days to get over him. That shouldn't stop you from going out there and having some fun. Nothing wrong with a bit of window-shopping. Lining them up for *if* you *do* want to get back on the horse.'

She just didn't get it. I didn't want to *get back on the horse*. I didn't want to line up my next boyfriend.

'I haven't got extra time off like you. It's my first day back at work tomorrow, so I'm just going to have an early night.'

Roxy lived on the other side of London, so rather than walking to the hotel like I normally did, I'd have to get a tube, then walk from the station. Which meant I'd need to leave at least an hour earlier than usual.

'Suit yourself, darling.' Roxy zipped up her knee-high boots, put on her leather jacket and then headed towards the front door. 'Don't wait up!'

I hardly slept a wink last night. I wanted to start my first day at work this year feeling fresh and motivated. Instead I felt like there were ten-tonne weights hanging from my eyelids. I was so tired. Every step I took as I made my way from the tube station to the hotel was like walking through quicksand. I'd had two coffees already this morning and I still wasn't feeling remotely awake.

At Roxy's I'd spent most of the evening watching TV. Well, trying to. But it was like the universe was conspiring against me. Every channel seemed to have something love- or romance-related.

I'd immediately bypassed the movie channels as they seemed to have all decided to play romcoms at the same time. Then I stumbled across the *My Fantasy Wedding* show I used to love. Just as it came up on the screen, there was a woman in a huge princess ball gown with a sweet-heart neckline. The kind that I used to go crazy over. But it did nothing for me. Unsurprising, really, given how gutted I was about not getting my fairy-tale proposal. Maybe it was more than that, though. After all, because of how busy I'd been at work and all the Christmas celebrations and other stuff going on, it had been weeks since I'd watched any bridal TV. Strangely I hadn't missed it. And now I was possibly about to become single again, I definitely wouldn't be watching more wedding-related series anytime soon.

So I'd skipped that show and decided to watch a money management programme, which I thought would definitely be a bridal-free zone. They had a financial guru who helped people get out of debt. And who was the person in need for that particular episode? A couple that were in trouble after spending too much on their wedding. They'd borrowed money to pay for an elaborate dress and ceremony and now were struggling to keep up with the loan and credit card repayments. They looked like they were on the brink of divorce.

After that, I watched one of those true crime shows. There was definitely no mention of romance or weddings in that. But it was so gruesome that it unsettled me for hours. Yep. Seeing how a murderer buried his victims probably wasn't the best thing to watch before bed. That combined with worrying about my relationship wasn't ideal for having a good night's sleep.

I put the key in the door. It was so quiet today. Goldie was still with the siblings at the new place in the country. It would just be Jada and me in the office today.

As I walked up the stairs, I could hear music playing. Jada always had a Spotify playlist in the background, especially when she was working in the office by herself.

'Morning,' I mumbled, dropping my handbag on the floor next to my desk.

'Happy New Year! Whoa...' Jada frowned as she caught sight of me. 'What the hell happened to you? I hate to say it but, girl, you look like shit.'

'And a happy New Year to you too.' I switched on my computer.

'No, seriously.' Jada crossed her arms. 'What happened?'

It was like she had pressed the *open the floodgates* button in my brain, because the moment Jada said that, I crumbled. I couldn't get my words or my emotions out fast enough.

I told her everything. Including the details of Conclude. The third C I'd conveniently left out when I was explaining my plan to her before.

'*Sweet Jesus.*' Jada slapped her forehead. 'So you threw a full-scale tantrum, just because Miles didn't meet a deadline that he didn't even know existed?'

'It wasn't a tantrum...' I winced. Who was I kidding? It totally was. A flashback of our argument popped into my head. 'I was upset. I didn't think about what I was saying. It all just kind of fell out. It was like I was vomiting the words. All those months of frustration just bubbled up inside of me and once I opened my mouth, I couldn't seem to close it again.'

'*Clearly*. I'm not gonna lie, sis: This is *bad*. Listening to advice from random strangers online who don't even know you. *Shit*. When you were getting tips from these so-called *experts*, did you ever think about what would happen if this day came?'

'Well, yeah... no... sort of... not seriously, though.'

'This is all because you got too impatient about waiting. Because people kept asking when you were gonna get married and that stupid bougie bitch Karen kept winding you up, isn't it? So instead of having confidence in your man to choose the right time to propose, you decided to give into peer pressure and force his hand by giving him an ultimatum.'

'I didn't give Miles an ultimatum. I…'

Jada didn't give me a chance to finish. She seemed really upset with me. There was such a look of disappointment in her eyes. As if I didn't feel crappy enough already.

'Did you think about what would happen when it all backfired, the relationship got ruined and you lost the love of your life, forever?'

Jada's eyes began to water. *Hold on.* Were we still talking about me and Miles or someone else?

Actually, was this about Jada? I couldn't be sure, but something told me that she was speaking from personal experience. It seemed like I'd touched a nerve.

'I knew it could be a possibility, obviously.' I hung my head, feeling like a complete idiot. 'But I was thinking positively. That's why I tried to make things as easy as possible for Miles. So that we could avoid it coming to this. I never wanted to force him. That was the point of the plan. I wanted him to propose by himself. Spontaneously. For it to be romantic.'

'I wish you'd told me everything about your plan earlier. Then I could have warned you. Ultimatums, deadlines, whatever you want to call them are bad news. Yeah, they can work sometimes, but when you've got a good man who is kind, loving and loyal, someone who does right by you, and you bust his balls just because he hasn't proposed, that can mash up your relationship. Permanently.'

'If you don't mind me asking, is that what happened to you?' I softened my voice. After the reaction at Christmas when I'd tried asking about Jada's love life, I knew I needed to tread carefully.

'Yep,' Jada sighed and tied her hair up into a bun. 'I ruined a perfectly good relationship because I pushed him into proposing. He did it. But because he felt like he had to. He wasn't ready and I forced him. Four months later, it was all over.'

Part of me thought, well, maybe there were cracks in their relationship anyway. Maybe it wasn't the proposal or the idea of marriage per se that made it break down. There could have been a million other reasons. But it would have been insensitive to say that.

'I'm really sorry.'

'Yeah. And before you start thinking that it was because the relationship wasn't solid, it *was*.' Jada read my mind. 'He grew resentful about being forced into something. When we broke up, he said he wanted to propose himself, in his own way, and was adamant that he would have done it, but I'd taken the opportunity away from him. Even a year later, it still hurts to talk about it, because I genuinely believe I'll never find a man as good as him again. *Please, Alex.* Don't make the same mistake I did. It might not be too late. Miles seems like he's still open to talking. Apologise to him. Do whatever you need to get him back. Otherwise you'll regret it. *Trust me.*'

I felt awful for Jada. I couldn't bear the thought of being without Miles, but I didn't see why I had to be the one who grovelled. He was the one who'd broken his promise, not me. He'd told me it would happen soon and it hadn't.

Okay. I could have expressed myself better. The way I'd got my point across wasn't ideal, but that was what happened when you got fobbed off. Eventually you cracked. I was only human. I was sure other women in my position would have reacted the same.

And I still wanted to get married. It was important to me. What was I supposed to do? Give up on my dream? Change my value system just because Miles had changed his mind? I was willing to compromise with some things, but if Miles and I had any chance of a future, I needed some sort of security. If we got married it would prove that Miles was truly committed and ready to go all in. Raising the kids I wanted to have wouldn't be easy, so I needed to know that he was in it for the long haul.

At the same time, like Jada had just said when she spoke about what happened to her, I didn't want our engagement to feel like an obligation. That was never my intention. If, say, I went to see Miles after work this evening and he got down on one knee, would I be happy, knowing that he'd only done it because I'd walked out on him? Then I'd spend the rest of the relationship feeling like he'd only proposed because I'd made him. Hardly romantic.

Whichever way I looked at the situation, it was clear. This was all one big giant mess. And I had no idea how to fix it.

CHAPTER THIRTY-ONE

Yet another night without sleep. The bags under my eyes were so big that Santa could have carried a sackful of Christmas presents in them.

After my conversation with Jada yesterday, I was even more uncertain about what to do, so I'd been mulling over my options, which wasn't exactly the perfect remedy for a good night's rest.

I hadn't focused on work as much as I should have today either, which wasn't ideal. This Friday, in just two days' time, we'd be announcing the winners of the competition, so there was a lot to do.

I'd been dying to speak to Stacey about my situation, but she was away on her babymoon and I didn't want to ruin her break with talk of my disaster of a situation. Especially since she'd warned me from the beginning that my plan could end in tears.

No. I had to figure this out for myself. Think about what was more important to me.

The way I saw it, I had three options. I could 'get my

own way' by effectively forcing Miles to marry me, just so that I could stay true to my values. But engagement by blackmail wasn't what I'd dreamt about for all these years. Plus then I'd have the cloud of knowing that he hadn't done it of his own free will hanging over me for the rest of our relationship. Which, if Jada's experience was anything to go by, might not even last that long, because he'd end up resenting me.

Or I could go back to Miles with my tail between my legs and say that actually, I didn't care about getting married anymore. So I'd basically be giving up on my dream. The trouble with that, though, was that I knew that I'd still always be hoping he might take pity on me and propose at some point. Which of course would mean that every time we went out, every time we went on holiday and every time he bent down to do something in front of me, I'd always be wishing and wondering if *this* would be the moment. That would drive me insane.

The other option would be to break up with him altogether. Admit defeat and leave Miles permanently to make way for a man who really was ready for marriage.

I'd read about a lot of women who took the big step to call time on their relationships, then ended up meeting and marrying their real Mr Right a few months later. Maybe that would be me too? The only way I'd know would be to walk away. Sooner rather than later.

My stomach plummeted just thinking about it.

I heard the front door slam and glanced at the clock radio on the bedside table in Roxy's spare room. 1.37 a.m. She must have had a good time.

Oh… there were voices in the hallway. She'd brought a guy home. Groans and moans followed. And not the kind that you made when you'd stubbed your toe against the wall by accident or were unhappy. The complete opposite. *FFS.* It was like these walls were made of paper.

I heard the bedroom door slam and their voices grew louder. There was a loud thud.

They had crashed onto the bed.

I knew because Roxy's bed was right against the wall directly behind mine. *Let's hope they keep the noise down.*

Who was I kidding? The thought barely left my mind before the squeaking started, then the thud of her headboard repeatedly hitting the wall.

God, no. Not tonight of all nights. I was finding it hard enough to sleep as it was.

The banging grew louder and faster, Roxy crying out with every thrust. Hopefully he'd be a two-minute man and this would be over quickly. They couldn't sustain that level of intensity for much longer, right?

Wrong.

I pulled some tissue out of the box on the table, ripped it up and started stuffing bits into my ears. *Didn't work.* I could still hear them as clearly as if they were screwing right in front of me.

Ugh.

I pulled the spare pillow beside me over my head and then the duvet. But it was as if they had a sixth sense, knew I was trying to block them out, so took it as a cue to go louder.

Aaargh.

I tossed the duvet and pillow off and pressed the radio's *on* button, then turned up the volume. God, I hated that song. I think I'd rather listen to Roxy's sex show.

I pressed the skip button to scroll through the stations. Too pop for me. I kept pressing and then…

I froze.

They were playing that song.

The song Miles had requested for me on the river cruise.

'All of Me.'

My heart flipped.

I immediately started thinking about that night. How Miles had surprised me with that date to make up for not going to Rome. Even though he'd told me to hold off from booking, so technically he didn't have to make up for it at all.

How we'd danced together, cheek to cheek. How he'd declared his love for me so publicly, and how deeply I'd felt it.

How other people had seen it too and commented.

Bang, bang.

How was it possible that they were getting even louder?

I turned the radio up a notch. I needed to hear this song. To listen to the lyrics. Somehow it helped me feel closer to Miles.

Roxy let out a scream so thunderous, you'd think she was giving birth to triplets. The man, whoever he was, finished seconds later.

Peace at last.

I listened to the last few lines of the song and went back into my trance. Thinking about Miles.

I thought about how patient he was with me. When I'd asked him to sit down and watch those romcoms whilst I paused them and gave him a blow-by-blow breakdown of the proposals, as if he wasn't capable of figuring out what was going on for himself.

He must have cottoned on to all the hints I'd been dropping. Known that I'd left the tab open for the engagement rings and been looking up wedding and engagement websites on his laptop, but yet he still didn't get angry or ask me if I'd lost my mind.

And the things I'd said to him before I left were *awful*. I'd told him our time together was a waste. How could I do that? My relationship with Miles had given me some of the happiest times of my life. Saying it was the best relationship I'd ever had wouldn't do it justice, because of my terrible past experiences. Even though I hadn't had loads of serious boyfriends, I knew that Miles was head and shoulders above the average man. He was caring, considerate, kind, handsome, sexy. I could literally fill a five-hundred-page notebook with how amazing he was.

He'd waited six months to sleep with me. How many men would do that? Introduced me to his friends and family not long after we'd first started dating. He'd asked me to move in with him. Spoke openly about the future and our plans. What we could do. *Together*.

He loved me. He really, truly, deeply loved me.

But he didn't just say it. He *showed* it. Every day.

How many times had I dreamt of having a man like him?

It was probably easier to find a needle in a haystack than to hit the jackpot with someone like Miles.

What the hell was I thinking?

I heard the front door slam. Must have been Roxy's fuckbuddy going home. She never let them stay overnight. *Wham, bam, thank you, man* was more her style.

A chill ran down my spine as I remembered how the men used to come and go through my doors too. The difference was that I wanted them to stay over, but they never did.

That was the life I used to have, and I'd hated it. But my life with Miles was a joy. We laughed, we talked, we hugged, we made love. Everything with him was so easy. So great. Until I'd spoiled it with my obsession about getting hitched.

Then it hit me.

I remembered what Babs had said. On the cruise. In the toilets. She'd told me that although they weren't married, Babs and her partner were madly in love and committed and that was the important thing.

It was.

She was right.

Miles *was* committed to me. We shared our lives together. We shared a home. We had a future. He loved me.

Yeah, marriage would be great. There was no one else I'd rather walk down the aisle to marry. But was it worth losing the love of my life over? Definitely not. I'd rather be with Miles and not be married than not be with him at all.

And Miles *was* a man of his word. If he'd changed his mind about getting married, he would have told me. It wouldn't be because he didn't love me. He did. I had no doubts about that.

Just because the reason he hadn't proposed wasn't immediately obvious to me, it didn't mean he didn't have a good reason. Maybe he was scared. It happens. He was going to explain to me, and instead of listening to him, I'd thrown my toys out the pram and stormed off. I was so wrapped up in my own feelings and my own obsession that I hadn't even given him a chance. Who would want to marry a woman like that? I was lucky he was still willing to speak to me.

I ran my hands through my hair. I saw it as clear as day now. What a fool I'd been. I'd fucked up. Big time.

I didn't need to get married. What I needed was to be with Miles in whatever form felt right for the both of us. It couldn't just be all about me and what I wanted.

If marriage was something Miles wanted in the future, that was fine. I'd wait until he was ready. I didn't care if we got married in two years or five or ten anymore. I just wanted to be with him.

We could be committed without marriage. We could have children without marriage. Just like Babs and millions of other couples around the world.

Love and commitment came in many forms, I finally saw that. And now I'd come to my senses, I needed to go to Miles and apologise.

Before it was too late.

CHAPTER THIRTY-TWO

I took a deep breath and pressed the call button.

I'd held out for as long as I could. If I could've, I would've called Miles at two a.m. once I'd realised how much I'd screwed up. But I knew if I disrupted his sleep, he might not be able to function properly for the rest of the day. So I'd tried to go back to bed, woke up, washed and dressed extra early, then waited until 7.15. By now he would have finished in the shower and be having breakfast.

It was ringing.

My heart thudded against my chest. I hoped he'd pick up. Just as I'd had time to think, Miles would have done the same. He could have decided that he wanted nothing more to do with me. I wouldn't blame him.

Still ringing.

Maybe this was a mistake. My stomach churned and sweat trickled down my forehead.

Please pick up.

Please.

I was tempted to cancel the call. But then I heard 'All of Me' playing in my head. The song that had brought me to my senses earlier this morning. And reminded me how important Miles was to me. I had to try. To know that I'd at least attempted to make amends.

Suddenly, I heard a voice.

'Hello?'

Yes! He'd answered.

'Hi!' I jumped off the edge of the chair in Roxy's spare room excitedly, then quickly slumped down on it again as I remembered that now he had, this was my cue. It was time for me to talk.

'Um, how are you?' I mumbled, racking my brains for what to say.

'I'm okay. You?' It was hard to read his voice. It was kind of neutral. Like he might have been a bit happy to hear from me, but at the same time I could sense caution. Like he wasn't committing to any form of emotion until he heard what I had to say.

'I'm okay, thanks,' I replied. Truth was, I was less than okay. I felt like a fool, I missed Miles like crazy. I was desperate to know if he still wanted to be with me. But I couldn't tell him all of that. I'd created this mess, so I couldn't expect him to feel sorry for me. 'I was wondering if we could meet later. To talk?'

'Sorry, I can't.'

Shit.

I was too late. He didn't want anything more to do with me.

'Oh.' My shoulders slumped. 'I understand.'

'I'm working late tonight and not sure what time I'll finish.'

So there might still be hope…

'Tomorrow, then?' I crossed my fingers and toes quickly. I needed all the help I could get.

'I've got some appointments tomorrow afternoon, then I'm working after that, so it could be another late one…' Miles paused.

This was not good. I *had* to see him. I couldn't bear for another day to pass with him thinking that I believed our relationship was a waste. There *must* be a way.

'What about if I came to see you at work—I mean, during your break or something?' I said.

Dammit.

As soon as the words left my mouth, I realised that tomorrow morning, Siobhan and the film crew would be coming to the hotel to film the winners. I'd been working on the competition for months. It was my project. I *had* to be there. That TV feature could transform the future of the hotel. Goldie and Jada were relying on me and I couldn't let them down.

But this was also important. I had to save my relationship.

'It would take you at least two hours to get to the hospital and back to work again, and you only have an hour for lunch.' Typical Miles, worrying about me. I could leave once filming had ended. Go and see him and come back to the hotel.

Then again, I'd planned to mingle with the winners afterwards and focus on preparing social media posts and a million other things before the show aired in the evening.

'I know, but I'll find a way to make it work. Or I can meet you after you finish?' I didn't care if it was midnight or three in the morning. I had to know I'd done everything

I could to put things right. 'I really want to apologise to you. In person.'

'That would be good. You said some pretty shitty things.'

Pow. I felt like a herd of elephants had just ploughed into my stomach. He was right, though. I could tell I'd hurt him. I wished I could see him now and throw my arms around him. Explain how much I regretted the things I said.

'I know. I'm sorry.'

'We'll both be tired then…' I could hear him thinking and I swear that waiting for him to speak felt like hours. I couldn't stand it if he said we couldn't meet until next week or worse still, not at all. I was desperate for him to give me a chance to make amends. 'Look, how about we meet for breakfast tomorrow. Before I go to my appointments?'

Thank God. He was willing to see me. But if he was working late, the last thing he'd want to do would be to get up early.

'You sure you won't be tired?' I said.

'Probably, but it's okay.'

Actually, that would be doable. If I stayed late at the hotel tonight to get a head start on some of the tasks I had to do tomorrow that could be prepared in advance, I could still get everything done. I didn't care if I only had a few hours' sleep. It would be worth it.

'Great!' I felt a wave of relief wash over me. We might still have a chance. 'I can meet you at the café by our house…' I paused. Was it still *our* house? 'By your… you know the one I mean.'

'Yeah. Eight a.m.?'

'Perfect.'

'I better go.' Miles sounded harassed. Like speaking to me had dredged up all the horrible words that had spewed from my mouth during our argument.

'Okay. I'll see you tomorrow.'

'Yeah,' he said quickly, then hung up.

I leant forward and put my head in my hands. I felt awful. Knowing I'd upset him was the worst feeling in the world. At least he was open to having a conversation, though. That was something.

But whether I'd be happy to hear what he had to say when we met face-to-face was another thing entirely…

CHAPTER THIRTY-THREE

I'd got here too early.

I was *so* nervous. My stomach had been cramping all morning. I'd had a nightmare that I'd slept through my alarm, woke up at nine and raced to the coffee shop, only to find that Miles had left and texted me to say he never wanted to see me again.

I bolted out of my sleep at that point, dripping with sweat. I didn't want to lose him. I couldn't. So I thought it'd be better to start getting ready.

After my shower I'd taken my time to do my hair and make-up. I wanted to make an extra effort for meeting Miles and greeting the competition winners later.

It didn't take me long to get dressed. Mainly because I hadn't taken many clothes with me when I'd left, so my options were limited. Borrowing an outfit from Roxy wasn't feasible either. Her wardrobe mainly consisted of short leather skirts and tight-fitting vest tops, which weren't really ideal for breakfast, early-evening TV or the cold January weather. I decided on my favourite blue jumper dress, some tights and my Chelsea boots instead.

I was sat at a white wooden table tucked away in the corner of the cosy coffee shop, sipping on my latte and scrolling through a newspaper someone had left on the chair to take my mind off things.

I wondered how I'd be feeling in an hour's time. Sad after Miles told me he couldn't bear to be with a wedding-obsessed evil woman like me or relieved that he was willing to give our relationship another chance? I'd tried to think about what I would say, but everything was kind of jumbled. In the end, I'd decided that I couldn't plan it. I just needed to speak from my heart and hope Miles saw how genuinely sorry I was.

One thing I *was* sure of, though, was that I wouldn't let our relationship go without a fight. Miles was the man for me. I was certain. I wanted to be with him no matter what.

It wasn't all about me. Miles had to feel comfortable too. So if he needed more time to think about whether he wanted us to get back together, I'd wait. Just like he waited to sleep with me, I'd wait for him. He was worth it.

'Hey.' I looked up and saw Miles standing at my table. He took my breath away. I could tell he was tired, but to me, he still looked gorgeous. His coat was undone and I could see that underneath he was wearing a cream jumper which clung to his chest. God, I missed resting my head on his beautiful chest. Miles smiled awkwardly. Normally when Miles saw me, he flashed a massive megawatt smile that could power a thousand lights. But the one he'd just given me would barely charge a mini bedside lamp. Not the warm welcome I was hoping for, but I supposed it was to be expected.

'Hi…,' I replied.

Would it be weird to hug him? I just wanted to throw my arms around Miles. To squeeze him. To smell his beautiful scent. Maybe it was too soon to make physical contact. It had only been a week since we'd last seen each other but it felt like months. How could we go from feeling so natural and affectionate around each other to struggling to say hello?

'Um, I was going to order you a coffee, but I didn't want it to get cold, so thought I'd wait until you were here. I got you a pain au chocolat, though.' I gently pushed the plate towards him.

'Thanks. It's okay.' Miles took off his coat and scarf, put them on the back of the chair, then sat down. 'I already had a coffee before I left to wake me up. I'll get another one in a bit.'

'Okay. So…'

God, this was awkward. It felt so cold and formal. I hated it. But what the hell. I couldn't overthink it. I just had to get my thoughts out there. Deep breath…

'I wanted to meet to tell you that I'm really, really sorry for all the things I said. I was just… I don't know how to describe it. Frustrated. Upset. I just felt like… well y'know. I've always wanted to get married and we'd said it would happen within a certain time frame—well, the proposal at least. But it didn't, and when I did bring it up, you said "soon" and nothing happened…'

I didn't want to sound like I was blaming him, but it was true. I felt like I was in a constant state of limbo. I tried to read Miles' face. It gave nothing away. He rested his chin on his hands and just listened.

'I thought that maybe "soon" meant you were waiting

for a big occasion like Christmas or New Year,' I continued. 'And when it didn't happen then either, I thought you'd just been fobbing me off. That you'd changed your mind. I think seeing you so casual about everything on New Year's Day made something inside of me snap. All my feelings just rose to the surface and I said lots of things I didn't mean. I'm sorry. I just want you to know that you are more important to me than getting married. If you're willing to give us another chance but don't want to get hitched anymore, we'll work through it. And if it *is* still something you want to do, then I'll wait. Until you're ready. Whatever it takes.'

I sat there in silence. Waiting for Miles' response. Without realising it I started holding my breath. I quickly pinched my hand to bring me back to my senses and to remind myself to breathe.

Come on, Miles.

Say something.

Anything.

Put me out of my misery.

'I get it,' he said at last. 'I do. I know marriage is important to you. It is to me too. But so is trust. You should know me by now, Alex. I keep my promises. So if I wasn't interested anymore, I'd tell you. Straight up. I'm sorry that things haven't happened yet. Sometimes life is like that. Things don't always go to plan or turn out exactly the way we want them to. But for a relationship to work, both parties need to believe in each other. So if I say I will propose soon, then I mean it. I told you. I just needed more time.'

'I understand.' I nodded. 'Like I said, I can wait. This has to be right for the both of us. I get that now. I just got swept away in all the wedding stuff. Especially with Karen getting engaged and social media being flooded with proposal posts at this time of year… it all kind of messed with my head. I know it's not an excuse, but I promise to try and do better. You mean so much to me. I love you, Miles.'

The corners of his mouth turned up into a little smile, but until he spoke, I didn't want to get my hopes up. My heart started pounding. I felt like I was a contestant in the final of *The Voice*, waiting to hear whether I'd won a recording contract.

'What you said… about our relationship being a waste,' Miles sighed, 'that really hurt…'

'I know. I didn't mean…'

'But I love you, Alex.' He reached across the table and took my hands in his. 'And I don't want to be without you. So let's try again, shall we?'

'Yes!' I shouted. A bit too enthusiastically as literally everyone in the coffee shop turned around to see what I was so excited about. I felt like I was Meg Ryan faking the orgasm at the table in *When Harry Met Sally*. I didn't care, though. My relationship wasn't over. Now I felt like I'd just won every talent show in the world *and* the lottery. I wanted to throw my arms around him. This was the *best* news.

'Let's take it slowly, though, shall we?'

'Sure.'

'Rather than you just coming back home straight away, maybe we can start with meeting somewhere neutral again first. See how things go…'

'Of course.' I was nodding so much, my head could topple off my body at any second. Truth be told, if I could,

I'd race back to Roxy's right now, get my stuff and move straight home with Miles again immediately, but I respected his wishes. 'We can do that. Did you have something in mind?'

'Yeah. I'm still up for meeting tomorrow if you are?'

Tomorrow? Did we already have something planned?

I racked my brains, thinking of what we were supposed to do on Saturday. *Oh yeah.* The action film Miles wanted me to come and see.

When it came to choosing an activity to help rekindle our relationship, spending two hours watching a bunch of adrenaline-pumped men firing bullets wouldn't be my first choice, but who cared? If it meant I'd get to spend time with him and start rebuilding what we had, I'd sit through the whole *Die Hard* series, all the *Terminator* films and every Quentin Tarantino film. *Twice.* If *that* wasn't true love, I didn't know what was. Miles was more than worth it.

'Course! What time shall I meet you there?'

'Eleven okay?'

'Yep.' As it was an early showing, maybe we could go for a nice walk afterwards and talk some more. Spend the day together. But like Miles said, we'd need to go slowly. Take things step by step.

'Cool. Okay. Well'—Miles moved his hands away—'I guess you better go. Isn't today the announcement of the competition winners? You must have loads to do, so I'm surprised you were able to meet me.'

He remembered. Wow. I didn't want to mention it to him because I knew he'd suggest that we meet another time so I could focus on the competition.

'It's okay. Meeting you was important. I worked late

last night, so I'll be fine.' I glanced at the clock on the wall. He was right, though. I did need to get going. It was 8.37 and the crew would be there in less than two hours. As excited as I was about the filming, I didn't want to leave him, though. I wished I could just sit here and talk to Miles. See him smile. Hold his hand. Hug him. Kiss him.

I'd told Jada I was meeting Miles this morning, and even though she knew it was an important day for the hotel, Jada said she understood I needed to fix things and would clear it with Goldie. *So kind.* Miles had a busy day ahead of him, though, and I reckoned we'd said what we needed to for today. Miles knew I was sorry and we'd agreed to start over, which was the important thing.

'Well, I'll see you tomorrow at eleven, then.' I got up and put my arms into the sleeves of my coat.

'Good luck with everything today.' Miles stood up and kissed me on the cheek.

It was only a gentle peck. His warm lips barely touched my skin for more than two seconds. But in that moment, during that brief exchange, I felt a surge of electricity race through me.

More than that.

It was like a shot of reassurance that told me that even though it wouldn't be easy to get things back on track, there was hope.

Somehow, some way, after talking things through calmly, something told me we were going to be okay.

Time would tell…

CHAPTER THIRTY-FOUR

It had been a whirlwind of a day. As well as meeting with Miles earlier, today the winner of our Hero Dog of the Year competition was announced.

Obviously we'd all known who the winner was since before Christmas, to give us time to get everything prepared, but this morning we'd invited the finalists down for the formal presentation. And true to her word, Siobhan turned up with a TV crew. She'd said with all the doom and gloom in the world, it was a nice happy, heartwarming story for the new year that they wanted to share with their viewers. Siobhan said it probably wouldn't be a long feature, but I told her we'd be grateful for anything.

Now it was almost 6.25 p.m. and I was in the living room with Goldie, Jada and the siblings, watching the show and waiting for our moment on TV.

'I bought some more biscuits.' Jada put the plate on the table.

'Excellent!' Goldie took one of her favourite vegan

biccies from the plate whilst Jada and I grabbed another chocolate digestive.

'Can't beat a biscuit with a warm cuppa.' I dunked mine into my fresh cup of tea. I was feeling much happier. Not just because things went great with the competition this morning, but also because it was amazing to see Miles and take the first step towards rebuilding our relationship. I couldn't wait to see him tomorrow. 'Oooh... I think we're up!'

We all glued our eyes to the screen. There it was! Siobhan was in our living room with the three finalists and their owners beside them.

'Today we're here at the Happy Dog Hotel in Clapham, South London to crown the winner of their Hero Dog of the Year competition...'

'Oooh!' shouted Goldie. 'We got a name check and everything.' Scooby rushed over to the screen, looked at it, glanced at Goldie, then back at the screen, and then flashed his big toothy smile. 'There's Jada! And, Alex—there you are!' Goldie jumped off the sofa in excitement and Lady Gaga started barking and running around in circles like she was possessed.

'The winner of this year's award was Monty, who saved his owners from a fire...'

I'd been bowled over when I'd read about the story of a border collie called Monty. When a fire had broken out in their house in the middle of the night, not only had he woken everyone up, but he'd also run back into the flames to save the other family dog and dragged it out of the house. We were all blown away by his bravery. It was amazing what dogs did when their humans were in danger.

'Clementine'—Siobhan was now interviewing Monty's

owner—'how does it feel to hear that Monty has been crowned the winner?'

'It feels wonderful!' Clementine grinned. 'There are so many fantastic dogs who do so much to help their families and others, so to have Monty recognised like this is brilliant. We owe our lives to him. We can't thank him enough.' She bent down and gave him a hug and a kiss. Monty barked with approval and wagged his tail happily.

'And, Goldie…' Jada and I screamed as Goldie appeared on the screen. Goldie suddenly became all shy and hid behind her hands. 'You're the founder of the Happy Dog Hotel and the organiser of these awards. What made you want to start this competition?'

'Well, it was Alex's idea, and Jada and I fully supported it. We absolutely adore all the dogs we take care of and we know how much they enrich their owners' lives. Dogs are heroes in so many ways. Whether it's a rescue dog, service dog, or our best friends at home, they are so precious. They're loyal companions you can always rely on. They do so many fantastic things for us and we all agreed this would be a great way to celebrate their achievements.'

'You've certainly done that. Congratulations also go to runners-up Sammy from Croydon and Bernard from Dulwich and all of the finalists…'

I was glad the others got a shout-out as well. Sammy, a golden retriever, had saved his owner from being hit by a car by pushing the girl out of the way, causing himself to be run over instead. Every time I thought about it, I teared up. So selfless. He'd loved her so much that he was willing to give up his own life.

Bernard, an Alsatian who was awarded third place, had

called 999 when his owner had a seizure and fell out of her wheelchair. Thankfully the dog had been trained to call for help by pushing a speed dial button on her phone with his nose. Talk about remarkable.

'Well done, Alex.' Goldie squeezed my shoulder. 'You did a brilliant job. I can't thank you enough.'

'She sure did!' added Jada. 'You worked so hard on this and it really paid off. So proud of you, sis.' She gave me a big hug.

Now I really did feel like crying. This was probably the only time in my working life that I'd been recognised or appreciated. So cool.

'Thanks, guys. I'm just so chuffed it all worked out. Just seeing how happy and proud the owners were made it all worthwhile. I really hope it helps spread the word about the hotel and leads to loads more bookings.'

'Girl, please. It already has!' said Jada. 'Ever since the competition launched we've been getting new clients. And after being in the local paper *and* on the TV, I reckon our phones are going to be ringing off the hook.' As if by magic, the phone rang. 'Looks like it's already starting… Good evening, the Happy Dog Hotel. Jada speaking, how may I help you?'

And just like that, I sensed that the fortunes of the hotel were about to change forever.

CHAPTER THIRTY-FIVE

I'd made it.

Despite allowing myself an extra half an hour contingency to get here, there were delays on the tube because of a faulty train in front of us or something.

I was already nervous enough about this morning, so the added worry of wondering whether I was going to arrive on time wasn't helping.

I pushed the white double doors open and raced through them. I looked up at the clock on the wall. Four minutes past eleven. Dammit. Could have been worse, though. At least I was here. Let's hope Miles was too.

I spotted him waiting in the foyer. *Phew.* My heart skipped a beat as I took him in from head to toe. Miles looked hot as always. In terms of sexiness, but this time also in terms of temperature. He had his phone resting between his shoulder and his neck and was fanning himself with his hand. Not surprised. He was wearing his big green puffer jacket, and although it was pretty cold out there, it was quite warm in here.

I loosened my scarf as I approached him. I probably could take my coat off too. I was wearing a pretty new aqua-coloured jumper that Roxy had bought me. Not only had she surprised me with it last night when I got back, she'd also invited a colleague round to do our nails.

I'd been so busy during the day with the competition that I hadn't had time to update Roxy on how everything had gone with Miles. I think that probably made her think he'd dumped me and that I'd need cheering up. Roxy acted all tough, but really she was such a sweetheart. We had a lovely girly night together. Now I was looking forward to another good day with Miles.

I loved this cinema. It was classic and old-fashioned, but with a modern twist. The entrance had been designed to look like an American movie theatre in the 1950s. It had a beautiful gilt-domed box office and the popcorn was stored in a retro machine. Even the ushers were dressed in smart red velvet tuxedo jackets and bow ties.

As I got closer, my heart started thumping. I wondered how Miles would act when he saw me. We seemed to have left things on a positive note yesterday, so I hoped he'd give me a warm smile. Then I'd know today would be okay. I crossed my fingers and took a deep breath.

'Yeah, that should be…' Miles caught sight of me and his eyes widened. I couldn't tell whether the expression was good, bad or shocked. 'Gotta go.' Miles hung up quickly. 'H-hi. You're here.'

'Hi…,' I replied. 'Sorry I'm late—had a nightmare on the tube.'

Miles was about to say something when his phone started ringing. He looked at the screen. 'I need to get this. I'll just be a sec…' He walked to the other side of the foyer and turned his back. I hoped he wasn't angry and that we wouldn't miss too much of the film. Pretty sure he would have given me the time the doors opened rather than the start time, so we should be fine. Still hated being late, though.

Miles was nodding. I wondered who he was speaking to. Maybe it was the hospital. He hung up, then started walking back towards me.

'Everything okay?'

'Yeah.' He mopped his brow. 'Think I'm coming down with something again.' That was the thing with working in a hospital. It was easy to pick up stuff, especially at this time of the year.

'Oh no. You need some of my special remedy.' I smiled.

When Miles was feeling a bit off colour, I'd make him some fresh honey, lemon and ginger. Jada suggested that adding some pepper, chilli and a generous splash of rum made it even more effective, so I'd been using her version lately and Miles said it seemed to do the trick. Wished I'd shared the recipe so he could've whipped it up himself or been around to help him feel better.

'So'—he glanced at his watch—'the film is going to start in a minute, but I need to go to the bathroom. Here's the ticket.' He reached into his pocket and pulled it out. 'It's screen two. I'll be there soon.'

'Okay. Do you want me to order anything? Popcorn? Maybe some tea or something warm for you?'

This cinema wasn't like the normal ones where you had to queue up for food or drink. Here, once you'd sat down in the fancy seats, you just pressed a button on the remote control that was built into the armrest and a waiter would bring everything to you. Proper hot meals, snacks, alcohol… whatever you wanted. Very posh.

'Thanks, but I'm fine.' Miles wiped his brow again.

'Okay. I'll wait for you there. Want me to take your jacket?' He'd sweat a lot less if he took it off.

'I'm alright. See you in a bit.' He walked quickly to the gents'.

I sighed. This was going to be difficult. I could tell. But hopefully if the film was good, it should relax him. I couldn't even remember what it was called, so hadn't managed to check it out online. But Miles was looking forward to it, which was the main thing.

I showed my ticket to the usher and walked through into the theatre. *Crikey*. It was like a ghost town. There wasn't a single soul here. Such a shame how no one went to the cinema anymore. The fact that it was Saturday morning probably didn't help. Even when Miles and I came here on a Friday night, it was never packed, but this was pretty bad.

So different to when I was a teenager. Back then, the cinema was always buzzing. You had to get there early or the good seats would be sold out and you'd be stuck on the front row, craning your neck and hurting your eyes because the screen was too close. No danger of that now.

I guess it was to be expected. These days with Netflix and so many streaming services, unless it was a mega blockbuster, people had less of a need to come here. Then when you factored in the cost of the tickets, food, drink, etc., it was easy to see why people preferred to curl up on the sofa at home and order a takeaway instead.

The trailers had already started. They were advertising some big-budget Hollywood film with loud explosions and a load of special effects that probably cost more than the net worth of a small country.

I sat down in our favourite seats on the back row. It was a special love seat: a soft red leather sofa. Much nicer than the hard, sticky chairs in the cinemas I used to go to before.

As I picked up the matching red cashmere blanket resting on the chair beside me and laid it across my legs, my mind flashed back to the time when Miles had first brought me here during my Six Months to Love challenge. I smiled as I remembered how we'd got hot and heavy snogging each other's faces off. The usher had brought our food over during a particularly passionate kiss and the poor boy hadn't known where to look.

Well, whoever came to take our order today wouldn't have anything like that to worry about, though. If the lukewarm reception Miles had given me in the foyer earlier was anything to go by, I'd be lucky to get another kiss on the cheek.

I looked at my phone. Miles was cutting it a bit fine. I picked up the menu and gave it a quick scan. He might not want anything, but I definitely did. I'd order some proper food later, but for now I'd just have some popcorn and a glass of wine. Calm my nerves a bit. I pressed the service button on the armrest, reclined the back of the chair then raised the footrest. I loved these chairs. They were so plush.

They're taking their time.

Not as if they could be rushed off their feet right now.

And where was Miles?

I hoped he was okay. I should go and check on him in

the toilets. I'd hate to think he was there being sick or something.

Just as I got up out of my seat and started walking up the aisle, the thick red velvet curtains slid all the way to the edge of the screen, indicating that the main film was about to start. Yep. Then came the message about switching off your phones. Unless there was a group of ghosts sitting in front of me that I couldn't see, there was zero chance of a ringing mobile disturbing anyone here.

I paused. Knowing Miles, he'd probably want me to tell him what he'd missed from the beginning, so I should stay and watch. But if he wasn't here in five minutes, I'd definitely go and check he was okay, just to be sure.

I walked back to my seat and pressed the button again for the usher. Actually, might be quicker to just have a quick peek out the door to see if I could see the lady who took my ticket. I got up and started walking up the aisle again.

Once upon a time, in a city called London, there was a beautiful young woman...

The voice boomed from the cinema speakers. I turned to face the screen.

This wasn't what we were supposed to be watching. It was some sort of cartoon. I'd gone to the wrong place. Then again, this was definitely screen two, like Miles had said, and the lady had checked my ticket, so it must be the cinema who'd mixed up the showreels. Easy mistake to make at this time in the morning. Kiddies' films would be more common for them to show right now.

I poked my head around the door. There was no one there.

One day she went to Fogg's Tavern to meet a young man...

How cool! I've been to that pub before. I turned back and glanced up at the screen. The Fogg's Tavern entrance was decorated in bright, colourful flowers. The animation was so vivid. It looked just like that in real life. That's where Miles and I had gone on our first date.

I shouldn't get distracted. I needed to go to the foyer and try and find someone who worked here. They could show me to the right screen too. But I supposed another minute wouldn't hurt. I'd love to see what this film was about. If all went well with us today, maybe Miles and I could come and watch it another time. I enjoyed Disney and Pixar films almost as much as romcoms, and this looked like a combination of the two. Really cute.

The couple, who were on their first date, had a wonderful time, laughing, joking and debating their favourite romantic comedies. So much so that they met again the following afternoon and went on a trip to the zoo.

My eyes were glued to the screen as the woman in the cartoon with long brown hair walked around London Zoo, hand in hand with the cute guy with dark cropped hair, gazing at the animals.

Awww. So sweet. That was where Miles and I had gone on our second date.

Hold on.

These two characters went to Fogg's Tavern on their first date and the zoo on their second? Just like we did? That was a bit of a coincidence…

The date was perfect and Miles knew from that moment

that Alex was the woman for him. In fact, he'd known it from their first date in the pub…

O.M.G.

No way.

Did the narrator guy just say Miles and Alex?

I walked further down the aisle so I was closer to the screen.

This is…

Was this…?

I squinted, trying to process what was going on.

It couldn't be…

I couldn't take my eyes off the screen.

Alex, however, took a little more convincing. But a trip to this very cinema, where they shared their first kiss, helped to seal the deal.

My mouth fell open and my eyes almost popped out of their sockets as it showed the two animated characters snogging in the back seat and a very startled cinema attendant fainting. *Hilarious.*

Over the past two years, they've enjoyed many special moments together. But the best moments in their lives are still to come…

On the screen, the male character dropped to one knee on the cinema stage and proposed to the female character, who now had much shorter hair. Just like mine. She threw her arms around him, they kissed, and as the scene faded out, rather than *The End* appearing on the screen, *The Beginning…* flashed up instead before the credits began to roll.

Suddenly the cinema lights came up and Miles appeared on the stage.

What the hell was going on?

'Hey, baby…' He flashed his megawatt smile, jumped down into the aisle and started walking towards me.

OMG.

As he did, a slideshow of photos appeared on the screen and 'All of Me' played from the speakers.

Wow.

My head started spinning. This was so much to take in.

My eyes darted back to the screen, where there were photos of us at Winter Wonderland last year, pictures taken in Paris, a selfie of us curled up on the sofa with Cuddles… so many wonderful memories.

I turned my gaze back to Miles, who was getting closer. I felt like someone had let off fireworks in my head and then spun me around like a spinning top. So many things were happening all at once.

Before I knew it, Miles was standing in front of me. He was staring at me. Smiling. I wanted to smile back. Or do something. *Anything.* But I was frozen to the spot. I couldn't move.

Suddenly Miles dropped down on one knee.

Jesus, Mary and Joseph.

Did he just…?

Is he about to…?

It couldn't be.

My hands covered my mouth.

My heart pounded like a hundred bongo drums.

Miles opened a little blue velvet box and glanced up at me.

Holy shit.

There was a ring inside.

Was I dreaming?

I had to be.

'Alex. You are the love of my life. Like my character in the film said, from the moment we met, I knew you were special. I *knew* you were the woman I wanted to wake up to. I wanted to see you first thing in the morning and last thing at night. *Forever.* Now I know I'm doing this a little later than expected, but somehow I got the feeling that when it came to proposing, the *setting* and the words had to be special.' Miles smiled. 'So I had to take my time to get it just right.'

Fuck...

'I wanted it to be unique. We're both fans of romantic comedies, and when we had those first dates, we always joked about starring in our own romcom, with each date being a different scene. Remember I used to refer to you as my leading lady? So I thought, why not create one for the actual proposal? I thought about using real actors, but I knew I'd never find anyone good enough to play you, so I decided an animation would be better. I didn't quite realise how much was involved, though, so it took longer than planned. A *lot* longer. It should have been finished last summer. Then it got pushed to September. I hoped it would be ready in time for our second anniversary so it'd mark one year of us living together, but then the animator got sick, and by that stage I'd come too far to give up. Shit. I'm rambling, sorry. I'm really nervous...'

Miles wiped his forehead and took a deep breath. I, on the other hand, was struggling to stay upright. My heart was racing so fast I was convinced I was going to keel over at any moment. This was so surreal.

'I could have proposed at a restaurant at the top of a building or at the Eiffel Tower, but I wanted the proposal to mean something to you. To *us*. And this is where we had our first kiss, so I thought it would be ideal. Anyway, you've waited long enough, so I don't want to keep you waiting a minute longer with my long-winded monologue. I just want you to know that you mean *everything* to me. Like I said yesterday, I don't want to be without you. *Ever*. So, Alex, will you do me the honour of becoming my wife?'

As soon as those words fell from his mouth, I swear I stopped breathing. Maybe the world stopped. Hell, I might have even died and gone to heaven. Anything seemed possible right now.

My arms fell to my sides.

'Alex?' Miles took my left hand and squeezed it gently. 'Are you okay?'

I was stunned.

Shocked.

Rooted to the spot.

I opened my mouth.

Nothing came out.

It was like my brain had shut down.

I held my right hand over my heart. Hoping that would calm it down.

I breathed in. Then exhaled.

Slowly, I felt the cogs in my brain starting to turn again.

There was no Hollywood action movie.

Miles had created a film. A romantic, animated film.

From scratch.

With us as the lead characters.

We'd starred in our own mini romcom, which was about our first dates.

Photos of us were now rotating on the giant cinema

screen, and that song from the river cruise was playing on the surround sound speakers.

Miles was in front of me.

Down on one knee.

He had just proposed.

Miles had *proposed.*

To me.

It had happened.

It had *finally* happened.

Oh. My. God.

Oh my God!

And now Miles was waiting for me to reply.

Shit.

Wake up properly, brain.

And say something.

Quickly!

'Yes!' I said, relieved that I'd regained the power of speech. 'Yes! Yes! *Yessss!*' I screamed so that everyone this side of London and probably in Wales, Scotland and Ireland could hear me too.

A massive smile spread across Miles' face and his shoulders relaxed. He took the ring from the box and slid it slowly onto my finger. As soon as he did, I started crying hysterically. Miles stood up and threw his arms around me.

'Hey…' He stroked my hair. 'I hope those are happy tears?'

'Of course!' I sobbed.

I couldn't believe this was happening. It was like a dream. The sweetest, most wonderful dream.

Miles pulled away gently, lifted my chin and looked into my eyes like I was the most precious woman ever created. Then he kissed me. It was just like in the films.

Long, passionate, full of emotion. My whole body tingled, my skin prickled with goosebumps and I felt my knees buckle. I was glad Miles had his arms around me to keep me rooted to the ground, because right now, I was floating so high that I could probably fly through the ceiling.

It was only when we came up for air that I noticed an usher standing at the front with another lady beside her, both in tears and a photographer and videographer on the left-hand side of where we were standing. Had they been there the whole time? I hoped so, as I didn't even remember half of what Miles had said. I was pretty sure that at one point I'd blacked out. If they told me I'd lost consciousness for a few minutes, I would believe them.

'Congratulations!' said another staff member, clutching two glasses of champagne.

'Thank you,' said Miles, taking one from her. I took the other, still in a daze.

'Thanks!'

'Can I have a look?' She pointed at the ring.

'Oh!' I paused, looking down at my left hand. *Holy shit*. There was so much going on I hadn't even checked out the ring. *Jeez*. It was bloody beautiful!

It was an oval aquamarine floral halo diamond ring. The light blue aquamarine centre stone was surrounded by diamonds in a way that made them form a ring of petals around it. It looked like a flower in full bloom. And it fitted perfectly. Miles did well.

'I know the rings you were hinting at were just classic diamonds, but I thought an aquamarine ring would suit your personality better. I mean, blue is your favourite colour, and when I looked at it, it reminded me of the clear water you see in a tropical paradise. Y'know, like how I imagine the sea to be somewhere like Bali or the Caribbean. And I loved that it looked like a flower. Sounds cheesy, but I thought that could be like a symbol of our love blossoming. Plus, you won't have to think about finding something blue on our wedding day. I hope you like it?'

Wow. He'd put so much thought into it. I felt like the luckiest woman in the world.

'I absolutely love it! It's the most beautiful engagement ring I've ever seen. Better than anything in my magazines, on Instagram, in fact, *anywhere*!' The design was so unique. In the most amazing way.

Then I remembered that the woman had asked to see it. My head was all over the place. I lifted my hand up to give her a better look.

'It's gorgeous!' she gushed.

'Phew!' said Miles. 'I was so nervous. The jeweller helped me design it. I wanted you to love it all. The ring, the proposal. I know how important it is to you. I wanted to get it right.'

'I do. I did. It's perfect! *Everything* is just amazing!' I threw my arms around him again, hoping the longer I held on to him, the longer this moment would last. I didn't want it to end.

I closed my eyes, still trying to take everything in and as I opened them slowly again, I noticed the photographer had come closer and was still snapping away.

I slowly unwrapped myself from Miles and smiled. She took that as a cue to come closer.

'Is it okay if I take some posed shots?'

'Sure.' I smiled, glancing up at Miles: my fiancé. I had a bloody fiancé. I was engaged! This was overwhelming, in the best possible way. My cheeks started shaking from all the smiling and my hands trembled. I was so excited I could scream.

Miles wrapped his arm around my waist and we clinked our glasses as the photographer took dozens of photos.

It was funny. I'd seen a million posed proposal shots on Instagram. Left hand held up in the air, arms draped over the partner's shoulders to show off the ring, clutching a 'she said yes' banner… Whenever I saw them, I'd always thought about what I would do to make my announcement to the world. In the end I'd planned to do something like a photo with Cuddles between us with my left hand strategically placed on her fur. Or with us holding hands and a sunset behind us. But somehow something had shifted inside of me. I felt different to how I'd imagined I would. Right now I wasn't bothered about getting the perfect shot. I just wanted to enjoy this moment.

Later, when I'd had time to take everything in, I would love to see the candid photos. The ones that captured this all happening. The surprise of it all, the ones that caught me off guard. I reckoned those shots would probably be my favourites.

After a few minutes of taking more photos and thanking everyone for their well wishes, the photographers and staff left Miles and me to enjoy some time alone.

Miles had apparently already ordered our favourite fish and chips followed by sticky toffee pudding for dessert, which would be served shortly whilst they replayed our film. I was so excited that right now, I wasn't even sure if I'd be able to eat anything.

'Wow!' I squeezed Miles tightly. 'That was some

proposal. I did not see that one coming. *At all.* Especially after, you know, what happened this past week…' I hung my head. I felt so embarrassed knowing that if I'd just held out for a few more days, everything would have been fine.

'Yeah, you had me worried! But I believed in you. In us. I knew we'd get through it. And I'd spent so long planning it that even if you hadn't called me when you did and asked if we could talk, I wasn't going to give up. I was still determined to try. If I had to, I would have gone to Roxy's and begged you to come to the cinema with me.'

'I'm so sorry.' I winced.

'Maybe if I'd done something less involved, I could have proposed sooner, but I wanted it to be right. To do something extra romantic. And so, even though I noticed you'd started mentioning marriage more often, I just thought you wouldn't mind holding on a little longer. But clearly I got that wrong… when you were screaming at me last week, I really wanted to tell you about everything, but then I thought: no. Stick to the plan.'

'Well, I'm glad you did,' I said, thinking of the mention of the word *plan*. Now I saw that I hadn't needed one after all. Miles had had a proposal in the pipeline for months. I didn't need to cook him fancy meals, convince him I was wife material or convey what I'd like. He already had it covered. All I had to do was trust him. 'This… everything was absolutely perfect. I couldn't have planned it better myself.'

'I'm so relieved to hear you say that! So did I get the *setting*, the *words* and the *sentiments* correct?' He chuckled.

'Definitely!' My cheeks burned with embarrassment

again. 'Sorry about all that too. I know I got a bit obsessed.'

'Just a bit…' He smiled, then took my hand to reassure me. 'It's fine. I knew you were just enthusiastic about it all. Was pretty funny, though, when you started talking about tall buildings and cliffs and all that. Not sure you'd thought that part through…'

'Me either.' I slapped my forehead. 'This setting was *much* better and safer than the top of a cliff. Thank you for being so patient with me and my constant hint dropping.'

'What?' Miles frowned. 'Did you drop hints to encourage me to propose?' He raised his hand to his mouth, pretending to be shocked. 'I hadn't noticed. I thought all those random engagement ads kept popping up on my laptop because I'd been researching rings in my sleep.'

'You realised, then…' I cringed.

'Of course! I never researched stuff like that on my laptop. The tabs you left open were particularly subtle.' He smirked. 'It wasn't all bad, though. Leaving that ring out on the table for me to find was really helpful. Before that, I'd been trying to tie a string around your finger when you were sleeping to get a measurement, but that didn't work too well. You kept moving.'

'You didn't?!'

'Yep.'

'Thank you for trying. And by the way, great idea to lure me here under the guise of us going to watch an action film. I never would have guessed.'

'What? That was true! This *was* an action film! No high-speed car chases and shoot-outs, admittedly, but there was drama, suspense, excitement, surprise, and enough adrenaline to fuel ten football teams.'

'There definitely was. Not to mention a happy ending, a stunning engagement ring and of course an even more gorgeous husband-to-be.' It really had been a roller coaster of a morning here, and I'd enjoyed every second. 'Yep, Mr Miller, my darling *fiancé*'—I kissed him firmly on the lips—'you really pulled it out the bag. This morning's entertainment was right up my street. Best film and best day *ever*. It was definitely worth the wait.'

CHAPTER THIRTY-SIX

I was still on cloud nine. I still couldn't believe it had happened. I was engaged. *Engaged!* And it felt fucking amazing!

After we'd watched *our film* on repeat several times whilst eating brunch, Miles and I had left the cinema hand in hand. He'd insisted we stand outside, then asked me to look up.

A personalised message was displayed on the cinema sign:

CONGRATULATIONS ON YOUR ENGAGEMENT
ALEX AND MILES XOXO

My heart melted for about the hundredth time that day and it was barely one in the afternoon.

We'd then gone for a walk in Hyde Park. Crazy to think that when we were here just over a week ago at Winter Wonderland, I was wondering if that would be the day. And today it was.

Even though it was cold, I only wore my glove on my right hand because I couldn't stop staring at the ring on my left. It was just beautiful.

'So, *fiancé…*' Saying that would never get old.

'Yes, my darling *fiancée*?' Miles grinned.

'What do you fancy doing next?' We were almost at the exit, so I thought it was a good opportunity to make plans.

'It's almost time for your next surprise.'

'Surprise?' My eyes widened. 'Another one?'

'*Mmm-hmm*. It's only early. This is our special day, so we have to keep the happy vibe and celebrations going!'

'Ooh!' I felt butterflies dancing in my stomach.

We stepped out onto the main road and Miles hailed a black cab. He pulled out his phone and showed the screen to the driver. 'It's a surprise, so I don't want to say where we're going out loud.'

'No worries, mate.' The cabbie nodded. Miles opened the door and I climbed inside.

'I'm very intrigued, but I won't even ask where you're taking me,'

'*Good*. I wasn't going to tell you anyway.' He smirked.

'It's fine!' I held up my hands. 'You've already proved your ability to organise the best surprises. If surprises were an Olympic sport, you'd be getting gold.'

'Awww.' Miles leant forward and kissed me. 'Surprise Organiser Olympic Gold Medallist. Has a nice ring to it. Think I'll add it to my CV.'

'You should!'

'Speaking of surprises, I have to say, *you've* surprised *me* today!' Miles rested his finger on his chin.

'Really?' I had no idea how.

'Yeah. We've been engaged for, what, almost three hours and you haven't told anyone yet.'

'Oh yeah!'

So funny. If you'd have asked me weeks ago what the first thing I'd do after Miles proposed would be, I would've sworn I'd be texting my friends and stopping random strangers on the street to show them my ring. Especially because I'd been so quick to tell everyone that I thought Miles was proposing loads of times, only to be disappointed when he didn't. But now it had actually happened, I was so happy being in this big bubble of joy that I hadn't wanted to step outside of it to think about anyone else but us. Even for a few seconds. I didn't want to break the spell. I just wanted this feeling to last forever.

Now we were in the taxi, though, it might be a good time to share the exciting news.

I pulled out my phone, held out my left hand and took a quick photo. So glad that Roxy's colleague had come round to give us a manicure last night. My hands had been looking so manky before, but the French polish went perfectly with my gorgeous ring.

A simple picture would say it all. I didn't want to spend ages taking loads of shots and scrolling through them picking the right one. The first pic I took was fine. I wasn't going to agonise over writing a message either. I wanted to get back to enjoying my day with Miles.

I wrote a quick caption.

Me

So… this just happened!

. . .

I started with firing off the photo to Stacey. If it wasn't for her encouraging me to do Laurie Love's challenge, I would never have met Miles in the first place. I owed her so much.

Next up was Jada. Even though we hadn't even known each other for that long, she already felt like a sister to me. She'd shown me so much love and support, and she'd been instrumental in helping me to see the light and what a fool I'd been with my Operation Proposal/three C's plan and walking out on Miles. I cringed just thinking about it. If I hadn't realised my mistake, I wouldn't be enjoying such a wonderful day now.

Hmmm. Who was next?

Of course, I had to share the news with Roxy. She'd probably tell me I was making a huge mistake and ruining my life by 'getting shackled to a man' and 'entering a prison called marriage', but I didn't care. Roxy was the closest family member I had in London and she'd supported me in her own unique way, so I wanted her to know all about my happiness.

I searched for Audrey's number and gave her a call. She wasn't big on texts. She answered after three rings.

'Hi, Audrey! It's Alex!'

'Oh, hello, dear. How are you?'

'I'm on top of the world, actually!' I smiled at Miles and glanced down at my ring again. It was so beautiful. 'I just wanted you to know that Miles proposed to me this morning. We're engaged!'

'Oh my goodness!' Audrey gasped. 'That's the most wonderful news. I'm so happy for you both. That Miles is a lovely young man. We'll have to celebrate. Perhaps you'd like to come round one evening next week and I can make a nice supper?'

'That would be great, thank you. Well, I better go. I just wanted to share the news with you.'

'Thank you, dear. And please pass on my congratulations to the lucky young man too.'

'Will do!'

My heart was so filled with love and happiness it could burst.

I quickly messaged my brother.

Even though she definitely wasn't my favourite person in the world and I still wasn't sure what was going to happen with our friendship, I supposed I should message Karen too. I fired off a quick text.

The replies came through thick and fast.

Stacey

OMG! OMG!

OMG!!!! CONGRATULATIONS!!!

Stacey

I knew it would happen soon. Miles is a keeper. You guys are going to be soooo happy together.

Stacey

Let me know if you need help with the wedding planning, dress shopping, etc. I'm a bit slower on my feet these days, but I'm here if you need me.

. . .

Stacey

Let's meet ASAP, so you can tell me how it all happened!! Congrats again!!

Awww. I knew she'd be over the moon.

It didn't take long to hear back from Jada either.

Jada

Whoop! Whoop! I knew he'd come through! Congrats, sis! So happy for you.

Jada

Enjoy your weekend together (which means no overthinking… Just be in the moment!) can't wait for you to tell me on Monday how it all went down. Xoxo

I loved her. I was definitely going to try not to overthink. So far so good. I hadn't quizzed Miles about where we were going like I had when we were on our way to the river cruise. I had just decided to sit back, relax and get ready to enjoy whatever was in store.

My phone pinged again. It was Roxy.

Roxy

Yay! About bloody time he pulled his finger out! Only joking. Congrats, darling. xxx

. . .

Roxy

Bet you're glad we had those manicures last night…

Roxy added a winky face. I was just thinking the exact same thing a minute ago. I was glad she was happy for me.

No word from Nick or Karen yet, but that was to be expected, given the time differences.

I wasn't sure about posting on Instagram. I'd told the most important people, which was the main thing. I'd think about it tomorrow, maybe, or next week, if I felt like it.

'And how about you?' I asked Miles as I replied to everyone with smiley face emojis. 'Aren't you going to tell anyone?'

'So far I've told Mum and Dad. That's who I was speaking to when you arrived at the cinema. They called to give me a final pep talk and calm me down. I was sweating so much.'

'I'm not surprised. Especially in that huge jacket. You should have taken it off.'

'Wish I could've, but I had the ring inside. It was the only one I had with pockets big enough to hide it. If I'd worn the other one, you might have seen the shape of the box. And I was worried if I took it off that the ring would fall out or something.'

'Ah! I see.' He'd really put a lot of thought into everything. 'Well, I'm glad the pep talk from them helped. They're so sweet. You really have the best parents.' I knew if I told my mum and dad they wouldn't be that bothered, so I wasn't going to. Ron and Mary, on the other hand, would be so chuffed. Looked like Mary would need to buy that hat after all…

'Yeah, I'm very lucky,' said Miles, staring out the window. 'We're here!'

The driver pulled up outside a glass building.

'Welcome to the Park Plaza Hotel,' Miles added. 'Our home for the next twenty-four hours.'

'Whaaattt!?' I squealed. 'An amazing proposal and a night at a five-star hotel? I really have died and gone to heaven!' I jumped up and down on my seat like an excited puppy, whilst Miles shrugged as if it was no big deal.

'If I'd proposed abroad, say in Paris or Rome like a certain lady had hinted, then we'd have had a night at a hotel, right? So I didn't want you to think that just because it happened in London, I was going to do it on the cheap,' Miles chuckled.

'As if I'd think that!' I pulled him into me for a kiss. 'I know I've said this a million times already today, but you really are the best. You've already done so much, I would have been happy just going home and chilling with you on the sofa.'

'It's not too late for me to cancel…' Miles winked.

'No, no!' I jumped in. 'That would be rude! Staying here is absolutely the polite thing to do.'

'Thought you might say that!'

Miles paid the driver and we walked through the revolving glass doors and up to reception.

'I've just thought—we don't have any clothes or anything…'

'Already taken care of.' Miles wrapped his arm around me. 'I packed a bag for both of us and dropped it off to the hotel on my way to the cinema. Roxy also packed up the stuff you had at her place and brought it here too.'

'Roxy? But how did she…?' Hold on a minute. The pieces of the puzzle all started to come together. 'Did you tell her you were proposing?'

'Yep.' He smirked.

Wow. She kept that quiet. 'When?'

'Yesterday afternoon. I knew you'd want your nails to look nice for the photos, so I asked if she could help me find a subtle way for you to get them done and also to get your stuff over to the hotel, because I wasn't sure if you'd need to have certain things with you. And when I told you we should take things slow, obviously I didn't mean it. I really wanted you to come home last night, but I knew it would be best if you stayed at Roxy's because I'd probably end up getting so nervous about the proposal, that you'd guess or something.'

Oh, wow. When he'd suggested that we not rush, it had seemed like a reasonable request, given the circumstances. And I hadn't suspected a thing when Roxy had said her colleague was coming to do our nails to get some practice. Or when she'd given me the new jumper.

Roxy knew how important the engagement was to me and she wanted to help me feel and look good. And she probably gave up a night of hot sex with her latest fuck-buddy to stay in with me too. Now *that* was love.

'You guys are worryingly brilliant at keeping secrets!' I poked him gently in his side. His abs were as solid as ever. *Yum*. 'I'm so grateful, though. It made the surprises even more special!'

'Glad to hear it.' He kissed me on the cheek. 'Anyway, come on, fiancée. Let me take you to our room.'

As we stepped through the door, my jaw fell to the floor.

There was a huge colourful bouquet of flowers on the table along with a bottle of champagne in a bucket, two glasses and a giant pink heart-shaped box of chocolates.

The bed was covered in rose petals, and the views—*Oh my God.* I rushed over to the huge windows and pulled back the curtains fully so I could see them in all their glory.

Directly opposite us was Big Ben.

Wow.

I wouldn't have to check my phone or ask Miles what the time was whilst we were staying here. All I'd need to do was look out the window and the answer would be right there in front of me.

I watched the cars and the red double-decker buses drive over Westminster Bridge. Then I looked to the right and saw the London Eye.

'Views okay for you?' quipped Miles.

'Just a bit! They're amazing!'

'Thought I'd squeeze in some extra "settings" points. Wanted to have all bases covered, so this should tick off the tall buildings and views brief…'

'I'm never going to live that down, am I?' I winced.

'It was cute! You wanted me to get the proposal right. I got it. At one point, though, I did think you were going to show me a PowerPoint presentation or give me a handout summarising everything you wanted me to do,' Miles teased.

'I did go a bit overboard…' I shook my head. 'On a less embarrassing note, look at all this.' I gestured around the room.

'Remind you of anything?'

'Our first night… *together.*' My body tingled as I remembered how Miles had decorated his place for the first time we had sex. After holding out for six months, finally doing the deed was extra special, so he'd made a big effort.

'They've used fake rose petals, though, so no worrying about staining the sheets this time.'

'I think I'll definitely brush them onto the floor before we get on the bed so I don't get them stuck up my bum like I did before!' I burst out laughing. '*Ah, memories!*'

'Yeah…' Miles stepped forward and stroked my cheek. 'How do you fancy creating some more *memories* right now?'

I ran my fingers down Miles' chest, then started unbuckling his belt.

'I thought you'd never ask…'

APRIL

CHAPTER THIRTY-SEVEN

The big day was finally here.

I'd fantasised about this ever since I was a little girl.

Waited decades for this moment.

It was my wedding day.

I didn't think I'd been so excited and nervous about anything in my entire life.

My stomach had been churning and fluttering all morning. If it wasn't for my amazing bridal party keeping me calm (and perhaps one teeny tiny glass of Prosecco), I would have been a complete wreck.

I couldn't believe that after all of the days, months and years of wishing and hoping, in less than half an hour, my dream of walking down the aisle and becoming a bride would become a reality. I would become Mrs Alexandra Miller.

Holy shit.

My big day was going to be light years away from

what I'd imagined, though. It was nothing like the cut-outs in my wedding folder.

That wedding was all about getting married in a castle, palace or some elaborate hall and wearing a big ball gown.

Everything about the wedding I *thought* I wanted was huge. Including the budget. But then I'd realised, being married wasn't just about having a big wedding. It was about the rest of our lives. What was the point of spending twenty grand on a fancy venue or breaking the bank buying a huge dress? Especially one that didn't suit me?

I could have asked my dad for money, but I hardly spoke to him, so it wouldn't feel right to call out of the blue to ask. We could have got loans, or whacked everything on credit cards, but I didn't want to start our married life with debt up to our eyeballs. Or end up like that couple I'd seen on TV who were on the verge of divorce because they couldn't keep up their repayments.

The woman who'd started the wedding folder all those years ago was different to the woman I was now. We wanted different things. When I'd first constructed the fantasy of having the perfect proposal, elaborate wedding and huge dress, I was unhappily single. The old Alex had seen those things as a symbol of what would bring me happiness. So when I'd actually found happiness with my Mr Right, I'd been too blind to fully appreciate what I had. But not anymore.

In the end, I'd packed my folder away and started from scratch. This wasn't just *my* wedding. It was Miles' too. It made sense that we planned it together. It was important that our big day reflected our shared vision.

First we agreed that, just like the proposal, we wanted our big day to be meaningful to us. The ceremony was a celebration of our love. We didn't need anything flashy. All we needed was to be surrounded with the people closest to us, somewhere that felt relaxed.

And we didn't want to wait a year to get married or have loads of restrictions about what we could or couldn't do. We wanted *all* of our family—including our furry four-legged friends—to be able to join us too. That's why Goldie's farmhouse was perfect.

I was so chuffed when she suggested it. It wouldn't be opening as a second site for another month or so, and now it was mid-April, the weather was warming up, making it perfect for an outdoor wedding.

Goldie refused to take any money from us for using her enormous garden. All we had to do was provide the seating for the ceremony and whatever we needed for the reception. Which was so much cheaper than paying venue costs. We'd saved a fortune.

Plus we got to choose the date (a Saturday, of course) without having to go on a waiting list, and we were free to have all of the siblings join us. It was perfect.

It wasn't just the venue that we kept simple. The same went for my dress. After getting engaged, I'd arranged appointments at different stores that were at the top of my suppliers list, including returning to the Forever Bridal Boutique. But even after trying on loads of dresses I'd saved in my Instagram folder, I hadn't found anything that felt like me. Which was strange, because I'd always thought they were all so perfect.

Stacey told me it was normal and that she'd spent months trying to find the gown that was *the one*. Which did make sense. But it was during a visit to Audrey's that everything started to click.

Audrey had said that she thought in many ways it was harder for people getting married these days because there was too much choice and loads of pressure for everything to be fancy. With millions of dresses to choose from, it was easy to feel overwhelmed. And then with all of the images of perfect brides and weddings we saw on social media, there was always a feeling that our wedding and our dress needed to be as good as or even better than what we saw online or in magazines.

I remembered when I was sat on Roxy's sofa, flicking through the channels, and stumbled on the *My Fantasy Wedding* show I used to love and thinking everything was just so elaborate. All the big dresses and ceremonies that had captivated me before no longer had the same appeal. That made me think: What if we stripped everything back? What if we just kept it simple, like it used to be?

When Audrey showed me her wedding photos, everything was low-key. The food was some sandwiches and nibbles, like sausages on sticks, that kind of thing. Yet everyone looked so happy. She said she had a fantastic day because she'd married the man of her dreams and was surrounded by the people she loved. *That* was what mattered.

Her dress was simple too, yet so beautiful. I couldn't take my eyes off it. It was then that Audrey turned to me and said:

'Have you ever thought about having a gown made for you that's more understated? Something like a slip dress would look very elegant on you.' My ears pricked up as Nancy had said the same. 'I made a few wedding dresses when I was younger. Including my own. I could make one for you if you like, dear,' she'd added casually.

Instantly I'd said yes. Something in me just knew it would be right.

Audrey wasted no time in measuring me up. We went fabric shopping the next day and in less than two weeks, she'd created the most beautiful slip dress. Minimal, sophisticated and chic, it was a bias-cut silk charmeuse gown with floral lace details at the top which made it look so unique, pretty and feminine.

It fitted like a glove and as soon as I put it on, I felt like a bride. And most importantly, I felt like me. All that time I'd had my folder I had been picking the same dress. 2010s ball gown. 2020s ball gown. And all that time it was the wrong dress for me. I didn't need to have a huge dress to glide down the aisle like a princess. I just needed something that made me happy. And right now, I felt amazing.

'You look stunning!' Stacey wiped her eyes for about the tenth time in ten minutes.

'Doesn't she just?' Audrey zipped up the back of my dress.

'Thank you!'

'I promise I'll stop in a minute. You've got me crying more than Maisie today and that's saying something!'

Maisie was Stacey's adorable little girl, who was only three weeks old. When Miles and I had decided on an April wedding, I wasn't sure if Stacey would still be able to be part of it. I'd already asked her to be my maid of honour, but now the date was going to be much sooner than planned, I didn't want to put extra pressure on her. I mean, surely the last thing Stacey wanted to do weeks after giving birth would be to walk down the aisle. But when I'd raised it, Stacey had said that even if Maisie was late and she had contractions during the ceremony, there was no way she was missing our wedding. She'd give birth in a field if she had to.

Brie, the make-up artist Roxy's friend Sophia had recommended, did a final check of my face. She'd kept my eyes neutral, shade-wise, but really emphasised my lashes. We were going to keep my lips neutral too, but then when she'd tried a pop of red, it had really worked, so I'd gone for it.

I'd been growing my hair since the end of last year, and now that it was just above my shoulders, my hairdresser, Jenna, had pulled it to one side to offset the floral details on my dress. Jenna attached the cathedral-length veil. Despite always wanting a tiara, in the end I'd decided that the veil was perfect on its own.

'You're all set!' she said.

Audrey and Stacey stood back to take me in and both started tearing up again.

'What's all this blubbing about?' Roxy walked in the room with Jada, clutching another bottle of Prosecco. 'This is supposed to be a bloody wedding, not a funeral! *OMG…*' Roxy paused as I turned to face her. 'Fuck! Alex. You look… *wow*! Jada. Pass me the box of tissues, please, honey. I'm about to mess up my mascara!'

Roxy had surprised me so much during my wedding preparations. As well as conspiring with, I mean, *helping* Miles with the proposal, she'd also arranged an engagement party for me. She said a guy she shagged who owned a bar owed her a favour, so she'd called it in to use to host the celebrations. It was nothing crazy. Just a small gathering with our nearest and dearest. Roxy had also helped organise my hen do, which was fun. She'd invited her friends Sophia and Bella, and along with Jada, we'd all had such a hoot.

When I'd asked Roxy why she was being so super amazing when she was anti-marriage and commitment, she'd said:

'I told you, darling. I just want you to be happy. You've been banging on about tying the knot for ages, so if this marriage malarkey is what floats your boat, then I'll support you. Miles seems like a good egg, so hopefully you two will make it work.'

Roxy was such a sweetheart. I was lucky to have her.

'Don't worry!' Brie reassured Roxy, who had now lost the battle to fight back the tears. 'The mascara is waterproof.'

'Sweet Jesus!' Jada gasped, dipping her hand in the tissue box before passing it to Roxy. 'Can't believe you got us bawling like this, Alex! Audrey, that dress is *on point*. You're a genius. And, sis, you are a *goddess*. I'd hug you, but you look so fine, I'm worried I might crease your gown.'

'You guys!' I fanned myself to try and keep it together. 'Today wouldn't even be possible if it wasn't for all of you and your love and support. I can't thank you enough. And you ladies also look amazing. Jada's right, Audrey. I know I've said it a thousand times, but their dresses are bloody gorgeous.'

With the help of a couple of seamstress friends, Audrey had also created ocean-blue off-the-shoulder bridesmaid's dresses for Stacey, Roxy and Jada. She'd even finished Stacey's at the last minute to make sure everything fitted and was comfortable for her. Audrey really was a diamond.

There was a knock at the door.

'I'll get it,' said Jada.

'Wow!' Ron walked into the room. 'Alex, you look knockout. Miles is going to have a hard time standing upright when he sees you gliding down the aisle.'

'Awww, thanks, *Dad*.' I smiled. I'd asked Ron to give me away today. Neither of my parents were coming. My so-called father had said he was away at some important work conference thing this weekend, and Mum was jet-setting with her new boyfriend. She'd said that it was too short notice to change her plans and that getting married was a waste of time anyway. I hadn't expected anything less.

Nick sadly couldn't make it either. He was gutted, but we'd set up an iPad on a tripod and Jada was going to put it on FaceTime so he could stay up with Cate and the kids to watch the whole thing.

Karen was a no-show. She said she'd got a new role in a 'huge' film and they couldn't give her time off. Funny, because she hadn't mentioned it on social media and she *always* announced everything on there.

After her lukewarm response to my engagement news, I wasn't surprised. It had taken her four days to reply to my announcement text. If I hadn't seen her posting on Instagram when I'd checked briefly, I would have worried that she was sick.

I think the fact that Chuck had also called off their wedding, or should I say *weddings*, plural, also had something to do with her not wanting to come. When the news had broken last month, she'd closed her social media accounts for two weeks, and when she'd relaunched them, all trace of him and everything wedding-related had gone. She was still refusing to tell me what had happened.

Funny to think that I had been jealous of Karen because she'd got a proposal so quickly. Just showed that even when it seemed like people were happy and living the fairy-tale engagement life, it wasn't always true. Of course, I was sure there were people who got engaged quickly and it worked out brilliantly for them. But now I understood that it was better for me and Miles to wait, rather than rush into things. This was what felt right for us.

I exhaled. I couldn't believe it. It was time.

We started making our way out into the garden. My heart was pounding and what felt like a million butterflies were happily dancing in my stomach.

I'd heard about people getting last-minute jitters. Worrying about whether they were doing the right thing. But I can honestly say I didn't have a flicker of doubt. I couldn't remember ever feeling so certain about anything in my whole life.

I took in the surroundings. Resting on the bright green grass were rows of wooden benches, with lovely blue-and-orange cushions on top. We'd picked them out especially to make sure everyone would be comfy during the ceremony.

The guests started to turn around and they all gasped, their hands going to their mouths. I saw Mary wipe her eyes. And then Miles spun around.

OMG.

He was a vision.

Miles was dressed in a gorgeous royal-blue tuxedo, and he took my breath away. He scrubbed up brighter than a shiny penny.

Miles' jaw fell open and Todd, his best man, reached in his pocket and pulled out a fresh tissue. Miles wiped his eyes. He'd always joked that he'd be the one in tears. I loved that he felt the emotions and wasn't afraid to show them. Looked like he wouldn't be the only one. I could feel myself wobbling again.

Don't cry.

Don't cry.

Sensing my thoughts, Ron squeezed my hand reassuringly.

Jada was standing with Scooby, Flapjack and Lady Gaga. They were family, so of course I *had* to get them involved in the ceremony.

They'd also got dressed up for the occasion. Their leashes were covered with flowers, which looked so pretty. Scooby was wearing a navy bow tie, which matched the groomsmen. I looked down at Lady Gaga, my honorary flower girl, and smiled.

'You look stunning, Lady G!' She had on a pink tutu and fresh flowers around her neck which matched mine. 'If I didn't know better, I'd think you were trying to steal the limelight away from me... I'll let you off, just this once.' She barked with approval.

Flapjack was wearing a navy doggy tuxedo and looked adorable. Thankfully he was behaving himself too. There wasn't a pair of socks or lacy knickers in sight.

'Thinking Out Loud' by Ed Sheeran started playing and Jada took her cue. She led Scooby, Flapjack and Lady Gaga down the aisle.

Stacey followed, then Ron turned to me.

'Ready to get married?'

'Definitely!'

This was my moment.

I took a deep breath, then stepped forward. It was so hard to concentrate on putting one foot in front of the other without worrying about tripping over and smile at everyone at the same time.

Just relax.

Enjoy the moment.

As soon as I'd had a word with myself, I started to let go and savoured every step as I got closer and closer to Miles: my hubby-to-be.

Before I knew it, I'd reached the bright floral heart-shaped arch, which represented our altar. We'd picked the colours out to match the flower design that was outside Mr Fogg's Tavern—the pub where we'd had our first date.

Miles took my hands and we faced each other.

'You look absolutely beautiful, baby,' Miles said. My stomach flipped.

'You look gorgeous too, darling,' I whispered.

'Ladies and gents, we are here today to witness the wonderful wedding of Alex and Miles,' boomed Goldie.

Yep, that's right.

Not only had Goldie offered to host the wedding here, she'd also suggested that she marry us. She'd got ordained especially. As soon as she had mentioned it, somehow, again, it just felt right. We wanted our wedding to be all about sharing our love with the people closest to us, and now Goldie was like family, it was ideal.

As Goldie spoke, it really started to dawn on me that this was actually happening. Miles was in front of me. Our favourite people were here to see us declare our love for each other. I wasn't watching someone else's wedding on

TV or on Instagram. This was real. We were getting married!

Miles squeezed my hand gently. He was about to read his vows. He took a piece of white card from his pocket with our initials printed on the back.

'My darling Alex, I've loved you from the night we first met. I love how kind and caring you are. I love your determination, your passion and your beauty. Every time I look at you, you take my breath away. Thank you for showing me what unconditional love feels like. When I'm with you, anything is possible. You make me feel like Superman, Iron Man and Batman all rolled into one! It's as if there's nothing I can't overcome or achieve. I mean, you even got me dancing all night on that cruise, and my friends will tell you that alone is a miracle.'

Todd and a group of Miles' friends chuckled.

'Seriously, though, there aren't enough hours in the day for me to explain how much you mean to me. You're the reason I wake up with a smile on my face, and every day I fall more in love with you.

'I promise to be there for you, through thick and thin, through the highs and lows. I promise to watch endless romcoms with you on a Sunday afternoon and to be there with a glass of White Zinfandel and a big hug whenever you need one. And I'm going to try *really* hard not to leave all the lights on in the house…' Everyone laughed. I was trying so much to hold it together, but my bottom lip was wobbling like crazy.

'When I was in my twenties, I always wondered how I'd know when I found the woman I wanted to marry. And a wise man, my amazing dad, said, "Son, you don't marry the woman you can live with—you marry the woman you can't live without." He was so right. The last two and a half years with you have given me some of the most precious moments in my life. I'm looking forward to us creating more memories. Thank you for making me the happiest man in the world. Even though I know a lifetime with you won't be enough, I can't wait to start the next chapter of our lives together. I will love you forever and always.'

Game over.

I was now blubbing like a starving baby. I didn't care that I had tears rolling down my cheeks. That was the nicest thing that anyone had ever said to me.

'Shit! That was beautiful. Oh crap!' I winced. 'I just swore at my wedding. Sorry, Audrey, Ron, Mary, Granny and Gramps.'

The guests burst out laughing, Miles' grandparents smiled, Mary waved her hand reassuringly as if to say not to worry and Ron gently patted my shoulder.

Todd reached in his left pocket, then a look of horror filled his face as he fumbled around.

Uh-oh...

He swiftly dipped his hand in his right pocket and relief washed over him as he pulled out the box and handed it to Miles. Miles slid the gorgeous gold ring that we'd designed together down my finger.

OMG.

My heart was melting and the tears wouldn't stop flowing. I had no idea how I was going to say my vows now. Ron passed me his handkerchief. I dabbed it under my eyes and on my cheeks, took a deep breath and tried to compose myself.

Stacey handed me the card with my vows.

Here goes…

'Miles… you truly are the love of my life. For years, I dreamt of finding my Mr Right. But never did I imagine finding someone like you. You're all that I wished for and more. You're kind, loving, incredibly patient and when we're together I feel so safe, secure, happy and totally loved. And you're pretty easy on the eyes too…' I smiled. 'Every day I pinch myself to check that this is all real and not just a fairy tale. I can't believe that I get to be this happy! I love you so much.

'I promise to be there for you in good times and bad. I promise never to take you for granted and to treat you to delicious pain au chocolat at least once a week. And I will love you no matter what—even when you leave the house lit up like a Christmas tree! Glad to hear you're going to try and address it, though.' We laughed again. Such a coincidence that we'd both mentioned his illumination habit in our vows. 'I read a quote the other day by a guy called Dr Seuss and it summed up how I feel about you. It said: "You know you're in love when you don't want to fall asleep, because reality is finally better than your dreams." Thank you for making my dreams come true. For making me feel so special. Today is the first day of the rest of our lives. And I can't wait to share it with you.'

Now Miles was the one wiping his eyes. We were like a couple of babies, but neither of us cared.

Todd passed the ring to me. My hands were shaking so much from the excitement. I better not bloody drop it. I slid it onto Miles' finger. It got a bit stuck halfway down, but I gave it a push. I glanced up to check I didn't hurt him. Miles flashed me his amazing smile and I knew we were all good.

'Beautiful vows, guys!' Goldie sobbed, then blew her nose loudly. 'Oops, sorry about that, folks. This is just *so* emotional. I love it! Oooh, we didn't do the *I dos*, did we? Bugger. Can't get married without that. I should have said it with the ring bit. *Doh.*' Goldie slapped her forehead.

'Don't worry!' I smiled. Miles and I kind of jumped the gun by putting the rings on after each of us said our vows instead of waiting. Must have been all the nerves and excitement.

'Sorry all. I'm a bit of a virgin. Not that type of virgin, *obviously.*' Goldie winked at Willy, who we *think* had now become more than a friend… 'I mean, it's my first time marrying people. Anyway, enough of my babbling. Let's do that bit again, shall we?' Miles and I were trying really hard not to burst out laughing. I kind of liked that everything hadn't been too scripted. Made it more fun and real. 'Alex, do you take Miles to be your hubby?'

'I do!' I grinned.

'And, Miles, darling, do you take the gorgeous Alex to be your wife?'

'I do!'

'Excellent! I think I've covered everything. No one had any objections, did they? No? Great. *Wonderful.* Now it's *finally* time for the really fun part. Miles: you can now kiss the beautiful bride!'

'Whoop, whoop!' Roxy cheered. 'Go for it, girl!'

'No tongues!' shouted Sandeep.

'Can't promise, mate,' Miles called back before pulling me in to him and giving me the sweetest kiss.

Yep. I definitely would be happy having these soft lips on me for the rest of my days.

'That's it, sweethearts! You're now officially hitched!

Congratulations, you two. Everyone, please give three cheers for Mr and Mrs Miller!'

Everyone whooped and the song '(I've Had) The Time of My Life' by Bill Medley and Jennifer Warnes played. *Of course* we had to choose a song from a romantic film. We loved watching *Dirty Dancing*, and the song featured in *Crazy, Stupid, Love* too, which was one of Miles' favourite romcoms. No chance that he was going to do the famous move where he lifted me over his head. Well, not right now anyway, but who knew what might happen later…

'We did it!' Miles grabbed my hand excitedly as we turned and walked back up the aisle. Everyone started throwing confetti and the photographer snapped away. I couldn't wait to see the pics later, as right now this still felt like a dream.

'I can't believe it!' I kissed him again. 'We're married!'

Miles had said earlier that I made him feel like Superman. Right now I felt like Lois Lane. Like I'd just been swept off my feet and was flying in the clouds with him. This really was the best feeling in the world.

~

We were a few hours into the wedding and I still hadn't made my way around to speak to everyone yet, but they looked like they were having a great time. They were chatting amongst themselves and all had a glass of something in their hands, so that was a good sign.

Some people were sitting on the sofas and haystacks we'd laid around the garden and covered in blankets.

Others were in the corner posing with the giant rings I'd made as photo props. I'd also bought a Polaroid camera and plenty of film. Much more cost-effective than hiring a photo booth, and we thought it was more fun too.

After we'd taken professional photos and done the speeches, everyone got stuck into the food. We'd hired an amazing food truck to serve fish and chips, burgers, sandwiches and salads, and it was a big hit with the guests.

Keeping the food and seating simple meant no worrying about seating plans, centrepieces, wedding favours, what colour napkins to choose and all that stuff. Which meant less stress leading up to the wedding and more time to enjoy ourselves today.

Another tradition we'd decided to buck was the bouquet throwing. I knew what it felt like to be single at a wedding and desperately longing to be the one who caught it, so I didn't want anyone who didn't to feel bad about themselves. Maybe I'd leave it somewhere later, though, in case someone still wanted it.

The dessert table looked like it was a winner too. A crowd had gathered to enjoy the mini cupcakes, donuts and sweet treats.

Displayed proudly on its own was our two-tiered wedding cake, which had been created by Chloe, a local baker that Audrey had recommended. Chloe worked with a charity that helped the elderly, which was where they'd met, but she also baked for coffee shops and private clients on the side. After tasting her creations, I knew I wouldn't need to use the companies in my folder.

I was so chuffed with the design. Rather than having round tiers, Chloe had suggested we mix shapes, so we had a large square carrot cake tier at the bottom and a red velvet round tier at the top. The cake was covered with ruffled white buttercream and decorated with pastel flowers. To represent our family, it had little figurines of Miles and me, which were inspired by the cartoon characters from our romcom, alongside a little cat to represent Cuddles. It was perfect.

'Congratulations!' Tabitha threw her arms around me. 'So he finally did it, then!'

'Yes!' I said.

'I knew he would!' she gushed. 'That night we saw you at Sandeep's birthday party, after you got back from Paris, I said to Jilly it would only be a matter of time.' It didn't feel like that was what she was thinking back then or during any of the other times they'd asked me when the wedding was. But at least we'd done it now. No more awkward questions, thank goodness.

'Congrats!' Jilly beamed as she approached us. 'Welcome to the wives' club!'

'Thank you.' I smiled politely.

'So…' Jilly grinned. 'When are you having kids?'

So much for no more awkward questions. Miles and I had barely been married for a few hours and she was already asking. *Give us a bloody chance, love.*

'Soon,' I replied, hoping that was true, then grinned again. Nothing was going to burst my bubble today. Not even Jilly and her probing. 'I better go and find *my husband*. Help yourselves to more food and drink. We're going to open up the dance floor, so I hope to see you both on it!'

As I walked away, Flapjack zoomed past me with a pair of boxer shorts in his mouth and Willy was chasing after him. So funny. I guessed that confirmed that he and

Goldie really were an item, or at least had been enjoying each other's *company*... Good for them.

There he is. My gorgeous husband.

I felt my stomach flip with excitement as I joined Miles at the outdoor bar Willy had built for us.

'So, Mrs Miller.' He wrapped his arm around my waist. 'Ready for our first dance?' He glanced over at the area we'd sectioned off in front of the DJ to use as a dance floor.

'Sure am. I'm ready for our first dance and our fiftieth.'

'*Whoa*. Fifty dances? You reckon we can do all of that and still have energy to enjoy our wedding night and get up in time to catch our flight?'

Tomorrow morning we were going to Rome for our honeymoon. Rather than go in March, we'd decided to save the tickets for a special occasion. Crazy to think that I'd originally planned to go there to get engaged. Now we'd be there as a married couple. Our first trip together as husband and wife.

'Hmm. Good point. But it doesn't matter how many dances we have today, whether we consummate our marriage tonight or if we're tired when we catch our flight tomorrow. We've got the rest of our lives to dance and make love. All that matters is that we have fun along the way.'

'I couldn't have put it better myself. I knew there was a reason I married you,' Miles chuckled.

'Although…' I smirked. 'I just remembered that Goldie mentioned she'd have the bedroom in the loft made up especially for us if we needed to slip away for some *privacy*, so maybe we could check it out later this afternoon…'

'What happened to those beautiful romantic words you just said about having the rest of our lives to make love?' He laughed.

'Have you seen how hot you look today?' I pulled him in for a kiss.

'I feel so objectified!' Miles fake-gasped. 'And I love it! You don't know how much I want to get you out of that dress. You look like a goddess. I have the sexiest wife in the world. I am one lucky man and I am *definitely* up for some afternoon delight if you are. Hopefully our guests won't notice if we're gone for half an hour…'

'Now you're talking. Who says we have to wait for our wedding *night*? We'll probably have zero energy left by then. A wedding *afternoon* sounds *much* more realistic and fun. Our wedding, our rules.'

'Can't wait. So…' He held out his hand. 'Mrs Miller, shall we have some fun on the dance floor? Then we can go and make love and who knows? Maybe we'll be lucky enough to make a baby too…' He winked.

'Oooh!' I said, my heart bursting with joy. 'I'm *definitely* up for that. Creating a mini Miller sounds like the *perfect* way to start our marriage…'

Want more?

Fancy finding out what happened on Alex's and Miles' romantic honeymoon in Rome?

Visit: https://BookHip.com/NCCQJBA to join my VIP Club and **download the *When's the Wedding?* Bonus Chapters for FREE!**

ENJOYED THIS BOOK? YOU CAN MAKE A BIG DIFFERENCE.

If you've enjoyed *When's the Wedding?*, **I'd be so very grateful if you could spare two minutes to leave a review on Amazon, Goodreads and BookBub**. It doesn't have to be long (unless you'd like it to be!). Every review – even if it's just a sentence – would make a *huge* difference.

By leaving an honest review, you'll be helping to bring my books to the attention of other readers and hearing your thoughts will make them more likely to give my novels a try. As a result, it will help me to build my career, which means I'll get to write more books!

Thank you so much. As well as making a huge difference, you've also just made my day!

Olivia x

ALSO BY OLIVIA SPRING

The Middle-Aged Virgin

Have you read my debut novel ***The Middle-Aged Virgin****?* It includes the feisty character Roxy from *When's the Wedding?* too! Here's what it's about:

Newly Single And Seeking Spine-Tingles...

Sophia seems to have it all: a high-flying job running London's coolest beauty PR agency, a long-term boyfriend and a dressing room filled with designer shoes. But money can't buy everything...

When tragedy strikes, Sophia realises she's actually an unhappy workaholic in a relationship that's about as exciting as a bikini wax. And as for her sex life, it's been so long since Sophia's had any action, her bestie has started calling her a *Middle-Aged Virgin*.

Determined to get a life and *get lucky*, Sophia hatches a plan to work less and live more. She ends her relationship and jets off on a cooking holiday in Tuscany, where she meets mysterious chef Lorenzo. Tall, dark and very handsome, this Italian stallion might be just what Sophia needs to spice things up in the bedroom...

But the dating scene has changed since Sophia was last single, and although she'd score an A+ for her career, when it comes to men, she's completely out of her comfort zone. How will Sophia, a self-confessed control freak, handle the unpredictable world of dating? And how much will she sacrifice for love?

Join Sophia today on her laugh-out-loud adventures as she

searches for happiness, enjoys passion between the sheets and experiences OMG moments along the way!

Here's what readers are saying about it:

"I couldn't put the book down. It's **one of the best romantic comedies I've read**." Amazon reader

"Life-affirming and empowering." Chicklit Club

"Perfect holiday read." Saira Khan, TV presenter & newspaper columnist

"Olivia has an innate knack for the sex scenes, which are very hot. **This book was steamy**, but with such a huge element of humour in it that when you read it **you will certainly giggle throughout at the escapades**." Book Mad Jo

"Absolutely hilarious! A diverse, wise and poignant novel." The Writing Garnet

Buy *The Middle-Aged Virgin* on Amazon today!

AN EXTRACT FROM THE MIDDLE-AGED VIRGIN

Prologue

'It's over.'

I did it.

I said it.

Fuck.

I'd rehearsed those two words approximately ten million times in my head—whilst I was in the shower, in front of the mirror, on my way to and from work…probably even in my sleep. But saying them out loud was far more difficult than I'd imagined.

'What the fuck, Sophia?' snapped Rich, nostrils flaring. 'What do you mean, it's over?'

As I stared into his hazel eyes, I started to ask myself the same question.

How could I be ending the fifteen-year relationship with the guy I'd always considered to be the one?

I felt the beads of sweat forming on my powdered forehead and warm, salty tears trickling down my rouged cheeks, which now felt like they were on fire. This was serious. This was actually happening.

Shit. I said I'd be strong.

'Earth to Sophia!' screamed Rich, stomping his feet.

I snapped out of my thoughts. Now would probably be a good time to start explaining myself. Not least because the veins currently throbbing on Rich's forehead appeared to indicate that he was on the verge of spontaneous combustion. Easier said than done, though, as with every second that passed, I realised the enormity of what I was doing.

The man standing in front of me wasn't just a guy that came in pretty packaging. Rich was kind, intelligent, successful, financially secure, and faithful. He was a great listener and had been there for me through thick and thin. Qualities that, after numerous failed Tinder dates, my single friends had repeatedly vented, appeared to be rare in men these days.

Most women would have given their right and probably their left arm too for a man like him. So why the hell was I suddenly about to throw it all away?

ALSO BY OLIVIA SPRING

Losing My Inhibitions

Have you read my third novel ***Losing My Inhibitions***? It includes Alex and Roxy from *When's the Wedding?* too! Here's what it's about:

Finally free and ready to have fun...

He's hot, single and off limits. She's just got her life together after a messy divorce. Should she risk it all for a forbidden fling?

A year after leaving her controlling ex, Roxy's divorce is finally official. She's got her confidence and career back on track and is ready to start enjoying some no-strings-attached fun.

But just when Roxy thinks she has her dating plan all mapped out, a hot younger single man unexpectedly appears. On paper, he sounds like exactly what Roxy's been looking for, until she's warned that he's strictly off limits. Getting involved with him will put her career, home and everything she's worked for in extreme jeopardy. There's a million reasons why Roxy shouldn't give into his charms. The trouble is, he's just too tempting...

Will Roxy take a chance and risk it all to pursue a forbidden fling? And if she does, can she find a way to let him rock her world, without turning it upside down?

***Losing My Inhibitions* is a sexy, laugh-out-loud romantic comedy with a modern twist. This story is about self-love, new beginnings, forging your own path in life and being true**

to yourself. It can be read as a standalone novel or as a prequel to *The Middle-Aged Virgin* and *Only When It's Love.*

Here's what readers are saying about it:

"All hail the new queen of funny, sexy romantic fiction, Olivia Spring. A brilliant read with cringe worthy moments captured perfectly and **genius comedy that had me laughing out loud.** I can't wait to see what Olivia Spring conjures up next but I will snap it up. **All we need now is a movie deal for all three books. Five stars." Love Books Group**

"Oh my word. Ladies **if you haven't already read this, you are missing out**. **It's steamy, it's sexy and it's very funny.** There is a part in it, of which I can't repeat, that had me doubled up laughing. Totally loved it. **Five stars.**" **Books Between Friends**

"The perfect mix of sexy romance, drama and comedy. I would definitely recommend this book! It's perfect for a summer read, chilled out in the garden with a glass of something lovely. Five stars." **Nicole's Book Corner**

"Well Olivia Spring, you've done it again. This modern girl's rom-com is about self-love, self-discovery, and to always be true to who you are. **I devoured it!" Girl Well Read**

"I really enjoyed reading this - some of the situations Roxy finds herself in **had me laughing out loud!** There's also a few steamier moments! Five stars." **Home Full Of Books**

"I read it in two evenings and it was brilliant!! **I couldn't put it down.**" **Head In A Book 18**

Buy *Losing My Inhibitions* on Amazon today!

AN EXTRACT FROM LOSING MY INHIBITIONS

Chapter One

At last.

I thought it was never going to end.

He'd been pounding away for ten minutes, grunting like a pig, and I'd been listening to the radio playing in the background, trying to figure out what advert the song before last was from. Was it the one advertising car insurance or the one for those panty liners that are supposed to keep you *cotton fresh all day long*? *It'll come to me…*

We should have just called it a night when he'd first struggled to get his machinery working. Based on tonight, it seems like what I'd read about some older men finding it difficult to get it up was true.

It was only about half an hour after he'd popped a little blue pill that he'd been able to get his little soldier to stand to attention, if you catch my drift. Which, unfortunately for me, was around the same time I started to sober up and wonder what the hell I was doing.

But by then, he was really excited, and it had been so long since my last time that I'd got myself worked up and was just as keen as him to give it a go. I mean, when I start something, I like to see it through. *Yep, I'm dedicated like that.*

I'd also read that there are lots of benefits of sleeping with an older guy. Apparently, after years of experience in the sack, they know their way around a woman's body better than a gynaecologist, so I thought I may as well give it a try. *Purely in the name of research, of course.*

But now I was really wishing I hadn't bothered. It was about as exciting as watching a hundred-metre snail race. And this guy wouldn't know his way around my anatomy if I gave him a map.

Still, at least it was over now. I was back in the saddle. First time since I'd left my ex-husband. Frankly, I hoped it got better from here. *Please tell me it does?*

I opened my eyes slowly and glanced up at his crepey skin and flaky bald head, which had tufts of grey at the side. His droopy man boobs hung above my chest, whilst the weight of his large pot belly pressed down on my stomach.

Dear God.

I must have had a lot more to drink than I'd realised.

Don't get me wrong. If I was looking for a relationship and this was a man I'd fallen madly in love with, then I wouldn't be so shallow. It was just that right now, I was looking for fun. To make up for the years I'd wasted with my ex. When I was dreaming of the day that I'd be free from Steve and with another man, this wasn't exactly what I'd had in mind.

I'd pictured a young, hot, sexy guy with abs that would

give a Calvin Klein model a run for his money, with a full head of dark hair I could run my fingers through. A stud who would have me screaming for more, rather than wondering when it would all be over.

It was Colette, my boss, slash landlady, slash housemate, slash friend, who'd set me up with him at my divorce party earlier this evening. Now that I was officially free, Colette said some male company might be good for me, so she'd invited Donald, her loaded sixty-two-year-old boyfriend, and he'd brought his fifty-five-year-old mate Terrence along.

I knew that I was ready to get back on the horse, and it was already under control. My cousin Alex had been helping me. She'd given me a crash course in online dating two weeks ago, and I wanted to set up my profile ASAP so I could get going on the whole swiping thing, but this big work exhibition kept getting in the way. I'd been burning the midnight oil every night and often over the weekends too, trying to get everything prepared, which didn't leave me with any time for extracurricular activities. And after another long, tiring and stressful day, a hook-up was the last thing I was thinking about. But I guess the booze I'd been drinking all night had made me relax a little too much, so when Terrence had started flirting, my libido had woken up, curiosity had got the better of me, and I'd hastily thought, *Why not just get it out the way now?*

Big Mistake.

Oh well. You live and you learn. We all do things in the heat of the moment that we regret. As long as I didn't do it again, then it was fine. Which meant I better start thinking about how I was going to get this big sweaty oaf of a man off me. *Now.* I'd heard the effects of those pills can last for hours, and I definitely couldn't endure another round.

No way.

Remind me never to drink alcohol again.

ALSO BY OLIVIA SPRING

Love Offline

Have you read my fourth novel ***Love Offline***? Here's what it's about:

Looking for romance in real life…

Emily's Struggling To Find Romance Online. Will Ditching The Dating Apps Lead To True Love?

Online dating isn't working for introvert Emily. Although she's comfortable swiping right at home in her PJs, the idea of going out to meet a guy in person fills her with dread.

So when her best friend challenges her to ditch the apps, attend a load of awkward singles' events and find love in real life, Emily wants to run for the hills.

Then she meets Josh. He's handsome, kind and funny, but Emily's had her heart crushed before and knows he's hiding something…

Is Josh too good to be true? Can Emily learn to trust again and if she does, will it lead to love or more heartache?

Love Offline is a fun, sexy, entertaining story about friendship, stepping outside of your comfort zone and falling in love the old-fashioned way.

Here's what readers are saying about it:

"**Masterpiece chick lit**. Incredibly funny and through the whole book I was laughing, crying, smiling and I even learned a lot reading this book about social media and self love. I couldn't put it down! Five stars." **Amazon Reader**

"This book just **makes you feel good and all fuzzy inside**. Five stars." **Barbs Book Club.**

"**Fun, flirty and fabulous**... I was laughing throughout the whole book. Five stars." **Reading In Lipstick**

"**Hilarious, sexy-romp with heart!** I adored the relationship Emily has with her best friend Chloe." **A Girl With Her Head Stuck In A Book.**

"This book spoke to me on soooo many levels!! **I loved the realness it shows!!!!** Five stars." **Once Upon A Book Review**

"If you are a fan of Sophie Kinsella and Lindsey Kelk, then this book is for you! *Love Offline* is **a romcom for the modern woman**." **Girl Well Read**.

"I loved the refreshing take on love and dating in this book....**Definitely recommend!**" **Nic Reads In Heels**

"**A sexy little chick lit read**...A lovely, modern story involving friendship and falling in love." **Mrs L J Gibbs**

"I loved Olivia's last book, but I think this one was even better. Five stars." **Hayley Jayne Reads.**

"**The perfect sexy, hot, modern day romance**… an **all out bloody fabulous book!** Five stars." **Nicole's Book Corner.**

Buy *Love Offline* on Amazon today!

ALL BOOKS BY OLIVIA SPRING

The Middle-Aged Virgin Series

The Middle-Aged Virgin

The Middle-Aged Virgin in Italy

Only When it's Love Series

Only When it's Love

When's the Wedding?

Other Books

Losing My Inhibitions

Love Offline

Box Set

Ready To Mingle Collection

All books available on Amazon.

ACKNOWLEDGEMENTS

Yay! If you've read any of my previous books, you'll know how excited I get about being able to thank all of the amazing people who helped make this possible.

First and foremost, huge thanks go to my wonderful mum. You're always the first to read my novels. Your very *direct* (that's putting it politely!) feedback is always spot-on and helps to make my work stronger. I appreciate you *sooo* much.

To my Mr Right, *muchas gracias* for listening to my character and storyline ideas, plus the endless wedding talk whilst I was writing this book. Your constant support and encouragement mean the world to me.

Shout-out to my brilliant editor, Eliza, proofreader, Lily, cover designer, Rachel, and website designer, Dawn. Thank you for making this novel the best that it can be, inside and out, and getting it ready to showcase to the world. You ladies rock!

I'm so grateful for my amazing wedding consultants: J&J and Mich. Thanks for sharing your beautiful love stories with me. Your insights into the proposal and wedding planning process were invaluable.

Sending heartfelt gratitude to my pet consultants, Lindsey and Jas. Thank you for letting me tap into your animal expertise. I loved hearing all about your furry friends and the funny things they do.

To Loz, Jo and Brad, thanks for taking time out of your busy schedules to read early drafts of this novel and for your great suggestions.

Candi: thank you for the delicious food. Having a *very* happy tummy kept me going when I was spending long days in front of the computer writing this book. No one makes paella like you! *Gracias por la comida tan buena. Tener la barriga feliz me ayudó a continuar en frente del ordenador en los largos días que estaba escribiendo este libro. ¡Nadie hace una paella tan rica como tú!*

Big hugs to the brilliant book bloggers, who are always so generous with their time. Thank you for continuing to read and review my novels. You're the best!

And the biggest expression of gratitude of all goes to *you*, dear reader. I am so lucky to have you. I know there are zillions of books out there, so I truly appreciate you choosing to read mine!

Right, novel number seven is calling me, so I best get back to it…

Until next time!

Olivia x

ABOUT THE AUTHOR

Olivia Spring lives in London, England. When she's not making regular trips to Italy to indulge in pasta, pizza and gelato, she can be found at her desk, writing new sexy romantic comedies.

If you'd like to say hi, email olivia@oliviaspring.com or connect on social media.

facebook.com/ospringauthor
twitter.com/ospringauthor
instagram.com/ospringauthor